FIRST CONTACT

RETURN

FIRST CONTACT
RETURN

David Hiers

For more information on this
or other books by David Hiers,
Go to: **www.dhiers.com**

Copyright © 2014 by David Hiers
All rights reserved.
ISBN: 0692266658
ISBN-13: 978-0692266656

Acknowledgements

I would like to thank Deborah and Catherine Deborah for their assistance, encouragement and patience throughout the creation of this book. Without their kind words, I would never have succeeded.

PROLOGUE

The third planet from the sun had almost completely circled its star, but still the watcher remained, hidden in a crater on a small asteroid between the fourth and fifth planets of this system. The inhabitants of the third planet called this asteroid 4 Vesta, one of the larger asteroids in their so-called asteroid belt, but the watcher neither knew, nor cared about this designation. The watcher's sole concern was to find and destroy her sworn enemies.

She stretched her lithe body, fur bristling and claws snapping out. This long period of inaction was maddening, cooped up alone in her small ship. But she would continue to wait for her enemy to reveal themselves. Then she would avenge her mate. She would destroy the enemy mothership and then the third planet where her mate had died.

CHAPTER 1

Fireball detection
IR sensors aboard US DOT satellites detected the impact of a bolide over central China on 15 August 2012 at 08:41:15 UTC. The object was traveling roughly east to west. The object was first detected at an altitude of approximately 110km at 31.13 North latitude, 121.28 East longitude and tracked down to an altitude of approximately 11 km at 24.53 N., 103.24 E. The impact was simultaneously detected by space-based visible wavelength sensors operated by the US Department of Energy. The total radiated energy was approximately 1.29x 10^ 12 joules.

Mark awoke with a start, the dream fresh in his mind. He had been hurtling through the blackness of space towards a small planet shining blue and white in the distance. Green and brown continents had taken shape as he drew closer until he recognized India on the horizon, with a quickly expanding China in the foreground. His vision blurred red upon entering the upper atmosphere, was replaced by landscape zooming towards him, a quick glimpse of jagged stone structures, then impact. Upon awaking, Mark could recall every feature of the stone structures: row upon row of tall, jagged, oddly serrated, stone pillars that looked like they had weathered millions of years. A beautiful, eerie, almost alien landscape.

Reluctantly, Mark peeked open an eye, focusing on the glowing numbers on his alarm clock: 3:46. Relief. He still had over two hours before his alarm would go off. He settled back into his pillow, wondering if he could replay his dream. Maybe this time he could control the flight and soar across the Earth. That would be fun. He lay in bed, willing himself to fall back to sleep, the dream fresh in his mind. But he couldn't recreate it. Instead he had a feeling that he was lying on the ground, waiting to be found. Maybe if he called out someone would find him...

The 6:00 a.m. alarm jarred Mark awake. He dragged himself out of bed, amazed at how just waking up once during the night had broken his sleeping rhythm. He felt like he had not slept at all. An hour and two cups of coffee later, he was still exhausted as he pulled into the back of a 1928 house that he and his law partner had renovated to make into an office. That was pretty typical in downtown Pensacola, where professionals who preferred working out of the old buildings were renovating the historic city center. Although there were some glass or brick hi-rises, there were only a few and the tallest was only nine stories, as Pensacola seemed determined to buck the overdevelopment trend of the rest of Florida. Mark was relieved that his partner's car wasn't in the parking lot. He really didn't feel like talking to anyone yet and his partner was a morning person, way too chipper for Mark's current mood. Mark's secretary knew to keep conversation to a minimum in the morning and would have a pot of coffee ready.

Mark walked in the back door, hung his keys on a hook in the kitchen, poured himself a cup of coffee, and grunted at his secretary as he walked into his office. His secretary had already started his computer and the screen showed his day planner. He glanced at it as he opened the Wall Street Journal, which was in its customary spot in the center of his desk. Beneath it were several files. He would look at them later. He glanced at his day planner and confirmed that he didn't have any appointments today, rather he would be drafting documents. That was a mixed blessing. Although he would not have to be civil, drafting legal documents was mind numbing on the best of days. He hoped that four cups of coffee would do the trick. It didn't. By noon he was still trying to draft a relatively simple trust provision for a will. He just couldn't concentrate and knew that he would have to recheck the conveyance language carefully.

He broke for lunch, placing a sticky note to himself on the file to recheck the trust provisions. Foregoing the local restaurants, he went to the downtown YMCA, hoping that a three mile run would energize him for the afternoon. His route was an easy one. He merely ran under the I-110 overpass up to Maxwell Street and back. The mostly flat, grassy, park area under the overpass allowed him to stay out of the Florida sun for most of the run, which was crucial if you intended to survive running at noon in August. Although most people opted for running along the edge of Escambia Bay in hopes of getting a breeze off the bay, there were too many busy streets to cross. Getting run over during lunch hour was not Mark's idea of good exercise. Besides, his solitary run allowed him to concentrate on office projects; the ultimate in multitasking, he always told himself.

But this run was different. No matter how hard he tried, Mark could not shake the dream. It consumed him. He turned around at Maxwell Street and started heading back. 'Half way,' he encouraged himself as he stared fixedly at the dirt path. It felt like he was running in an oven. Wiping sweat from his eyes, he glanced up to judge his distance and saw a towering stone pillar. He stumbled, but somehow managed to catch himself. He staggered to a halt and bent over, hands on his knees, as he gasped for breath, beads of sweat falling from his head like rain to the dry dirt at his feet.

Stone pillar? He was under the interstate. There were no stone pillars. After several deep breaths, he looked up again and saw a double row of uniform cement columns holding up the interstate. That was more like it. After a few more deep breaths, he stood up and began walking back towards the YMCA. Overheated, Mark told himself. Hallucinating. But what an hallucination! He had seen the stone pillar in every detail, down to every crack on its surface. It was the same stone pillar from his dream.

Mark walked the rest of the way back to the YMCA, warily glancing at the cement columns as he passed them. The stone pillar did not reappear. Matt took a cold shower, followed by a Gatorade. He was still sweating when he put on his suit and headed back to his office. At least I am sweating, Mark reasoned. That rules out heat stroke. But heat exhaustion did not explain the hallucination.

"I had the worst day at work," Mark complained to his wife, Beth, over dinner that night. Beth Williams was Mark's wife of twenty-seven years. She was an accountant in a local firm. They had met when she was an expert witness in a case he had tried. They had hit it off and started dating shortly thereafter. Twenty-seven years and three children later, they were facing "empty-nest syndrome" as their youngest headed off to college. "I just couldn't concentrate all day and then I had the oddest hallucination while running at lunch time."

"I told you not to run at noon," Beth interrupted. "It's way too hot. You'll get heat stroke for sure."

This was Beth's favorite mantra. A morning person, she worked out early, before it got too hot. But Mark was not a morning person and the thought of getting up, let alone doing so to exercise, was repugnant. No, he would take his chances with heat stroke. "I had a dream last night," Mark continued. "Woke me up around three and then I couldn't get back to sleep. All day today I have been dragging. And then during my run today, when I made the turn at Maxwell, I had this vivid hallucination that I was running towards a stone pillar. I saw it plain as day. It was really weird."

"Would you like some more pasta?" Beth asked as she helped herself to some more.

"No, thanks," Mark replied. "It was the same stone pillar from my dream," Mark continued. "It was so real."

"This morning you said the dream was in space," Beth said.

"Yes, approaching Earth and then impacting somewhere in China," Mark said, a bit surprised as he had not thought his wife had been paying attention that morning.

"Maybe it's left over from one of those visions last year," she replied.

Mark thought about that for a moment before replying. "No, I don't think so," Mark replied hesitantly. "Those visions occurred when I touched that alien artifact."

"The cube," Beth said.

"Right. The memory cube. Then I became the alien who sent it, seeing, touching, feeling, what he felt. In this dream I was not an alien. I just saw the Earth approaching. It was as if from a meteor's perspective."

"But you also had visions last year when you weren't touching the cube."

"That's true. But those were very different. Fast, fleeting. And even in those I was an alien, had an alien body. And when the vision was in space, I was still in an alien's body in a space ship. This is different."

"Maybe it's PTSD," she said. "You were almost killed and came home all burned and bruised."

"I don't think so," Mark said. "Granted, I did have some nightmares, but they were more general and stopped over six months ago. No, this is totally different. It's probably just a dream. It's just odd that it's hanging on so long."

The dream haunted him the rest of the evening. When he finally fell asleep, he dreamed of an alien landscape, with valleys filled with stone structures, rising up, jagged and sharp, climbing up in nonsensical piles above the valley floor. And through it all was a call: *"Come find me."*

"How was your day?" Beth asked when Mark got home late the next night.

"Exhausting," Mark said. "It was just like yesterday. I just couldn't..."

"You didn't have another hallucination, did you?"

"No. I didn't..."

"You didn't run did you?"

"No, I didn't run today," Mark finished saying. "I was just tired all day. Couldn't concentrate with that dream lingering in the back of my head all day. Took me forever to finish a simple trust. That's why I'm so late getting home."

"Why don't you have a glass of wine and go to bed early tonight?"

"That sounds like a great idea," Mark said. "Maybe I'll have two glasses."

But later that night, Mark still lay wide awake in bed while the call, *"Come find me,"* kept swirling through his consciousness. Finally, he climbed out of bed and took his laptop into the den. "Just out of curiosity," he muttered to himself as he searched the web, typing in a Google search for recent meteor sightings. He perused a number of hits, none of which satisfied his curiosity. He was about to exit when an entry caught his attention. Clicking on it, he saw a brief reference to a reported meteor in China Wednesday afternoon. He almost skipped past it as his dream had been early Wednesday morning, but then he remembered that China time would be hours ahead of him. He checked the world time on his cell phone. China was thirteen hours ahead of him. He re-read the entry. It merely mentioned that a number of people reported seeing a meteor streak through the late afternoon sky near Shanghai, heading west, and there was speculation as to whether the meteor had actually impacted or burned up in flight. Could that be it? Mark wondered. If only he knew the exact time, then he could be certain. 'The North American Aerospace Defense Command would have it,' he thought. 'Like he could call NORAD and ask them for information on a meteor,' he chided himself.

"This is stupid," he said aloud as he closed his computer and headed back to bed. But sleep would not come. The continuing command to "*Come find me*" kept him awake. 'What if I did dream about that meteor over China? So what?' Mark thought. But he knew there was only one answer to that question: a vision. Succumbing to the inevitable, he started to get back up.

"You getting up again?" Beth asked.

"Can't sleep," Mark said. "I keep hearing that call. I'm starting to wonder if you were right. Maybe it is some type of vision."

Beth rolled over to face him. "How could it be?" she asked. "You said the cube stopped working when the alien ships were destroyed."

"It did. But maybe this is a new one," Mark said without any real conviction. "A different type."

"Think about it," Beth said. "Last year NORAD tracked that alien ship when it landed in the Mariana Trench. Don't you think they would contact you if they thought this meteor was another alien ship."

"But what if they didn't see it?" Mark said.

"NORAD tracks everything. You told me that yourself after one of your debriefings."

"True."

"And besides, even with that genetic coding of yours, you still had to touch the cube, or be close by in order for the aliens to send the visions to you. You knew nothing about them until the Navy flew you to the *USS Ronald Reagan*. So just how can you be receiving a vision from a meteor half-way around the world from us?"

"Your talents are wasted as an accountant," Mark said as he lay back down. "You would make a great lawyer."

"I would settle for some sleep," Beth replied.

They lay in silence for a while. "How can you explain my dream about a meteor at the same time and place that an actual meteor landed?" Mark broke the silence.

"What?" his wife asked sleepily.

"Landed. That's the key," Mark said. "I need to determine whether it actually landed and confirm the time. If they match my dream, then that is just too coincidental. It would have to be related to the blue-grays."

"Why the blue-grays?" Beth asked.

"Because they were the ones who sent the last visions. It's their technology. It would mean that they survived the wormhole's collapse and are back. I need to learn more about that meteor."

"Well, do it quietly. I need to sleep," Beth replied as she rolled over.

Mark got out of bed and went back to the den to turn on his laptop. Now, how to confirm the time? He couldn't call NORAD. They didn't even know who he was and he doubted they would take calls from civilians asking about meteors in China. How about Space Watch, the folks who mapped approaching asteroids? He remembered a reference during a briefing last year that Space Watch had actually spotted the meteor before NORAD. He started with Space Watch's web site. When that didn't yield any further information, he checked the Department of Energy website, where he found a number of meteor entries, but none recent enough. He always wondered why the Department of Energy monitored meteors.

He found the U.S. Meteor Society and then jumped to its international counterpart. Finally he found a time entry hidden within the text of a blog on the Chinese meteor. A quick calculation confirmed it was within minutes of when he had awakened. But what about the coordinates? It took him another fifteen minutes on the computer before he found a site that would translate the latitude/longitude findings into something he understood. It was in the southern portion of China, heading east to west.

A cold chill went down Mark's spine. He had dreamed of approaching Earth and crossing China from east to west about the exact time this meteor had been sited. It had to be a blue-gray artifact. There was no other explanation for the dream. But had it landed? Try as he might, he could not find any confirmation that it had landed.

What should he do? The last time he had not known about the blue-grays until the Navy transported him to the South Pacific and he touched the artifact. But this time he felt like he was being called personally. So what should he do? Whom should he call? Who would believe him? Could he call the President? And what would he tell him? I dreamed of a meteor? Could he even get through to the President? And what if he was wrong? He would look like the ultimate fool. But what if he was right and did nothing? What if a blue-gray artifact had landed in China? What would happen?

The questions would not stop. And no answers were forthcoming. He finally decided that he would have to alert someone. He could not live with himself if something happened and he had done nothing. But whom? Last year the President had called him personally after Mark refused to believe the local navy officer's story of a strange meteor that appeared to be of alien origin. Should he call the President? Who else could he call? The whole event last year had been hushed up, not many people even knew about it.

But how does one contact the President of the United States? He finally decided he would have to do it the same way he did last year, when he needed to confirm that he was in fact talking to the President of the United States and not some friend of his trying to fool him with a very good impersonation. So, feeling rather like Chicken Little, he called the contact number for the White House listed on the government website.

"This is the White House, how may I help you," a chipper female voice answered. How could someone sound so chipper at one in the morning, Mark wondered?

"Yes," Mark replied. "Ah, yes, this is Mark Williams…" The last time he had said that, he had been patched right through to the President. But that time the President had called him first and was expecting his return call. That was a year ago. This time they weren't expecting him.

"Yes, Mr. Williams, what can I do for you?" the operator repeated, still chipper.

"Please give the President the following message," Mark continued. "Tell him that Mark Williams called and he thinks the blue-grays have returned. Ask him to call me." After having her repeat the message, Mark finished by leaving his cell phone number and then hung up, feeling very foolish and wondering if the message would be delivered or merely placed in the crank call log. If the message was delivered, he would receive a return call immediately. But would they wake up the President for a message they did not understand? Probably not. Not unless his name was on some important person list. Mark chuckled, unlikely. Five minutes passed, then ten. Nothing. Okay, let's assume that didn't work, Mark thought. What should be the fall back plan?

Now that he had decided to take some action, he could not wait for morning. Who were those two Navy officers that had come to his office last year? He remembered they came from Corry Station, but could not remember their names. He wondered if Captain Peters was still commanding the *USS Ronald Reagan*. They had become friends during Mark's short stay and Captain Peters knew all about the blue-grays. A quick Google search confirmed that Captain Peters was still in command and the carrier group was still stationed in the Pacific. He could help, Mark decided. The trick was getting a message through. Now how to do that?

Mark decided the best way would be to go to the Navy base and send a secure message to the carrier. He decided to go to Corry Field since it was a Naval Intelligence and Cryptology station, while Pensacola NAS was only a training command. Also, the two officers who had contacted him before were from Corry. So with some misgivings, he went back into his bedroom to get dressed, while trying not to wake up his wife.

"Where are you going?" a sleepy voice asked after he dropped his shoe the second time.

"Can't sleep," he replied. "I'm still thinking about that meteor. I'm going to run down to the Navy base and send a message to Captain Peters, have him check it out."

"Ok, don't let the cat in," Beth replied as she rolled over and fell back to sleep. Mark was always amazed at how fast she could fall asleep. In all likelihood she had never awakened and would not remember this conversation in the morning. He chuckled as he thought he should have answered: "A UFO landed in the back yard so I thought I would hitch a ride to Pluto for a pizza." Better leave a note on the kitchen counter, he decided as he headed for the door.

He drove down to Corry Station, arriving at the gate close to 2:00 in the morning. Not having a military I.D., Mark knew he would have trouble getting on base and probably even more trouble getting his message sent. But his time in the Army and experience in life had taught him that if you acted like you were in charge and knew what you were doing, people usually assumed that you did, particularly military personnel. Mark pulled up to the front gate. "I need an escort to the Communications Duty Officer," Mark said officially as he handed his driver's license to the armed gate guard.

"What's the nature of your business?" the guard asked unimpressed.

Mark was ready for that response. "Classified." He merely responded. The guard hesitated. "Do you have any military identification?"

"I am not in the habit of carrying military identification for everyone to look at," Mark answered, hoping that the guard would assume that more was implied in that sentence.

The guard was still not impressed. "Are you expected?"

"No," Mark responded, now ad-libbing. "An unexpected event has occurred and I need to send a secure, classified message out ASAP. That's all I can tell you. So if you will hurry and have someone escort me." The guard still hesitated. "Listen," Mark added forcefully. "You do not want to be the one responsible for holding up this communiqué. So I suggest that you get on the horn before you end up guarding a sand dune in the Mojave desert."

The last threat did the trick and the guard stepped into the guardhouse and made a call, while another armed guard watched him suspiciously. A minute later the first guard came back. "They want to know what this is all about."

"Well, you tell them that I am not going to explain it to a gate guard. Either they will have to come here or you can take me to them. I'm not trying to blow up your base. I can leave my car here and you can have ten guards take me to them. I don't care. But we have to do something now. We are running out of time." Mark glanced at his watch for emphasis.

Clearly undecided, the guard went back into the guardhouse and got back on the phone. When he returned he said, "Okay, park your car over there and we will escort you."

"Thank you," Mark replied and pulled his car into the indicated parking spot. A military van pulled up and Mark got in the passenger side while the second guard drove him onto the base. Mark glanced into the back of the van. They were alone. Mark chuckled to himself. If he were really a terrorist he could disable the lone driver with a quick blow to the head and then he would be on base, unsupervised, with the guard's weapon. Now how secure was that? The driver stopped in front of a nondescript, three story, 1940's era building and escorted Mark inside. After traveling down several corridors they arrived at a room marked "Duty Officer." One more hurdle to go, Mark thought to himself as a young Ensign looked up from his desk.

"What's this all about?" the officer asked.

"I have a coded message that needs to be sent by secure transmission to Captain Joseph Peters on the *USS Ronald Reagan*."

"What is the message?"

Mark looked at the guard and then back at the officer. "Let me have a piece of paper." The officer complied and Mark wrote:

Mark Williams is at our location. He says the blue-grays have returned. Wants you to contact him immediately.

"You will have to add your contact information to the end of that," Mark instructed. I will wait for his reply."

"What does this mean?" the duty officer asked.

"That's classified," Mark responded.

"I have a top secret clearance."

"That's not high enough for this," Mark replied calmly.

"How do I know you're not some nutcase off the street?" the officer asked.

"You don't," Mark answered. "And like I told your guard at the gate, you don't want to be the one who holds up this message. You can couch it with anything you want to cover your butt, but just get that portion of the message I wrote down through, now. It's about 1500 hrs. ship's time, I'll wait for the response. If he doesn't know who I am, then you can have me prosecuted for interfering with the military or any other charge you want. But if I am right…" Mark let the last part hang in the air.

The officer hesitated, trying to figure out what to do. He tried to size Mark up, fifty something, fit and trim, graying hair, civilian clothing, casual, yet expensive looking. He had an air of confidence and a sense of authority about him. Not someone who looked like a lunatic. If he were in uniform, he could easily pass as a Captain. The last observation did it. "Wait here," the officer commanded. "I'll get your message sent. But I'm warning you, if this is some type of joke, you'll be in big trouble."

"Make sure it is sent secure," Mark instructed, ignoring the threat. Mark glanced at his watch and sat down and waited while the guard stood by the door. 'I give it fifteen minutes,' Mark thought. 'I should have a reply by then.' The reply actually came back in twelve.

The young Ensign rushed into the room. "Captain Peters is on the comm," he stated breathlessly. "He wants to talk to you. Come with me." With that he escorted Mark down another hall to a communications center and motioned to a telephone. He's on that line."

"Is this line secure?" Mark asked.

"Yes, it is."

As Mark reached for the phone he pointed to the guard and said, "He needs to step out of the room."

"Of course," the Ensign answered and motioned the disappointed guard out of the room.

"You, too," Mark said. The Ensign paused for just a moment before complying, stationing himself outside the glass door where he could watch.

Mark picked up the phone. "This is Mark Williams," he said.

"Mark, Joseph Peters. I didn't expect to hear from you again." Came the friendly reply. Mark had wondered what type of reception he would get from Captain Peters. He had spent the majority of his time as Captain Peters' "guest" onboard the *Ronald Reagan* and had hit it off quite well. But when he left he had not been able to say goodbye, as Captain Peters was too busy trying to get his ship seaworthy after the alien attack. It had actually been adrift for a while, its nuclear reactors in jeopardy while they desperately tried to get the electronics back on line.

"I didn't expect to be calling either," Mark answered. "But I think I've had a new vision and I can't contact anyone over here. Probably because it's past midnight. So I need your help to confirm it."

"Your message says the blue-grays are back," the Captain remarked.

"I think they might be," Mark clarified and then told the Captain the details of his dream and his continuing feeling that he was being contacted again. "I tried to confirm it on the Internet," Mark concluded. "But I could only get bits and pieces, but what I did find was a reference to a meteor in China within minutes of when I was awakened by this dream. That and the continuing sense of contact made me feel that I just couldn't ignore this any longer, the potential ramifications are too great if the blue-grays have come back.

"So, can you contact NORAD and see what they have on it, particularly whether it landed? I think they track this sort of thing. If I'm wrong and it was only a dream, then I owe you dinner the next time you're in Pensacola. But if their satellites confirm what I saw at the same time and place and particularly if it landed, then my only conclusion is that the blue-grays are back and I don't know why. Or for that matter, how. I thought they were gone for good after the wormhole collapsed."

"Okay," the Captain responded. "I'll check with NORAD. Where can I get back to you?"

"Hold one moment." Mark said as he waived at the Ensign who was watching through the glass door. "Captain Peters has to check on something and will call me back. Can I wait here?" Mark asked.

"I suppose you can," the Ensign replied.

"I'll wait here for your answer," Mark told the Captain. "I assume you know how to contact me here, or do I need to put this officer on?"

"You said you were having a little difficulty on that end?" the Captain asked.

"Yes. You know how it is with us civilians. No respect."

The Captain chuckled, "Let me speak to the duty officer."

"He wants to speak to you," Mark said to the officer as he handed him the phone.

"This is Ensign Johnson," the duty officer said and then straightened up as he listened to the Captain.

Mark did not know what Captain Peters said to the young officer, but the change was dramatic. After the call it was all "Sir, this and Sir, that. Do you need anything, Sir?" This was more like it Mark thought.

"Do you have a cot or a sofa?" Mark asked. "It's rather late and I haven't had any sleep. I don't know how long this will take and I wouldn't mind getting a short nap." Mark was shown to a sofa in the XO's office with assurances from the Ensign that he would be contacted the moment Captain Peters called back. Mark looked at his watch. It was past three in the morning. Now that he had taken some action, he was exhausted. He lay down on the sofa and quickly fell asleep.

Mark was awakened several hours later by a commotion outside the door. "What do you mean there's a civilian sleeping in my office?" a very irate voice was shouting. The answer was lost as the door burst open and a senior officer stormed in. "Just what do you think you're doing?" he bellowed.

Mark sat up slowly and rubbed his eyes. "I was sleeping," he replied.

This was not the answer the Commander expected and after a moment of shocked silence, he went off.

Mark just sat back and smiled. It was nice being a civilian, no fear of rank. Mark ignored the tirade and when the Commander took a breath, Mark turned to the Ensign cowering in the corner and asked, "Has Captain Peters called back yet?"

"No, Sir," the Ensign replied timidly.

"Just what is going on? Who do you think you are…" the Commander went off again while Mark continued to sit on the sofa.

"Are you the commander here?" Mark asked during a lull in the tirade.

"I'm the XO," came the reply. "And you have a lot of explaining to do."

"I'm afraid I can't do that," Mark replied calmly. "My mission is classified."

"Classified? Let me assure you, I have clearance. This is the Center for Information Dominance. So what is going on?"

"It's classified," Mark repeated.

"And I told you, I have clearance."

"Not this high." Mark said. The XO started to sputter, threatening to put Mark in jail and "other" threats.

"Look. I'm not trying to give you a hard time," Mark continued. "Why don't you contact Captain Peters on the *Ronald Reagan*? He can decide what information to share with you. I can't."

This answer was not satisfactory to the XO. He shouted some more and then called for security. "You're going to the brig!" he declared.

"Might I suggest that you contact Captain Peters, first?" Mark calmly asked again. "He can probably clear this up real fast."

"I am not going to be intimidated by your fast talking," the XO raved. A minute later a military policeman arrived and was instructed by the XO to handcuff Mark and take him to the brig.

Mark stood up and calmly presented his wrists. As he did, he turned to the Ensign, "Please make sure that Captain Peters knows where to locate me." He then turned to the XO. "I'll say it one more time, if you will contact Captain Peters you can avoid making a very poor career choice here." The minute Mark said that, he knew he had phrased it wrong. It was like pouring gasoline on a fire. The military policeman had to stand aside while the XO screamed in Mark's face, while Mark calmly stood there handcuffed.

As he was winding down, a sailor burst into the room. "Sir, Sir, Sir!"

After three attempts, the XO turned on the unfortunate sailor. "Don't interrupt me…"

To his amazement, the sailor did, "Sir, the President is on the line!"

"The President? The President of what?" the XO sputtered.

"The President of the United States," the sailor responded.

"The President is calling for me?" the XO asked in disbelief.

"No, Sir. For him," he said, pointing to Mark.

Mark tried to suppress his smile. He held up his handcuffed hands to the military policeman as he quietly said, "I probably should take that call."

CHAPTER 2

Mark's call to Captain Peters had the desired effect. Captain Peters contacted NORAD and confirmed the time and location of the reported meteor two days before, NORAD having tracked its entry across southern China. After confirming Mark's report, Captain Peters sent a classified flash traffic message to CINCPAC (Commander in Chief, Pacific) summarizing his findings and noting that the President had personally requested to be informed of any new developments.

This was a bit of a reach. The President had requested immediate notification, but that was a year ago during the first blue-gray incident. Since everyone thought the blue-grays had been killed, either by the other aliens or the collapsing wormhole, it was debatable whether the President's request still stood.

But Captain Peters had not risen to his present position by playing too safe, so he sent the message knowing that without this notation his report would be shuffled along from department to department, wasting precious time. Meanwhile, Mark's phone message to the White House was placed in the crank call category, never to be seen again. Captain Peters' report was delivered to the President when he woke up and the President demanded a personal conference with Mark Williams. It was this call that kept Mark from having to visit the Navy brig that morning.

Mark described his dream and experience of the last couple days, along with his attempts to verify it to the President, concluding with his opinion that the intensity of the call and the timing indicated that this had to be another vision from the blue-grays.

"I thought the blue-grays were dead," the President said.

"So did I," Mark responded. "The ones that landed on the *Ronald Reagan* were killed by the cats, we saw that. And then both alien ships disappeared when the wormhole collapsed."

"Are you sure it collapsed?" the President asked.

"Yes. The information I received from the cube confirmed that."

"Then how can they be back?"

"I could only guess."

"Then guess."

"Either they survived the collapsing wormhole and came back here," Mark answered.

"Or?"

"Or there are more of them."

"How can there be more of them? You told us last year that two alien ships, one cat and one blue-gray, were locked in battle when they both got caught in a collapsing wormhole that accidently transported them to our time. You said they were not time travelers. So how could there be more of them? They are from sixty-five million years in our past," the President said, the tone of his voice clearly indicating that he was upset. "Are you saying that you were wrong?"

"They are not time travelers. The blue-grays' personal cube, the one I got from the dead blue-gray, confirmed that. I have been considering this very carefully," Mark continued. "We know that the first cube they sent, the memory cube, was created solely to get us to help the blue-grays fight the cats. So the information in it, the visions they sent me, may or may not be accurate. But the blue-grays' personal cube was not edited or altered for us. The information I learned from it was accurate. From it I confirmed that they were not time travelers and that only two ships were accidently transported to our time. Or to be completely accurate, I should say the dead blue-gray was only aware of two ships being transported here. Which is probably the same thing.

"The problem is the ships. Last year I described the cat's ship, the one I saw in the visions, as being a jagged, circular shape, like two circular saw blades, lying on their sides, one above the other, connected by some spoke in the center. But the cat ship that attacked the *Ronald Reagan* had only one blade, not two, to use my analogy. Some people theorized that it retracted one blade when it entered our atmosphere. Other people just assumed that my memory of a second "blade" was wrong. I have no idea how cat's ships work. I never received that information in any of the visions.

"As for the blue-gray ship, I was always inside. I never saw it from the outside so I don't know what it looked like. Now I did see a couple blue-gray ships in the memory cube visions. A cat destroyed one, and the other I landed on when inside some type of transport or shuttle. But those ships did not look anything like the ship that landed on the *Ronald Reagan*. Now it is possible that the ship that landed on the *Ronald Reagan* was the same type of ship that escaped from Earth sixty-five million years ago when the cats attacked. You will recall that was the vision when I was drugged and lost most of the vision. I don't know what that ship looked like."

"Don't you know from the dead blue-grays' cube?" the President asked.

"No. I only had contact with that cube for a very short time, so I only accessed a very small part of its information. Which I have already told you about." Mark added, hoping the President would not catch his half-truth.

"But if only two ships came through the wormhole, how could two different ships appear on the *Ronald Reagan*?"

"The cat ship may be the same ship, I don't know. It is very similar. The last blue-gray ship I saw from the outside, the one I landed on in the memory cube vision, was much larger than the ship that arrived on the *Ronald Reagan*. If the ship I landed on is the same one that came through the wormhole, and I am saying 'if' because I don't know if it was or not - the visions skipped on occasion - but if it were, then it is not the one that landed on the *Ronald Reagan*. It was much bigger. The ship on the *Ronald Reagan* could have come from it, like a shuttle or something."

"Which means the blue-grays still have another ship out there. A larger one," the President concluded.

"Yes. A mothership."

"That's a disturbing thought."

"Yes it is," Mark agreed.

"Getting back to this meteor you saw. You think it's calling you?" the President asked.

"I don't know," Mark answered. It's calling, asking to be found. I can hear it even now, faintly. It may be calling anyone who can receive it. After all, why land in China rather than Florida if it's for me?

"They landed in the Pacific last time," the President noted.

"Yes, but they were hiding from the alien cats in the bottom of the Mariana Trench, and then only after getting our attention by coming down on top of a carrier task force," Mark said. "This time they are on land, so why not land in Florida if they wanted me? Remember what I learned from my contact with the blue-gray's personal cube last year, although they requested contact with me, anyone with the same genetic coding should be able to receive their communications. I just happened to be the one they found first. I have never understood that," Mark added. "Maybe they're trying to contact someone else this time. Their contact with me last year was pretty much a failure. I would guess that they're trying to contact a Chinese with the same genetic coding. With China's population, statistically there should be a better chance of finding someone with the requisite genetic code. But I'm just guessing as to all of this," Mark conceded.

"Is there anything more?"

"No. That's it, just a call or command to be found."

"And you don't know what it is or what it wants?"

"No, Sir. But if it is the blue-grays, we will probably find out before too long." The conversation ended with the President indicating that someone would be contacting Mark later that day.

The first thing Mark did when he left Corry Station was to call his wife and tell her about his night.

"You actually were handcuffed?" Beth asked.

"Yes. They had to remove the handcuffs so I could take the President's call."

"I would have liked to have seen the look on the Commander's face during that conversation," Beth said.

"It was priceless," Mark said.

"It's a good thing you left me a note," Beth said. "Or I would have put those handcuffs back on you."

"I did tell you that I was leaving, but I didn't think you would remember the conversation."

"I have a vague recollection of it," Beth said. "So they are taking your call seriously."

"For now anyway. I just hope I'm not Chicken Little yelling the sky is falling. That would be real embarrassing."

"Be careful what you wish for. You really want the blue-grays back?"

"Right. You have a point there. I should just hope that I'm making a big fool out of myself."

"It's not like anyone will know, it's all classified."

"Only the President of the United States, probably the Joint Chiefs of Staff, NORAD, and who knows who else," Mark said. "I will be a laughing stock."

"And we socialize with those people all the time," Beth said. "How will you face them at all the parties?"

"Okay, I get your point," Mark said.

"The worst that will happen," Beth continued. "Is that next time the President will not return your call."

"And we will probably not be on his Christmas card list," Mark laughed.

"What if they ask you to go check it out?" Beth asked seriously.

"How?"

"By dragging you to China, you imbecile. How else? Last time they flew you to the Mariana Trench. What if they ask you to go to China?"

"I hadn't thought of that," Mark said.

"You were never big on planning."

"It makes sense though," Mark said. "I guess we'll just have to wait and see what they want to do."

"But if they ask, what will you do?" Beth persisted.

"I don't know," Mark said. When his comment was met by silence, he continued. "Well, what do you think I should do?"

"I think you should stay home where you are safe and not worry about it," Beth said.

Now it was Mark's turn to be silent. Finally, he said, "Where are you now?"

"I'm on Palafox, heading for the office."

"Meet me at The Coffee Cup, and we'll talk about it there," Mark said, referring to an old time coffee and breakfast shop on Cervantes Street that was an icon in Pensacola, having been there as long as anyone could remember.

The smell of bacon and eggs wafted over Mark as he entered The Coffee Shop. He spotted Beth at a small table near the windows and walked over to join her. A waitress was pouring a cup of coffee for her and he ordered one as well. When the coffee arrived, he ordered grits, eggs and bacon as the tantalizing smells awoke his taste buds and reminded him that he had not yet had breakfast. When the waitress left with his order, his wife jumped right to the issue.

"You want to go, don't you?" she said.

Mark hesitated before answering. "Yea, I guess I do," he admitted. "But just to see what it is. I would be safe," he added lamely.

"You said that last time," Beth countered. "You were on a United States aircraft carrier, surrounded by warships and you almost got yourself killed. In fact," she continued, when Mark tried to interrupt, "you were the only one injured in the entire battle group. Now if you can't stay safe there, how are you going to stay safe in China?"

Mark thought of many responses, but none seemed adequate. His food arrived, buying him some more time. Finally, after their cheerful waitress left, he said, "The problem is that I am the only one who can hear it."

"The only one here, maybe," Beth said. "There may be a million Chinese who can hear it."

"True."

"So let them find it," Beth said. "Let them get caught up in an alien war. It's not your fight. You said the aliens considered us insignificant, why get involved? Let them kill each other and we will just stay out of it. You said they were way too advanced for us. We should just stay out of it."

Mark waited until Beth had finished her tirade. He took a big bite of grits while he considered her remarks. Admittedly, everything Beth had said was true. The aliens did consider humans insignificant. And the only reason the blue-grays had tried to contact the humans last year was because their ship was a science vessel that was outgunned by the cats. They had hoped the human warships could either destroy the cat ship or at least distract it long enough for the blue-grays to escape. Of course that didn't happen. The cat ship had attacked, disabled the *U.S.S. Ronald Reagan*, killed the blue-grays, and almost Mark in the process. It was only when the cat ship was leaving that the wormhole had collapsed, taking both alien ships with it. Mark had assumed and certainly hoped the collapsing wormhole had destroyed the aliens. The passing of a year with no further contact from either species had increased that possibility. But now more than ever Mark was convinced he was receiving visions again. And the visions, or at least the past visions, were all from blue-gray technology. There was no reason for the cats to send these visions. Mark had to laugh at that reasoning. He really knew nothing at all about the cats and very little about the blue-grays, even after having had telepathic-like contact with the blue-grays.

"So why should you get involved again?" Beth's question interrupted Mark's reverie. "It's not like you're some expert."

"Actually I am," Mark said. "At least compared with anyone else. I have had contact with these aliens and I have seen them, even been them during the visions. I can at least put some of their actions in context."

"But the visions you saw occurred 65 million years ago," Beth protested.

"Which to these aliens was last year," Mark said. "And not all of the visions were that old. The last ones were recent. And no one else on this planet, not even the Chinese, have the perspective that I have."

Now it was Beth's turn to be quiet. Mark ate his grits and waited. Finally, Beth replied. "Well, let's wait and see what they decide." Mark managed to suppress his smile. "But you have to promise that you won't volunteer to go. They have to ask," Beth finished.

"I promise," Mark said solemnly, as he wiped up some egg yolk with his toast.

The expected call came from the Pentagon early that afternoon, asking if Mark could be available for a secure conference call at Corry Station in one hour. This time when he arrived at Corry Station they were expecting him and had an escort waiting. He was taken to a conference room where a secure video link was established, much like he had experienced onboard the *USS Ronald Reagan*. He repeated his description of the events of the last three days, focusing on the timing of his dream to the known meteor in China, along with his continuing sensation that something was 'calling' him. There were a number of skeptics in the conference, some more verbal about their disbelief than others. A Colonel from NORAD finally took over the questioning.

"Mr. Williams," he began. "I wonder if you could provide me some details?"

"I'll answer what I can."

"Perhaps you can give me the details of your dream, exactly what you saw. Every detail that you can recall. That would help me compare it to our findings."

Mark paused to consider his response. "My dream," he began, "started in space. It was like a movie, without sound. Visual only. I saw a planet hanging in black space, with stars in the background. I can't tell you what the constellations were, I just saw stars. The planet was bright blue with white clouds. Lots of clouds. It was smaller than the moon is at night. But it approached quickly, very quickly, and got larger and larger until it filled my view. For most of this time, I only saw blue ocean and white clouds. Finally some land began to appear on the horizon. I couldn't recognize it at first, but then I recognized India on the horizon. I orientated myself to that and realized I was traveling west across the Pacific, approaching the Asian subcontinent about level with Korea. I was coming in very fast now. The whole dream probably lasted about a minute or two, or so it seemed to me. It looked like I was approaching China, the southern half. As the view of China filled my vision everything blazed red. I am assuming that was when I entered the outer atmosphere. When the red cleared I was much closer to the ground and saw a landscape streaking beneath me incredibly fast. I was still pretty high, judging from the dotted landscape below. I would say higher than 30,000 feet."

"How do you know that?" the Colonel interrupted.

"Because on a recent commercial flight I took the Captain announced that we were at our cruising altitude of 30,000 feet and I remember what the ground looked like. I was sitting in a window seat. And the landscape in my dream was smaller or farther away than that. Anyway, in the dream I was streaking across the landscape very fast. Much faster than the commercial flight, which seemed like a turtle in comparison. And then as I got close to the ground I saw mountains and these fantastic stone sculptures that rose up hundreds of feet from the valley floor. Row after row, like teeth or trees of solid rock. I must have decelerated significantly, since these last features weren't blurred by speed. And then impact.

There was a momentary vision of brown, like dirt, like I was buried. That's when I woke up. Since then I keep having a feeling or sensation that I am being called. I really can't describe that any better. And occasionally I 'see' a fleeting image of a huge stone pillar rising up above me. Its like a still snapshot and then it is gone. That's about the best I can do for you," Mark concluded.

"Can you describe the stone sculptures better?" someone asked.

"I could draw them better," Mark responded, prompting someone to hand him a pad and pen. "Remember," Mark explained as he drew. "I saw them only for an instant. They were near a mountain range and on low hills. They were like a forest of jagged stone teeth or trees, rising up a couple hundred feet. The last vision I have is just one stone pillar rising up, like a jumble of stone blocks. It looks something like this," Mark finished, holding up the writing pad for the camera. "But imagine hundreds of these side by side."

"How's that compare with your findings?" someone asked the Colonel.

"It tracks all right," the Colonel responded. "We don't have anything as far out as he describes. We don't have any radar reports. The only thing we have is visual and energy readings. We picked it up first at thirty-one point thirteen point forty-nine North ..."

"English," someone interjected.

"We picked it up first about a hundred and ten kilometers over the southeastern portion of China, near Shanghai, to give you a bearing. It was headed west, but decelerating quickly. It traveled in a descending pattern across China until we lost it east of Kunming, which is the capital of Yunnan Province, which is southwestern China. At its last known trajectory it could have impacted, assuming it did impact rather than burned up, in Yunnan Province or even possibly Burma. It's hard to predict."

"That's a pretty wide impact point?" someone else stated.

"I really can't give a better one with any degree of confidence," the Colonel answered reluctantly.

"Why not? Can't you track meteors and predict their impact points?"

"Well, this thing was acting all wrong."

"Wrong?"

"Yes," the Colonel explained. "It made some course changes, not large ones, but course changes nonetheless and it decelerated."

"Don't meteors do that? Doesn't the interaction with the atmosphere and their breaking up cause them to decelerate and change course to some degree?"

"Not like this," the Colonel answered. "When it came in, we thought it was a meteor. But when we received Captain Peters' request, we analyzed the data closer and realized that the parameters were wrong. And the kicker is that we estimate the size of this at about a meter in diameter, and that never changed. It never burned up, at least not while we were able to monitor it."

"So you're saying it is not a meteor?" another voice asked.

"I would have to say, no," the Colonel answered. "Certainly not one that follows any characteristics that we have seen in the past."

"Are you saying it was a ship?"

"I can't say that for certain. It is possible that the course deviations and deceleration were caused by interaction with our atmosphere. But those, coupled with the fact that its size apparently never changed.... well, it is very odd. It could be explained by saying it is a craft of some type. I can't rule that out. But not anything that we have. I don't know," the Colonel admitted.

"What's your best guess?" an authoritative voice asked.

"If I hadn't been briefed on last year's incident," the Colonel began, "I would be at a loss to explain this. But in light of last year's events, I would have to say that in all likelihood this is an alien device. It can't be either of the ships we saw last year though," the Colonel continued. "They were much larger and we are confident in our assessment that the size of this object is no more than a meter in diameter. What it is, I don't know. But I would say that based upon all the facts known to us, we have to assume that it is of alien origin."

"Thank you, Colonel. Any other comments?" the authoritative voice asked the group.

A number of voices broke in, some objecting to the Colonel's conclusions, while others supported it. The general consensus was that for the time being it would have to be assumed to be of alien origin and that further investigation was warranted. There was some discussion of notifying the Chinese authorities, which was quickly withdrawn for a multitude of reasons, not the least of which being that they had no hard information to provide. They finally determined that the best approach would be to send a small team to the area to investigate. Naturally this team would have to be clandestine. Then came the question that Beth had predicted: whether Mark would be willing to accompany the team. It really made sense since he was the only one who could "hear" the call and the theory was that as he got closer, he should be able to pinpoint its location.

Surprisingly, the actual request made the whole thing much more real. Nonetheless, he agreed to be part of the team, which he assumed was probably all CIA. The conference lasted about two hours and upon its conclusion it was determined that Mark would first fly to Japan to get closer while they tried to narrow down the search area and assemble a team. "So how do I get to Japan?" Mark asked, remembering last year's six-hour supersonic flight in the backseat of an F/A - 18 fighter jet.

"We can have a Gulfstream 550 at Pensacola NAS in about two hours," was the reply. "It can take you directly to an Air Force base in Japan, which will be your staging area while we try to narrow down the probable impact point."

That didn't give Mark much time to get home, get his passport and quickly pack, not to mention explain to Beth that she had been right and that once again he was flying off in search of aliens. He called her as he soon as he got to the car.

"Hey honey, its me," Mark said, realizing that Beth's caller I.D. and ring tone would have already told her that, but old habits were hard to break.

"So did they ask you to do to China?" Beth asked without any preliminaries.

"Yes," Mark answered sheepishly. "You were right."

"It was obvious," Beth said. "If they believed you, it is the only logical choice. So where are you now?"

"I'm headed to the house to get my passport."

"Okay. I'll meet you there. Wait for me," Beth said.

Beth met Mark at home and then drove him to Pensacola NAS, where they were directed to a hanger at the edge of the airfield where a Gulfstream G550 was being refueled and serviced. A pair of Navy Officers that Mark recognized from the earlier conference escorted them into the hanger. Mark carried a daypack over his shoulder into which he had thrown his toilet kit, a change of clothes, passport and a book for the flight. They had told him to pack light as they would outfit him for whatever he needed and he hoped they were correct. After a few preliminary instructions, he was ready to leave. Beth hugged him tight as he stood at the boarding ladder for the Gulfstream, reminding Mark of a similar scene one year ago when he had been flown to the *Ronald Reagan*.

"Be safe," Beth whispered in Mark's ear. "No heroics."

"Heroics?" Mark said. "I'm fifty-six years old. I'm not going to do any heroics."

"Promise me," Beth said.

"I promise. No heroics."

"And come back safe."

"I will, promise."

CHAPTER 3

"Déjà vu," Mark thought as he looked out the window of the G550 at the land far below. It was a Friday afternoon last year when a Navy officer had arrived at his office and informed him that a UFO had landed in the Mariana Trench and for some reason appeared to be requesting his presence. That had been the beginning of the strangest nine days he had ever experienced, nine days that he had almost not survived. Now, one year later, he was once again traveling halfway across the world in search of aliens. Knowing that these aliens were hostile made him wonder how safe this trip would be. Last year he had flown in a fighter to the super carrier *Ronald Reagan*, where he had spent his entire time under the protection of the U.S. Navy. Even then he had been shot by an alien and almost sucked into a collapsing wormhole. This time it looked like he would be on a hastily planned clandestine mission to China with only a couple support personnel. He was glad he had not explained that portion to Beth.

While he was enjoying the luxuriousness of the aircraft, the flight attendant told him that he was wanted on a conference call. The attendant situated Mark at the built in desk, positioned the monitor and explained how the videoconference controls worked. He gave Mark an earpiece and activated the conference call. Once Mark was on line, he checked the security settings and then told Mark he could be contacted in the front cabin should Mark have any questions. With that, the attendant left.

After some quick introductions, one of the attendees started the conference. "Mr. Williams, I think we may have narrowed down our search area substantially. I need you to look at these pictures and tell me if they are anything like what you saw." He flashed some pictures on the screen.

"That's it!" Mark responded excitedly. "It's not exact, but that is what I saw when I was zooming over the ground. Where is that?"

"It's in Yunnan Province, China, which is in the southwestern portion of the country. North of Vietnam to give you some bearings. What you are looking at is called the Stone Forest and is considered by many as the first wonder of the world."

"That should narrow it down a lot," Mark remarked.

"Yes and no," the briefer answered. "It narrows it down to a country and region. But the Stone Forest encompasses about a hundred square miles. It was a seafloor two hundred and fifty million years ago. When the sea receded, the limestone eroded over time leaving the karst formations that you see here. There are several of these formations in China and Vietnam, but the one closest to the last point identified by NORAD is in Yunnan Province. Now if you could recognize a particular formation, then we could really narrow down our search."

Mark studied a series of pictures. "No. I can't say I recognize any specific formation. These pictures all show the general shape of what I saw. The last vision I saw was from ground level. But I don't see that in any of these pictures."

"I can download a lot more pictures. I'll send them to you later or show them to you when you arrive here in Japan. Maybe we can narrow the search down that way. But you are sure it landed in this type of formation?"

"As sure as I can be about any of this," Mark said.

There followed some discussion about narrowing the search and it was finally determined that they would focus their efforts on the Stone Forest area. Even then, there were not a lot of assets to use, particularly since this was located in China.

"Too bad it didn't land in Burma, that would have been much easier," someone complained.

"It's not Burma anymore, it's Myanmar," someone else corrected.

"Even Vietnam would have been easier," another said.

"Vietnam is south of the flight path," someone objected.

"I don't think you would have gotten me to go to Vietnam," Mark interjected.

"Vietnam is not our enemy anymore."

"That may be true," Mark replied. "But old memories are hard to ignore."

"Okay folks, let's focus," a voice scolded. The conference continued for another 45 minutes before they disconnected, promising to call back after they had worked out some more details.

Mark was sleeping when the attendant woke him up for the next conference. It took Mark a few minutes to orientate himself. He glanced at his watch: 1:00. Why were they calling at 1:00 a.m.? Of course, he did not know what time it was for the caller. After splashing some water on his face from the little sink, he followed the attendant to the desk where the conference call was set up. This time there was only one other person on the call.

"Here's the plan," the caller explained without preamble. "You will fly into Japan as planned. There you will transfer over to a civilian plane and fly into Shanghai, where you will make a connection to a domestic flight to Kunming, which is the capital of Yunnan Province. You will meet up with your team there and set out by car to search the Stone Forest. Hopefully, by the time you get there, we will have been able to narrow the search area."

"So how do I go into China?" Mark asked. "Just walk in and say I'm a tourist looking for aliens?"

"Actually, it is really quite simple," the agent explained to Mark. "We aren't changing anything. You will be flying in with your own passport and background. Don't change anything. The only thing that we have added is that you signed up for a hiking tour of China from a travel company you found on the Internet. You will meet your fellow tour members once you arrive in China, which will explain why you don't know anyone else. The goal of this travel package is to explore and hike portions of China, some of which are tourist attractions and some of which are not. That will provide you with flexibility during your travels.

"We will have travel brochures available for you when you arrive in Japan along with a Chinese Visa. You will have to look at your passport stamps so you will be able to say how you travelled commercially to Japan. Otherwise, everything is simple. The best cover story is the truth," the agent ended triumphantly. "Oh, one other thing," the agent added. "We had to put a rush on the Chinese Visa. Normally they take ten days or more. If anyone asks, you booked this trip months ago. The paperwork we will give you confirms that. However, you forgot about the visa requirement and had to do it at the last minute."

"So I shouldn't have any trouble getting in, even with the visa issue?" Mark asked a bit nervously.

"No. None at all," the agent assured him. "Stuff like that happens all the time. China is a huge tourist destination now and since ninety-nine per cent of your cover story is true, this will be a piece of cake. Just go in, take care of your business, and come back out."

"So who am I meeting up with?" Mark asked instead.

"We are currently assembling the team. You will meet them in Kunming."

Mark assumed that meant the other personnel would all be CIA, assembled at the last minute. 'Why did this sound like a bad spy novel?' Mark asked himself. "What about clothing? Hiking boots? Luggage? I don't have anything but what I'm wearing right now," Mark stated.

"We are putting that together for you now. You'll get it once you arrive."

"I hope it fits," Mark said, louder than he intended.

"Don't worry, it will," the agent answered as he wrapped up the briefing.

It seemed to Mark that he had just fallen asleep again when they landed at Yokota Air Force Base in Japan. "It's 1:18 a.m., Sunday morning, local time," the flight attendant announced as Mark collected his few items and was whisked to some nondescript conference room in a nondescript building on base. There he was met by a group of nameless civilian-looking individuals, who briefed him on the upcoming mission and provided him with the promised travel documents and brochures, taking his passport so they could get the required stamps. They had him read over the travel brochures and prepped him on how to answer questions about finding the company online and deciding to try out their tour. Mark noticed that one of the documents even showed the cost of the tour, with confirmation that it was paid with his Visa card about five months ago.

"Boy you sure handle the details," Mark said, looking at the Visa charge. "That's my Visa number!"

"Yes," one of the agents replied. "And your account has the charge posted to it also."

"You charged my account?" Mark asked surprised. "You really think it's necessary to have a Visa debit charge on my account?"

"Better to be safe than sorry," the agent replied. "I doubt that anyone will check, but if they did it would blow your cover story and since your cover is otherwise bulletproof, it would be really foolish to skip such an obvious detail."

"I hope you also thought to post a payment for that charge," Mark added, somewhat seriously.

"Yes, we did," the agent replied.

"You think they are going to check that kind of detail?" Mark inquired nervously.

"Normally not," was the reply. "They would only check if somebody came up on their radar. Consider it an insurance policy."

"An insurance policy?"

"If they get suspicious. If so, this may be enough to allay any suspicions. You are easy to research. You're all over the net. And best of all, it's all true. The perfect cover."

"So how would I show up on their radar?" Mark asked, getting more and more nervous about entering China on this mission.

"You shouldn't. Your paperwork and cover is clean. This is in case you do something over there that raises some suspicion."

'Such as talking to aliens,' Mark thought, but did not say. Hard to explain to a Chinese official why an alien ship was landing in their country and he was talking to them.

"So what do I do if we find the blue-grays?" Mark asked.

"Blue-grays?" the agent asked puzzled.

"You were briefed on this mission, weren't you," Mark asked confused. "Why I'm going into China?"

"Certainly, I was told that an unknown object is believed to have landed in China and you're going in to retrieve it."

"Well, that's basically it," Mark replied, none too optimistically. "So what do I do if we find it? What's the plan then?"

"Your handlers have that information. They'll take care of it."

'Great,' Mark thought. 'This is getting better all the time. I wonder what the plan is if it really hits the fan and we're in the middle of China? Probably deny all knowledge and leave us there. Like *Mission Impossible*, except I'm not Tom Cruise and I don't know the script! Would they be considered spies? The CIA agents probably were spies!' That thought was not comforting. But there was nothing he would be spying on, nothing Chinese anyway, Mark reasoned. He finally decided to ignore that line of thinking or he would scare himself to death before the mission even started.

When Mark finished the briefing, he was taken to another section where they outfitted him. "Here's your luggage," an agent explained as he pointed to a backpack. "We chose this backpack as it is easy to carry if you have to hike anywhere, yet will also pass as luggage, particularly with your hiking cover story. This part detaches and can be used as a daypack. This is a money belt. Wear it inside your shirt. Keep your money and all important papers, such as your passport and visa in here, particularly when out and about. This is high tourist season, prime time for pickpockets. In your luggage are several changes of clothes, hiking shoes, sandals, hat, and personal items such as toothbrush, toothpaste, soap and a razor. These sandals are for the showers. Don't walk into the showers barefoot. You need to familiarize yourself with these so the first time you see them won't be in customs. We have a first aid kit with basic supplies: Band-Aids, aspirin, tweezers, that sort of thing. There are also water purification tablets, anti-diarrheic tablets, insect repellant, wet wipes, and toilet paper. Except for the big hotels or restaurants, you will need the toilet paper. Now this is important. Don't drink the water! Ever. Don't drink anything that you don't see them break the seal on. Not unless you want a bad case of the trots. Now, if you do get the trots, here's some medicine that will help. An anti-diarrheic. But the main thing is prevention. If you get the case of the trots, make sure to stay hydrated. These pills, mixed with clean water, will help."

The agent pulled some other items out of the pack. "It's summer-time, so it will be hot. They say you're from Florida, so you understand that. Wear loose clothing, hat, sunglasses and drink plenty of fluids. Clean fluids. We're going to give you hepatitis A and B shots, but otherwise your shots are current. These are anti-malaria pills. Your handlers will tell you whether you need to take them."

Mark was beginning to have second thoughts about this whole adventure when the agent wrapped up his briefing. "And we have the obligatory tourist stuff, Chinese travel book, travel brochures, Chinese language phrase book..."

"Wait a minute," Mark interrupted. "Chinese language phrase book? I don't speak Chinese."

"Of course you don't, that's why you have the phrase book," the agent replied as if talking with a slightly stupid person.

"You expect me to have to speak Chinese?"

"No, your handlers speak Chinese. It just looks better for you to have a phrase book. You can at least try to speak the language." Mark felt a little better. For a minute there he thought they were sending him in without anyone who could speak Chinese. The agent finished his briefing, "And finally we have binoculars, camera and a compass."

With that Mark was given two shots, his passport was returned with the appropriate stamps and he was handed over to another agent who escorted him to a waiting car. "Where are we going?" Mark asked the new agent as they climbed into the back of the car and the driver pulled away from the building.

"Narita International Airport," Mark's nameless escort replied. "You'll catch a flight there to Shanghai."

"By myself?" Mark asked, nervously.

"No. Your tour guide will meet you at Narita and escort you through security and take you to Shanghai."

Mark was relieved. He didn't think he was up to doing it by himself. He couldn't even read the street signs. "What time is it?" he asked, looking at his watch, which was still on Central time.

"4:52, local time. The sun will be coming up shortly."

"What day is it?" Mark asked, feeling a bit foolish.

"Sunday."

"I think I lost a day somewhere," Mark complained, feeling exhausted.

"You can make it up. We have a two hour drive to the airport and it's several hours to Shanghai."

"Narita," Mark tried the pronunciation.

"Yes, you got it," the agent said. "It's just east of Tokyo."

"We're in Tokyo?" Mark asked surprised, looking out the window.

"Why, yes. Narita is sometimes called Tokyo International. Yokota is west of Tokyo. We will skirt south of the city. Hopefully, we will not pick up too much traffic this early. Now remember," the agent added. "Once you get out of this car, you are a tourist traveling to China. Always stay in character, unless your handlers tell you it is okay to speak openly. Don't mention the mission, Yokota, your flight here, anything that is not consistent with you being simply a tourist. China is a police state and you don't know who may be watching or listening. So always stay in character."

"You trying to scare me to death?" Mark asked, thinking that he was already doing a good job of that.

"Just trying to ensure you have a successful mission."

They ran through the details of his cover story again as Mark watched out the window. But soon it looked like any other foreign country, except of course the street signs, which were a dead giveaway. As they approached the airport, his nameless escort made a cryptic phone call. Upon arriving, he escorted Mark into the concourse, while the driver stayed with the car. They walked towards the ticket counter, where Mark was turned over to yet another individual. This man looked to be in his early 40's. He was a tall, thin, fit, rugged looking man, dressed in khaki outdoor clothes, with a daypack slung over one shoulder. Mark thought he looked like a stereotypical outdoorsman right from the cover of an L.L. Bean catalogue.

"My name's Bob," the man introduced himself to Mark. "I'm with World Wide Tours and I'll be taking care of you on this trip."

'Bob?' Mark thought. 'What kind of spy name was Bob? What ever happened to Bond, James Bond?' Mark almost said that before remembering the warning to stay in character. So instead he stammered, "Uh, pleased to meet you. Looking forward to the trip."

"Good, we have a great trip planned," Bob continued, sounding like a tour guide. "Now come with me. We have to clear security and then it's China Eastern Airlines to Shanghai." Mark followed Bob through security and then to the gate. They had another hour wait after they cleared security, during which Bob talked incessantly about the tour package Mark had purchased. "Of course, some of the trip is really up in the air right now. It will depend on the weather and what areas the group decides to visit. Like the brochure said, each trip is unique and individualized for that particular group. I'm sure you will enjoy the spontaneous nature of our tour package."

"That seems to be me," Mark ad-libbed. "Every trip I've done recently has been spur of the moment."

Bob glanced at Mark before picking up his conversation. "Great. You're going to have the trip of your lifetime."

Mark didn't like his choice of words. "As long as it's not the last trip of my lifetime," Mark mumbled, too quietly for Bob to hear. A short time later they boarded China Eastern Airlines flight MU 272 for the four-hour flight to Shanghai. During the trip, Bob never broke character, telling Mark about how the company researched its travel sites and how he was going to enjoy his hiking adventure. Mark's responses were muted as his anxiety rose the closer they got to China. Beth was right. He had no business doing this. At home it seemed like fun, an adventure. But as he flew towards China the reality of the situation started to overwhelm him. What was he doing? He wasn't prepared to meet the blue-grays. He didn't have a clue what was going on? He leaned his head against the cabin wall and closed his eyes.

Unbidden, the events of last year swirled through his mind. Landing on the *Ronald Reagan*, touching the alien artifact, which turned out to be a memory cube. The visions from the memory cube and the dead blue-gray's personal cube had provided Mark with some of the alien's history. He had witnessed the blue-grays experimenting with velociraptors 65 million years ago when they were attacked by an alien species Mark referred to as the cats, who attacked by crashing asteroids into the Earth, devastating the planet and causing the extinction of the dinosaurs.

He had watched as a cat ship and a blue-gray ship were caught in a collapsing wormhole, propelling them to present day Earth, where the age-old battle continued. When the blue-grays tried to contact Mark on board the *Ronald Reagan*, the cats attacked, killing the blue-grays and shooting Mark. They tried to leave through a wormhole, only to have it collapse, taking the cat and blue-gray ships with it. Mark thought they were gone for good. But now they seemed to be back...

"You air sick?" Bob's question broke into Mark's reverie. "You're awfully quiet."

"Oh," Mark stammered, realizing he ought to be very excited about his upcoming trip. "Oh, just tired. It's been a long flight getting here. Just jet lagged."

Bob seemed pleased by Mark's response. "Sure. I understand. You'll get a chance to rest in the airport. This flight arrives in Shanghai at 12:53 local time, which will probably be too late to take the next flight to Kunming, which leaves at 14:20. An hour and twenty minutes won't be enough time to get through customs, change concourses, get through local security and onto the next flight. That means we have to catch the late flight, which leaves at 21:00 hours, that's 9 p.m. So you will have plenty of time to catch up on some rest."

"Okay," Mark answered unenthusiastically. Sleeping in airports had never been his idea of a quality rest.

Mark did not know what he had been expecting, but Shanghai Pu Dong International Airport was not it. It was huge and modern. He could have been in any international airport in the world as he walked down the giant concourse, done in glass and steel, listening to flight announcements in Chinese, French, German and English, to name the languages he recognized. China's customs made Mark nervous, but there really was nothing to it. He had no contraband and was not, he told himself, on any clandestine mission against China. There was nothing that would make him suspicious going in unless he suddenly started shouting, "I confess, I confess!" Getting back out might be different; it all depended on what happened.

"We need to go to the national section of the airport," Bob said after they passed through customs. "There we will catch our flight to Kunming city, which is the closest airport to our destination. We will meet the rest of our tour group there, except for one, who is just flying in and should meet us on this flight." Bob led Mark through the airport and checked them in for the new flight, before directing Mark over to a nearby waiting area. As Mark walked to the indicated chairs, he looked up and saw a familiar face walking towards him.

"Jeffreys!" Mark shouted, barely avoiding adding Sergeant as he ran over and gave Jeffreys a big bear hug. "What are you doing here?" Jeffreys had been Mark's Marine escort on board the *USS Ronald Reagan* one year before. Although initially just an escort, as Mark's visions became more intense, Jeffreys ended up protecting Mark from himself and saved him from being killed by the cat. Although the experience lasted only nine days, the bond between them had grown quite strong.

"I couldn't let you have all the fun by yourself," Jeffreys responded. "After you told my... boss," he avoided saying Captain in public, "...he thought I might like to join you on your next exotic vacation." Mark did not miss the sarcastic inflection.

Mark laughed. "Now I know I'm going to enjoy this trip. I was a bit concerned not knowing anyone. But now it should be fun. Although I recall you can be quite a drill sergeant at times," Mark couldn't resist adding. "I remember last time we must have hiked thousands of miles and gone up at least 1 million staircases."

Jeffreys laughed. "Just trying to keep everyone in shape," he added easily.

"Watch out for this guy," Mark said to Bob. "He can hike you into the ground three times over and still want more. He's an absolute fitness fanatic." Mark did not know what Jeffreys' cover story was so he did not say anything about the Marines.

"Welcome to the tour," Bob said, shaking Jeffreys' hand. "I'm Bob. I'll be your tour guide."

"I'm William Jeffreys. But most people just call me Jeffreys."

"Ok, Jeffreys," Bob responded. "I trust you didn't have any problems getting here?"

"None at all," Jeffreys responded. "Your associates did a good job."

"We aim to please," Bob responded. "Our flight is not until 9 p.m., so you both have time to rest. Let me know when you get hungry and we'll get something to eat before the flight."

It was frustrating for Mark to be with Jeffreys all afternoon and not be able to ask him what had happened after he left the *Ronald Reagan*. He was also careful not to ask any personal questions, as he did not know Jeffreys' cover story. Bob must have picked up on the awkward silence. "Have you been on a tour together before?" Bob asked.

"Yes. A year ago," Sgt. Jeffreys responded. "It was quite eventful."

"That's an understatement," Mark agreed.

"I would love to hear all about it," Bob said. "But right now you both should probably get some rest. It helps with jet lag. We will have plenty of time to share stories once we meet up with the rest of the group."

Despite Mark's lack of sleep, the hustle and bustle of the airport and his keyed up nerves kept him from resting. He had still not slept when they finally boarded their flight and had an uneventful three and a half hour trip to Kunming Changshui International Airport.

"I can't believe how nice these airports are," Mark said after they had landed. "I don't know what I expected, but these airports are state-of-the-art."

Bob laughed. "It should be. This airport was opened January 2012 as a replacement for the old airport, Kunming Wujiaba."

A short taxi ride took them into the city of Kunming. It was 1:30 in the morning and even Bob's attempts to be the enthusiastic tour guide were muted by fatigue. Kunming was a large, modern looking city, complete with neon signs and non-stop city life. So far, China was nothing like Mark had expected.

They stopped at a nondescript hotel where the other three members of the team were already set up. Bob made the introductions as they walked into the room. The three new members of the group were composed of two Asians and one Filipino. The Asians were Hwang and Chin and the Filipino was Juan. Mark doubted those were their real names. To Mark's uneducated eye Hwang and Chin looked like the hundreds of Chinese that he had passed in the airport during his trip, they could blend in perfectly. Juan was easily spotted as Filipino with his darker skin and island look. Bob, Jeffreys and Mark cried out 'American', or at least European. There would be no blending in for them. That was the reason for the hiking tour cover story. Fortunately for Mark's nerves, the airports had been full of tourists of all nationalities so he had not felt too conspicuous. He could only hope that would continue as they got closer to their destination.

"Is the room clean?" Bob asked as they settled in.

"As far as we can tell, yes," Hwang answered. "Swept it twenty minutes ago."

Mark glanced at the floor and then tried to play it off as he realized they were talking about electronic bugs, "Good, pull out the map and give us your report," Bob instructed.

"Don't these people ever sleep?" Mark whispered to Jeffreys as he glanced at his watch. "It is almost two a.m.!"

Hwang spread a map out on the table. "Ok," he proceeded. "We are here," he pointed on the map. "Our search area is the Stone Forest, here. He circled an area with a grease pencil. "This is a huge tourist attraction, so parts of this area are real crowded. Other parts are rural. It all depends on where we go. Now, we have traveled these roads," again pointing to the map, "and talked with several people on the streets and at local shops. We have tried to keep our inquiries circumspect, casually bringing it up in conversations so as to prevent anyone picking up on the fact that we were interested. So far, nothing. No meteors, nothing unusual, nothing."

"It's worse than trying to find a needle in a haystack," Chin complained. "We don't know what we are looking for, what it looks like, or where it is. As far as I'm concerned, it's a huge waste of time and resources. You wouldn't believe the project they pulled me off to come out here. Nine months of work lost, just because some lunatic wants us to find some space junk."

Mark noticed Jeffreys surreptitiously cast a worried glance at him. 'Probably remembering my short temper last year,' Mark thought with a chuckle. Instead of blowing up, Mark simply smiled at Chin and said, "I happen to be that lunatic."

His comment was met by an awkward silence, followed by Bob quickly changing the conversation. "Ok, well, you two probably need to get some rest and then we can decide what to do next." He ushered Mark and Jeffreys to a back room. "Do you mind doubling up here?"

"Not at all," Mark replied.

"Sure," Jeffreys chimed in.

"Why don't you get some rest while I talk with the other guys and get updated," Bob suggested. "We will have an early start in the morning."

"Well that was a refreshing change," Jeffreys said laughingly after Bob left the room.

"That we get a chance to rest?" Mark asked.

"No, that you didn't beat the daylights out of that Chin character after his last comment."

Mark laughed. "I'm not getting those type of visions. But who knows, this trip is young. I might take a shot at him, yet."

"So what type of visions are you getting?" Jeffreys asked.

"What have they told you?"

"Not much really," Jeffreys admitted. "Only that you received some type of vision and thought that the blue-grays had landed in China. Actually, I wouldn't have been here at all except that the Captain took me aside and told me that you had contacted him and that you may be searching for blue-grays again. Since I had been your escort last time, he asked whether I would be interested in accompanying you."

"Probably thought I needed your help to survive," Mark interjected.

"Something like that," Jeffreys admitted, much to Mark's surprise. "Well, you got to admit," Jeffreys explained when he saw Mark's look. "You needed a lot of help last time, and that was in the comfort of the carrier. The Captain figured that since I had first hand experience taking care of you during the visions..."

"And since you're a Marine," Mark interrupted.

"And since I'm a Marine," Jeffreys continued. "The Captain felt that you could probably use my help."

"He's probably right," Mark agreed. "And I am really glad that you came along. Its nice to have a familiar face along." A moment later Mark added, "Tell me. Did they order you to accompany me?"

"Order? No. Once they told me about it, there was nothing short of a Court-Martial that would keep me away. Why do you ask?"

"Well... just in case things go bad. I wouldn't want it on my conscience that you were ordered to be here with me. After all, it did get a bit dicey last time..." Mark let his sentence drift off.

"Dicey? You mean when that cat thing shot you, or when you had a cardiac arrest during one of the visions, or when the wormhole collapsed and nearly sucked you into it?" Jeffreys asked sarcastically.

Mark laughed. "I was referring to the fact that I could never get enough to eat!"

"Right!" Jeffreys agreed laughing. "So what type of visions are you getting now?"

Mark told him about the dream and the events that followed. "So you see," Mark concluded. "This vision, if that is what it is, is very different from last year. This was visual only, with no feeling of a body. No other 'channels,' if you will. And then there is this constant call. I am assuming it's the blue-grays; because, well, what else could it be? It is certainly not from the cats, there are no emotions."

"Emotions?"

"Yes," Mark said. "The visions from the memory cube where I was a blue-gray didn't have any emotional channel. Just the five senses. Those brief visions I received after the contact on the submarine, the ones where I was a cat, were overwhelming because they contained very strong emotions. They were hard to recover from."

"Those were the ones that set you off," Jeffreys said, rather than asked.

"Yes."

"You never told anyone in the briefings that you were the cat in the vision, just that you had seen them," Jeffreys noted.

"You're right. I never told anyone. I was afraid the Captain would lock me in the brig if he knew some of the visions kind of overwhelmed me. Probably would have if you had not covered for me."

"I figured it was something like that."

"I thought you had, or at least suspected."

"Can we make a deal on this trip, though?" Jeffreys requested seriously.

"What?"

"Since we are in a hostile country, rather than the relative safety of the *Ronald Reagan*, will you promise not to keep anything from me? I will agree not to tell the others. But if I am going to do my job, I really need to know everything that is going on."

Mark thought for a minute. "You're right. You've got a deal."

"Thanks," Jeffreys said. "Hopefully, it won't matter. But just in case."

"Right, just in case," Mark agreed.

"So, are you still getting anything?" Jeffreys asked. "Any new visions now that you are in China," Jeffreys added when Mark didn't reply.

Mark paused. "Let me concentrate for a minute." Mark sat on the bed and closed his eyes. Up until now he could feel the call, like background noise it was there, but he had to concentrate on it. Now that he was closer, he could feel it much clearer, calling him, urging him on. Mark turned his head left and right to confirm. Yes, he could sense its direction now. He was certain. Mark opened his eyes and saw Jeffreys watching him closely.

"I guess it's time to get this show on the road," Mark said as he stood up and headed to the other room. Mark interrupted a hushed conversation among the other four members of the team when he walked in with Jeffreys close on his heels. "Hope I'm not interrupting anything," Mark said, although it was clear that he was. "I thought that since we will be working together, we might as well put all our cards on the table." Mark's comment was met with silence. 'Great,' he thought when that didn't work. "Ok, why don't you tell me what you all know and I'll fill you in on any details you may have missed?" More silence as the other agents glanced at each other. Mark started to wonder if these guys had been briefed or whether the spy mentality kept them from opening up. Either way, it was not helping his confidence level. "All right, why don't I start," Mark finally said. "Do you know about the incident on the *Ronald Reagan* last year?"

After a moment of silence Bob answered. "We, or at least I," he glanced at the others for some type of confirmation. It didn't come. "I was informed that there had been an incident, but I am not sure of the details."

"Is that the same for you?" Mark asked the other three.

"Basically," Juan replied. Hwang merely nodded and Chin sat stone-faced.

Mark swore under his breath. "This is absolutely intolerable!" Mark said. "Not your fault," he quickly added. "But you have no idea what you are getting into.

I can't believe it. Well, I'm probably going to break every rule in the book. But if we are going to work together and have any chance of getting out of this in one piece, you need to know all the facts. Let me start with introductions. I'm Mark Williams, that's my real name. And I'm nobody. Not CIA, not State, nothing. I'm just a civilian who got pulled into this mess last year by shear chance. Actually, by the luck of the genetic lottery. I'll explain that in a moment. This is Staff Sergeant Jeffreys, U.S. Marines, currently assigned to the *USS Ronald Reagan* in the South Pacific. Jeffreys was my escort during my stay on the *Ronald Reagan* last year and has personal knowledge of what I am about to tell you, because he was there and he saw it. What I am about to tell you is classified so secret, I don't even know what they call it. And, let me warn you, I doubt you will believe anything that I am about to tell you," Mark continued, specifically looking at Chin, "because I didn't believe it until I finally saw it first hand."

"Last year NORAD tracked what they thought was a meteor approaching the Earth. Its point of impact was near the *USS Ronald Reagan's* task force, so a couple of fighters were sent to observe it. They videotaped it with their gun cameras as it made its descent towards the Pacific Ocean. And then, right before impact, it stopped and hovered in mid-air before landing in the ocean and disappearing. The hunter/killer submarine *SSN Louisville* was attached to the task force and tracked the object to the bottom of the Mariana Trench. Shortly thereafter the object began transmitting a message to the submarine. That's when I was called." Mark neglected to mention that it was his web site that was being transmitted to the submarine; the story was unbelievable enough as it was. "It seems that for some reason I have the right genetic makeup that allows me to receive communications from the blue-grays."

"The what?" Hwang interrupted.

"Are you saying these are aliens?" Chin asked in disbelief.

"Yes," Mark responded simply. "And I didn't believe it either until I saw them." Mark ignored Chin's snort of derision and continued. "To make a long story short. There are actually two alien species that we know of, the blue-grays and the cats. Those are names that I made up for them simply because one species is blue-gray colored and the other is somewhat feline in shape. We have not been able to successfully communicate with them, so we have no idea what they call themselves.

"Anyway, the blue-grays and the cats are at war with each other and their war spilled over to the Earth last year when two of their ships entered our solar system. The blue-grays' ship was damaged and was hiding in the depths of the Mariana Trench, while they tried to enlist our aid in helping fight the cats. As I said, communication was difficult. The blue-gray finally landed its ship on the *Ronald Reagan* and we were about to make first contact when the cats attacked. They disabled the *Ronald Reagan*, killed the blue-grays and left, taking the blue-gray ship with it and leaving the *Ronald Reagan* adrift in the Pacific. Although rumors spread, the event was hushed up. You may have heard the cover story about damage done by a reentry vehicle." Mark looked for some type of confirmation. When there was none, he simply continued.

"That brings us up to today. For a year, nothing happened. Then Wednesday afternoon, China time, NORAD tracked a meteor crossing China and disappearing near here. The meteor's flight characteristics were abnormal and they believe it is of alien origin. Once again it is sending out a signal, a signal that I can hear, which is why I am here."

His comments were met by silence. "You expect us to believe that?" Chin asked finally.

"No," Mark answered realistically. "I said that I did not expect you to believe it. But ask yourselves: Why did they put together this team so hurriedly? And if you can, call your boss and ask them. Although they might not be in the loop either. I don't know." More silence followed.

"So what do you expect from us?" Hwang asked.

Mark was surprised by the question. "I didn't think I was running this show. I thought you were." Mark turned to Bob, "What are your orders?"

Bob answered for the group. "We were told to assist you in finding some space debris that is believed to have crashed in this area and to be very discreet about it as the debris is classified."

Now it was Mark's turn to look surprised.

"What are your orders?" Chin asked Jeffreys.

"My orders are to protect Mr. Williams," Jeffreys answered simply.

"Okay," Mark broke the ensuing silence. "How about this? You don't have to believe me. I understand that it's an unbelievable story. But you do know that something landed here from space, that's straight from NORAD. The question is: What is it? There are only three options: it could be a meteor, a piece of space junk, or, if my version is correct, something alien. Either way, our mission is to find it and to do so before the Chinese do. Now I am not going to ask you to believe me. Jeffreys didn't believe me at first, not until he saw it first hand. But what I am asking is that you remember what I've said, so if, or rather when it turns out that I am right, you will be able to react quickly and appropriately. Remember, the blue-grays are only here to use us in their fight against the cats. And the cats hate the blue-grays and probably us now as well. The cats are fast and deadly. They will not hesitate to kill you on the spot."

Mark saw Chin glance skeptically at Hwang at that remark. "Don't believe me," Mark addressed Chin directly. "That's okay. Just be prepared in case I'm right. I'm trying to keep all of us from getting killed during this little adventure."

Mark paused. The long silence that followed was finally broken by Bob, who Mark considered the leader of the group. "Well, now that we are here. What ideas do you have on how to find this...," Bob paused, "...object? We have been making inquiries and have come up with nothing."

"I told you, I can hear it. I can tell you what direction to look." Mark ignored Chin's raised eyebrows. Instead, he closed his eyes and concentrated on the signal. He turned and opening his eyes, he pointed. It's this way. Now where's that map of yours?"

They spread the detailed topographical map out on the table and Mark had them orientate it with a compass and show him where on the map they were located. Once orientated to the map, Mark closed his eyes again to confirm the signal and then looked at the map. He pulled off his belt and laid it in a straight line across the map. "It's in this direction," Mark explained. "I don't know how far, but I am sure of the heading. Mark's belt cut almost straight across the grease marked circle outlining the Stone Forest.

"That certainly narrows the search parameter," Jeffreys noted, looking at the map.

"Yes, but look at this area," Hwang complained. "They call it 'Stone Forest' for a reason. Huge, jagged stones jutting straight up. This isn't pastureland or even plain forest. You could hide an infantry company in there."

They studied the topographical map. Hwang removed the belt and drew a line with a grease pencil where the belt had been. "How narrow is this heading of yours?" he asked Mark.

"Narrow?"

"How wide a corridor does it cover?" Hwang added.

"I don't know."

They studied the map some more. "Are you sure you saw jagged peaks?" Hwang asked.

"Yes, lots of them."

"Then we should start here," Hwang said, pointing to a spot on the map near the line he had drawn. "It's near your heading and it has a large concentration of stone peaks."

"What is it?" Bob asked.

"It's Naigu," Hwang explained. "It's northeast of Shilin, which is considered the main entrance to the Stone Forest. There is a town around it, but it's less touristy than Shilin."

"Why not start at Shilin?" Juan broke his silence.

"Too far south of the line," Hwang explained.

"What are the odds that it is located in this area?" Jeffreys pointed to the part of the map showing pastureland between the outcroppings of stone.

"With my luck, I'd say zero," Mark answered. "I saw a lot of rocks right before impact. I'm afraid I have to agree with Hwang.

"Ok, then it is decided," agreed Bob. "That's about sixty or seventy miles away, so we will start early in the morning."

"And hunt for aliens," Chin added sarcastically.

"And hunt for aliens," Bob said seriously.

They broke up, Mark and Jeffreys heading to the back room to rest.

"You sure have mellowed," Jeffreys joked as they closed the door. "I barely recognize you."

"You mean Chin?" Mark asked. When Jeffreys nodded, Mark continued. "Yea. He's a jerk. But I've dealt with jerks before. You just ignore them. But he better hope that I don't get a cat vision when he's around or he will be in for it!"

CHAPTER 4

The next morning came too early. It was still dark when Bob shook Mark awake. Jeffreys was already up and dressed. "Don't you ever sleep?" Mark complained to Jeffreys.

"It's morning! Time's a-wasting," Jeffreys responded brightly.

Mark resisted the urge to hit him. "It's not morning until the sun comes up and right now it's dark."

"I'm a Marine, we get more work done before most people wake up, than they accomplish all day."

"No, you got that wrong," Mark grumbled. "That's actually an Army saying and the true version is: 'we waste more time before most people wake up, than they waste all day.'" Despite his complaining, Mark rolled out of bed and got dressed.

"Here's the plan," Bob said, when Mark entered the main room. "We'll take the SUV to Naigu. It will be a tight fit with the packs, but we should do all right.

Mark looked around the room. "Where are the others?" he asked, when he noticed that Hwang, Juan and Chin were missing.

"They already left," Bob explained. "Consider them the advance scouting party. They took the other car."

Bob led them out of the hotel and down an alley to a blue Daewoo Matiz SUV. Even though it was a four door, it was a tight squeeze getting all three of them and their gear inside.

"They call this an SUV?" Mark asked as he squeezed in. "I think it's smaller than a VW bug!"

"It beats taking the bus," Jeffreys stated from the back, where he was sharing space with three backpacks.

"Now remember our cover story," Bob instructed as he navigated the tiny SUV out of the alley onto the main road.

"I know, I'm here on a hiking trip I found on the Internet," Mark interjected.

"Right," Bob agreed. "But we can be more specific now that we have a goal. The goal of the trip is to hike portions of the Stone Forest. That's why we have that area circled on the map and have detailed maps of the region. We will tour some of the standard tourist areas, but we will also explore some of the lesser traveled areas. This is high tourist season so there will be a lot of people. That should be a sufficient explanation for us traveling back roads if the need arises. Just pay a lot of attention to the different stone formations. You have a camera in your backpack. Take lots of pictures of the stone formations when we head out. Oh, and don't take any pictures with any of us in them. You and Jeffreys can be in them, but no one else. That's real important. Now you can nap if you want. We have about an hour and a half drive. When it gets light, we'll stop and grab some breakfast."

Mark leaned his head against the window and watched the sleeping city pass by. The city quickly turned into farmland as they headed out on highway G78 to Naigu. Mark dozed fitfully. He didn't have any more visions, but he could still feel the alien call, so he knew they were headed in the right direction. They stopped at Yiliang at first light. Mark and Jeffreys stayed with the car, while Bob went to get some food. In less than 15 minutes they were crammed back into the little car heading to Naigu as Bob did not want to waste any time.

"Here you go," Jeffreys said to Mark as he handed him a bag containing rice and some type of fish. "Enjoy your breakfast," he chuckled, knowing Mark's penchant for good food.

"What is this? Aaggh, you have got to be kidding. You were supposed to get some food, not raid a dumpster!" Mark complained.

"This is...," Bob explained. Mark didn't understand the Chinese word for their meal, although he had a few choice words for it, none of them flattering. "Fish is very common here and very nutritious," Bob continued.

"Then you can have mine," Mark offered. "I'll eat the rice."

"You think that is bad? Check this out," Sergeant Jeffreys said, laughing as he reached into the bag and pulled out a skewer that he handed to Mark.

"You are not serious!" Mark exclaimed as he looked at the skewer, holding it as far away from him as he could in the small car for fear it would bite him. "Is this really a scorpion on a stick?"

"Looks like several," Sergeant Jeffreys said.

"And you expect me to eat this. You sure this is not some type of Special Forces' weapon?" Mark continued.

"It's actually a delicacy," Bob answered. "It's quite a popular food."

"Good," Mark replied. "Then you can eat it, too. I don't intend to be killed by my food, even if it is already dead." Mark handed the skewer to Bob who proceeded to eat it like a shish kabob, right off the stick.

"That's real gross," Mark said as he watched in disgust as Bob ate.

"You are such a food snob," Jeffreys said.

"Why couldn't the blue-grays land in France? Or Italy?" Mark said. "Then we could have some real food. At this rate I might even be willing to eat at McDonald's."

"They do have McDonald's in China," Bob replied. "But probably not in Naigu, that's too far out.

"See, we don't have to worry about aliens taking over the world, Jeffreys quipped, "McDonald's already has."

"I'm not sure which is worse," Mark laughed, "the aliens or McDonalds."

"I've never known McDonalds to kill anyone," Jeffreys answered. "But those cats are pretty mean."

"There is that," Mark agreed. They drove on in silence. As they neared Naigu they started spotting some rock outcroppings.

"Is that what you have been seeing?" Jeffreys asked.

"That's similar," Mark said. "But a lot of them."

"Just wait till we get to Naigu," Bob said. "You'll be seeing a lot of those. It's not much farther now."

Twenty minutes later they pulled into Naigu and parked the car. Hwang and Juan met them in the parking lot. "Chin is up at the entrance," Juan reported. "We've been asking around, but no one has seen anything." They took a couple of light daypacks, but left the rest of their gear in the SUV. They walked to the top of the small hill that the town was built upon. At the top, the Stone Forest began.

Mark stopped, stunned. "This is incredible!" he said as he stared out at the huge stone outcroppings that rose up hundreds of feet, row after row of incredible shapes. Even Jeffreys stood in awe.

Bob interrupted the mood. "Perhaps you have a suggestion as to which direction you would like to explore first?"

It took Mark a minute to realize that Bob was asking if he could still sense the direction of the call and was phrasing it circumspectly since there were other tourists around who might overhear him. Mark closed his eyes and concentrated. He could hear the call all right and it seemed to be louder. He opened his eyes and pointed. "Straight in," he said, realizing that he was pointing right to the main gate. "I don't know how far, but it's clearly this way."

"Okay folks," Bob commanded. "Let's be tourists." They headed for the entrance to Stone Forest, where they met with Chin who had obtained tickets for them. "Don't forget your camera," he added to Mark. "You want to have plenty of pictures for the folks at home."

It was not hard to act like a tourist. They walked in and were immediately struck by the majesty of the huge stones jutting straight up hundreds of feet. The paths between them were narrow and winding, giving a feeling of being on an alien planet. Only the trees that grew between the stones, or sometimes out of them, provided any sense of normalcy. It was magical, forbidding, and alien all at once. They walked in silence, staring up at the stone structures rising above them.

"This could get real awkward if a blue-gray or a cat showed up around one of these corners," Jeffreys whispered to Mark, "particularly with all the tourists here." Indeed, despite the early hour the paths were packed with tourists, so thick that at times they had to wait before taking the next path.

"That wouldn't be good," Mark whispered back. "Although with all these people here, it doesn't appear that anything out of the ordinary is happening."

"Not yet anyway," Jeffreys added, still in a whisper. "Have you figured out what you're looking for yet?"

"No. But it's in this direction," Mark added, pointing down the path.

When the path started to twist back, Mark stopped the group, indicating that they were starting to move away from where he wanted to go. Chin pulled out his map, which showed that they were at the end of this particular grouping of stones and that the path would be taking them back to the starting point. Mark looked at the map. "We need to go this way," he said.

Chin studied the map. "Not on this path, you can't. We can't start climbing here, not with this crowd," he indicated the passing tourists.

"What's on the other side?" Mark asked frustrated.

"This goes on for a short while, then there are some pastures or open fields and then there is another karst formation, a lot bigger than this one, but less touristy," Chin responded.

"I think we'll have to go there," Mark decided. "If we get to the other side, I should be able to tell which direction to go from there."

"Okay," Bob agreed. "Let's finish our tour here. And remember to take some pictures. Can't be a good tourist without photo evidence."

"Oh, yea," Mark said. He had forgotten all about the camera. On their way back to the entrance Mark made a point of taking several pictures and had Jeffreys take a picture of him standing next to one of the rock formations. When they got back to the car, they gathered around the map to plan their next move.

"That next formation is about three kilometers long and covers this hillside," Chin explained, outlining an area on the map. To get there we have to go back down the road we came in and then head north on highway zero-six-eight. That will take us up the west side of the formation. Now to get to the exact other side of where we just walked, we will have to go down these dirt roads and then hike across these fields. There does not appear to be any structures there, but we better have some explanation ready if a local farmer comes by and we are walking across his field." They drove the route Chin had outlined and before long were off the main road and driving down a dirt road between pastures.

They stopped in a valley and Bob turned to Mark. "Up that hill is the back of where we just walked," he said pointing. They got out of the car and Mark closed his eyes while Jeffreys surveyed the area with a small, but powerful set of binoculars.

"It's not there," Mark said, opening his eyes. "It's coming from that direction," he added, pointing to the karst formation on the second hill. "Somewhere in there. Can we get up in there?" Bob motioned for the team from the second car and they got out and spread the map across the hood, while Bob told them what Mark had said.

"Those are dirt roads," Chin stated. "If they are not too bad, we can certainly make it in our vehicle." Mark glanced at Chin's car, which looked like a Jeep Wrangler knock-off. "Whether you can make it in that SUV, I can't say. I told you we needed two Jeeps," Chin added pointedly to Hwang.

"And I said we didn't want to look like a military convoy," Hwang defended.

"We have what we have," Bob interrupted the quarrel. "The question is how to use the resources we have."

"We can all fit in the Jeep," Jeffreys pointed out.

"But what about the backpacks?" Juan asked.

"Either leave them with the SUV or strap them to the roof rack if you're afraid they'll be stolen," Jeffreys stated. "Either way, we can come back for the SUV later."

"I don't want to leave it here," Bob objected.

"You think someone will steal it here?" Mark asked, surprised.

"No. My concern is that someone will report it abandoned. The last thing we want is the PSB checking on us," Bob explained.

"PSB?" Mark asked.

"Public Security Bureau," Bob explained. "It's their police force." A cold chill went down Mark's spine. In the excitement of the hunt he had forgotten that he was in China with a bunch of CIA agents. "Here's what we'll do," Bob decided. "We'll go with Chin in the Jeep up the mountain. Juan, you take the SUV around here and we will meet you on the other side. That's only a couple kilometers, so we can keep in radio contact if necessary, but keep the power down, we don't want to be broadcasting all over the place."

"You have radios?" Mark asked surprised. He hadn't seen any.

Bob paused before reluctantly answering. "Our cell phones have radio capability. It's not a function we like to advertise. It allows us to communicate within short distances without our signal getting picked up by the cell towers where it might be monitored." Mark wondered what other gadgets they hadn't mentioned, his curiosity almost getting the better of him as he thought of all sorts of James Bond devices. "Can you tell how far it is?" Bob's question broke Mark out of his reverie.

"Uh. Oh, no. It's that direction," Mark said pointing again. "And it feels stronger. But I can't tell distance."

"Could it be on the other side of this formation?" Bob asked, pointing to a field and lake on the map.

"I don't know," Mark confessed. "I had visions of these formations, so I doubt it would be in a field or a lake."

"Let's hope it's not much farther," Chin stated. "Once we get past that lake we get into the mountains."

"That would be just my luck," Mark said quietly to Jeffreys.

"Okay," Bob concluded. "We stick with our plan. Juan, you might as well check out the other side while we take our trip up this hill. We'll keep in touch." They transferred the backpacks into the SUV, but took their daypacks with them. Then Juan took the SUV back to the main road, while Chin headed up the hill towards the karst formation with the others in the Jeep. Bob opened up his tablet PC and a satellite view of their surroundings appeared, along with a dot representing their location. "Go down this road here," Bob instructed Chin while pointing down a dirt lane. "We have to go through this field, then we can pick up a better road on the other side that will take us right up the center of this karst formation. It winds about a little, but it beats walking."

"I'll bet you anything that we start walking any time now," Mark said under his breath to Jeffreys.

"Jeffreys, can you get this gate?" Bob interrupted as they came to the edge of a field.

Jeffreys jumped out of the Jeep and ran over and opened the gate. The Jeep passed through and Jeffreys closed the gate before getting back in.

"Back home a farmer would shoot you for trespassing," Mark whispered to Jeffreys as he got back in and they started driving down the field.

"Chinese don't carry guns," Chin grunted from the front. They passed through the field and after passing through another gate got on the "main" road that would take them through the karst formation. It was a dirt road, not much bigger than a lane wide.

"Good thing we didn't bring the SUV," Sgt. Jeffreys commented as they bounced over another pothole. They drove up the small mountain, while Bob monitored their process on his laptop.

"Is that a real time feed?" Jeffreys asked, eyeing the laptop display.

"It will be," Bob answered hesitantly. "It's a little extra program we buried in the software. Again, not something we want to advertise to the locals. They don't like our satellites hanging over them, spying on them."

"Can the sat's see what's up ahead?" Jeffreys asked.

"The satellite just came up on the horizon a few minutes ago," Bob said. "I should get their feed any moment now." As he said it, the screen flashed, to be replaced with an almost identical screen, but with additional details. "Here it is," Bob explained as Jeffreys and Mark leaned over the seat to view the laptop. "Ok, here we are," Bob pointed to a moving square on the screen. "We appear to have some locals up ahead," Bob stated as he pointed to some dots on the screen. "They appear to be on foot. No sign of anything... alien," he concluded.

"The blue-grays don't show up very well on satellite sensors," Mark said a bit defensively.

"Convenient," Chin simply stated as he concentrated on driving.

"Not very friendly," Mark commented as he waved to an elderly couple that they passed as they continued up the hill.

"Foreigners in a noisy, polluting car, interrupting their hike in the country," Bob explained.

"That will be the least of their worries if the blue-grays are here," Mark whispered to Jeffreys.

They rounded another corner before Bob announced, "We are at the top now, any ideas?

"Can we stop?" Mark asked. "I can't get anything while we are bouncing around in the car." They stopped and Mark got out of the car. Closing his eyes, he slowly turned a complete circle in order to confirm his sensation. Ignoring Chin's contemptuous snort, Mark opened his eyes and pointed. "It's this way. And I have the distinct impression that we are close." Jeffreys orientated them on the map while Bob studied the satellite display on his tablet.

"The road turns the wrong way here," Bob remarked. "And it does not come back to your heading until after we leave this karst formation. You did say that you saw this type of formation in your vision?"

"Yes. Very similar to these," Mark agreed, eyeing the majestic stones rising above them.

"The next formation is not until here," Jeffreys said, indicating on the map he was holding. "That's a pretty good distance away. If you feel that we are close, then it's going to be in this area here, which is only about a half a mile wide as the crow flies."

Bob considered for a moment. "Ok," he decided. "Chin, park the Jeep. It should be fine here. Grab your packs and lets go for a hike. Jeffreys, you and Mark lead. Chin, Hwang and I will follow. Do you need a bearing?" he added to Jeffreys.

"Already have it," Jeffreys said as he grabbed his pack and slung it over his shoulder. He pulled out a compass and then with the map in one hand and the compass in the other he waited for Mark to get his light daypack on. "This way is the point you indicated," he said to Mark as he pointed to a path between two of the towering rocks.

Mark closed his eyes for a moment to confirm his bearings before heading in that direction with Jeffreys at his side. They walked in silence. Jeffreys scanning the terrain like the Marine he was and Mark torn between the grandeur of his surroundings and the increasing call sounding in his head. They wound their way through the maze of giant stones, Mark choosing his way by closing his eyes and listening to the call in his head, while Jeffreys checked his compass bearings.

They traveled for about fifteen minutes, before Jeffreys touched Mark's arm. "You sure it's this direction?" he asked softly so as not to be overheard by the others when Mark started to take a path to the left.

"Why?" Mark asked puzzled.

"Your compass heading would have us go this way," Jeffreys explained. Mark closed his eyes to confirm his direction.

"This is the right direction," Mark stated.

"Ok," Jeffreys said as he took the new compass bearing. "Lead on." They traveled another ten minutes winding through the giant stone structures when Jeffreys stopped Mark again. "Your course is drifting left," Jeffreys explained, pointing to his map and showing Mark how they were deviating from first the original course and now the new course.

Mark closed his eyes again and frowned. He turned back and forth before opening his eyes. "It's this way," Mark stated while pointing left. "I'm sure of it."

"What's going on?" Bob asked as he caught up.

"Just checking the course," Mark explained.

"We're off course," Chin stated, holding out his compass.

"What's on the satellite?" Jeffreys asked Bob, who was carrying his tablet.

"Can't get any detail inside the formation here. The angle on the satellite is too great. But we are heading to the road. We'll pick up more detail when we get there," Bob answered.

"Just chasing our tails," Chin muttered.

"It's this way," Mark insisted to Jeffreys. "I can feel it. It's strong and close."

"What direction?" Jeffreys asked. Mark closed his eyes before pointing to his left. "You sure?" Jeffreys asked, looking at his compass.

"Absolutely," Mark said.

"Then it's moving," Jeffreys stated. "Because a minute ago it was over there," Jeffreys pointed a few degrees to the right of where Mark had last indicated.

"That way goes to the road," Bob noted.

"Then we better get to it before they do," Mark said and headed off at jog. Jeffreys quickly caught up with Mark as they wound their way through the stone formations.

"If we are really close and it is the blue-grays, or worse, the cats," Jeffreys said to Mark when they slowed to get around a boulder, "we might not want to just run up to them." Mark responded with an irritated look. "Remember, they weren't really friendly the last time we met and we didn't part on the best of terms. I seem to recall you shooting at them."

Mark paused. "Good point," he conceded as he slowed his pace to a fast walk. "Keep your eyes open."

"Always," Jeffreys muttered. They hadn't traveled 100 yards farther before Jeffreys grabbed Mark's arm and pulled him down. "Something is moving up ahead," Jeffreys whispered in Mark's ear. Keep down." Jeffreys started moving forward in a crouch. Mark couldn't help but follow, trying to mimic the Marine's actions, as the call in his head seemed to get louder. Mark looked back and noted that the others must have realized something was up as they were crouched down as well. A moment later Jeffreys waved Mark up to his position. "It's a local," Jeffreys whispered. "Appears to be by himself."

"We need to get past him," Mark explained quietly. "We are close, real close. I can feel it. We need to hurry."

"Then let's just walk by him," Jeffreys stated. "We're tourists. We can do that."

"Okay," Mark agreed and they stood up and picked up their pace. They quickly closed the distance with the Chinese, who was threading his way slowly and slightly unsteadily through the formation. They were almost upon him when he noticed them approaching. He turned, shouted out in alarm, and ran away back down another trail.

"That's not good for public relations," Jeffreys said jokingly. "But he's out of our way now. We can pick up our pace." He started moving out, but stopped when he realized Mark was not following. Mark stood still, staring back in the direction of the departing Chinese. "Come on," Jeffreys said. "It's okay, we didn't do anything wrong."

"No," Mark answered. "It's him. He's got it. What ever it is. He's got it."

"You sure?" Jeffreys asked.

"Yes," Mark continued. "The call is coming from him. We have to catch him!" With that Mark started running down the trail the Chinese had taken.

"The local has it," Jeffreys yelled back to the others, who had stayed back a bit. Then he quickly caught up with Mark who was weaving through the maze of towering stones. At one point Mark stopped and looked around confused, before heading off in a slightly different direction.

"This guy's fast," Mark gasped as he slowed to negotiate a fallen rock.

"He can't be too far ahead," Jeffreys replied. "I can probably catch up with him."

"He keeps changing course," Mark objected. "And then we'll be separated and lost in this maze."

Jeffreys considered that and stayed with Mark. After all, his mission was to protect Mark and they had already lost the others with all their course changes. They rounded another fallen boulder and were coming upon a recognizable trail when a bright red glare filled the sky above their heads. Without hesitation, Jeffreys grabbed Mark and pulled him to the ground. "Quick, over there!"

Jeffreys said in a whisper as he rolled under a low rock outcropping, dragging Mark in with him. Huddled under the ledge, Mark panted for breath. Red light bounced strange shadows among the rocks.

"That's the same red light we saw..." Mark started.

"...when the cats attacked the ship," Jeffreys finished in a whisper.

"You have quick reflexes," Mark whispered back.

"I'm a Marine," Jeffreys whispered. "What do you suggest we do now? If that is the cats, they almost killed you last time. And you don't have a vest on and I'm unarmed."

Mark craned his neck to try to look out from under the ledge. The red glare had faded and then disappeared. "Do you think they're gone?" Mark asked.

"I wouldn't count on it," Jeffreys replied. "If it's the cats and they pinpointed this thing from space, they shouldn't have any trouble finding it here."

"I can still feel it. It is close. That direction," Mark added, pointing down the trail. "Let's see if we can get closer," Mark said as he cautiously started crawling out from under the ledge. A loud arcing sound filled the air and Mark collapsed.

Mark opened his eyes. The solid rock ledge was inches above his head and someone was holding him tight from behind. Claustrophobia started to engulf him when Jeffreys' voice whispered in his ear, "Quiet!" Mark froze. He strained his senses, trying to figure out what was going on. There was nothing, not even the sound of birds. After several long minutes passed, the birds started chirping again, a sure sign that what ever had been there was now gone. A few minutes more passed before Jeffreys released Mark.

"Are you okay?" Jeffreys whispered.

"Yes," Mark whispered back. "What happened?"

"What do you remember?"

"The last thing I remember is an arcing sound. And then I woke up with you trying to suffocate me."

"You collapsed right after the arcing," Jeffreys said. I dragged you back under the ledge. What happened to you?"

"It was like a shock. A psychic overload," Mark tried to explain, still whispering. "I could feel the call. It was loud, and close. And then suddenly it was hugely amplified like a clap, or a cymbal."

"Can you hear it now?"

"No. It's gone," Mark answered puzzled. "It was this way. But now it's gone."

"I guess we better check it out," Jeffreys said. "But carefully. Did you see something go past us when we were under the ledge?"

"No," Mark answered. "What did you see?"

"Something went by. I heard soft padding and thought I saw a blur of something. It was too quick to really see."

"What do you think it was?"

"My guess is a cat."

"You mean a cat alien?" Mark asked.

"Yes. It wasn't a kitty cat."

"Great," Mark said sarcastically.

"And I heard two shots," Jeffreys continued. "Two arcing type shots that the cat used on the *Ronald Reagan*."

Cautiously they crawled out from under the ledge. Jeffreys bent down and picked up a fist-sized rock as they started down the path.

"What do you think you're going to do with that?" Mark asked.

Jeffreys smiled ruefully. "A rock against a cat armed with a gun that can shoot lightning?" Jeffreys said. "Probably nothing, but it feels good to hold it."

They cautiously crept around the next rock formation and emerged in a small clearing. The unmistakable stench of burned flesh filled their nostrils. Looking around, they spied a burnt corpse lying sprawled on its back on the other side of the clearing.

"Stay here," Jeffreys whispered before creeping around the perimeter of the clearing, stopping at the corpse. Looking around nervously, Mark cut across the clearing to stare at the corpse. It was the Chinese they had been following. The corpse lay on its back, face contorted in agony, arms missing and chest and abdomen blown apart and burned.

"That confirms it was a cat," Jeffreys said quietly, breaking the silence. "Same type of wound as the blue-gray."

"And probably what I would have looked like if I didn't have that Kevlar vest on when the cat shot me," Mark added.

Jeffreys merely nodded. "So, what do you think he had?" Jeffreys asked, studying the dead man.

"Hard to say," Mark replied. "What ever it was, the cat got it. Probably destroyed it. I don't feel it anymore."

"He was probably holding it in his hands when he got hit," Jeffreys speculated. "Do you suppose it was a cube? Like the one the blue-gray was trying to give you last year when the cats attacked?"

Mark thought back to the events on the *Ronald Reagan*. The blue-gray standing in front of him. Reaching for the cube. The flash of psychic power that knocked him back. The overwhelming urge to touch the cube. Everyone thought it was another memory cube. It was not. It was a control cube. Designed to control whoever touched it. The same type of cube the blue-grays used to control the velociraptors and countless species before them.

Two things had saved Mark that day. The control cube was too strong, having been untested, and the arrival of the cats. Otherwise Mark would have been under the blue-grays' control. Could the blue-grays be sending control cubes to China? That was a terrifying new idea.

"Possibly," Mark answered when Jeffreys repeated his question. "But what ever it was. It's gone now."

"It may be for now," Jeffreys comment interrupted Mark's thoughts. "But this confirms that both the blue-grays and the cats are back. Somehow they survived the collapsing wormhole and they are continuing their war here on Earth." Mark merely nodded his agreement. "We need to find Bob and get this information back to Washington," Jeffreys continued.

"What about him?" Mark asked, glancing at the corpse.

"We'll let Bob decide. It's his show." They headed back along the trail the way they had come. They could have called out, but both were nervous about advertising their presence, just in case. They traveled slowly and warily, carefully looking around the giant stone pillars before committing to a path.

"You sure we're headed the right way?" Mark asked after walking for what seemed an eternity.

"We're headed to the road," Jeffreys answered from his position in front of Mark.

"How do you know?" Mark asked suspiciously. "I have a pretty good sense of direction, but I'm completely turned around in here."

"I have a compass," Jeffreys said, turning and holding out the compass.

"Oh," Mark replied sheepishly. They traveled in silence for a while longer and emerged on the road within 100 feet of their parked jeep.

"Still locked," Jeffreys said after trying the door handle.

"You suppose they got lost?" Mark asked.

"Might have," Jeffreys agreed. "There is a lot of territory out there and we made a lot of twists and turns during our chase."

"You don't have a cell phone on you by any chance?"

"No such luck."

"I guess we could yell for them," Mark suggested a bit reluctantly.

Jeffreys pondered that for a moment. Finally he said, "I guess we don't have a choice. But lets find cover first, just in case our unwelcome friend is still around." They moved down the road away from the car and found some places to hide. Then Jeffreys went back to the car before he started yelling out for Bob. He yelled three times and then sprinted down the road and hid. They waited for ten long minutes. When nothing happened, Jeffreys repeated his yelling and hiding. After another long ten minutes passed Jeffreys said, "That's not working. We'll have to go back in and find them."

Before going in, Jeffreys made a point of orientating Mark on the map and making sure Mark had his compass and knew the compass heading to get back out. "No sense getting everyone lost," he said. Reluctantly they went back into the Stone Forest, trying to retrace their route as best they could.

"Now I know how they could get lost," Mark said as they consulted their compasses yet again when trying to decide which path to take. "I am completely lost."

"This is not the same way we went," Jeffreys admitted. "But the compass bearing is true. We should be able to find our way."

"We're going to have to yell for them, though," Mark said. "They could be off course by fifty feet and we will miss them. And they don't have a compass bearing to go to." Jeffreys reluctantly agreed so every few minutes they yelled out Bob's name, hoping that the cat had left. The closer they got to the clearing, the more reluctant they were to yell out. When they got to the clearing the corpse was still there and Mark had to force himself to yell out for the others. "Any ideas?" Mark asked when no one responded. Jeffreys thought for a while. "Let's head back to the Jeep, but take a slightly different route so we cover more territory."

"And if we don't find them?"

"We deal with that when we get there."

"I hope you know how to hot-wire a car," Mark continued. "We probably have about an hour or two of light left and I really don't like the idea of spending the night out here."

"This is supposed to be a camping trip, isn't it?" Jeffreys said, actually bringing a smile to Mark's face. Jeffreys chose another path out of the clearing and led them around a huge rock outcropping. He travelled about fifty feet before taking a compass bearing for the road. "BOB, CHIN, HWANG!" he yelled, pausing to listen for a response. Receiving none, he checked his compass and headed down a different path. "BOB, CHI..." Jeffreys froze. Crouching, he waved Mark to get down.

Mark's heart was in his throat and he wondered if he would die from a heart attack before the cat came around the corner. Jeffreys waved him forward. 'Can't be a cat,' Mark reasoned. Jeffreys wouldn't be waving him forward. His heart beating in his ears, Mark inched closer. Jeffreys was pressed against the rock, peering cautiously around the corner. Finally, he straightened.

"Stay here," Jeffreys whispered and slid around the corner. Mark waited; crouched down against the rock face, heart pounding, while imagining all sorts of horrors. Mark almost yelled out when Jeffreys came back a minute later. "I found them," Jeffreys said quietly. It's not pretty. The cat found them first." Mark followed Jeffreys around the corner. In the middle of the path lay Bob,

Chin and Hwang, about ten feet apart and in about the same condition as the dead Chinese back in the clearing. "They didn't have a chance," Jeffreys was saying. "Caught in the open."

Mark looked down at the charred corpses as Jeffreys started to search the bodies. He found a set of keys on Bob and located three cell phones, all fried. They found pieces of Bob's tablet computer strewn across the path. It had taken a direct hit. When Jeffreys finished his inventory, Mark asked, "Now what?"

"We take some pictures and get the hell out of here," Jeffreys said. "We can meet up with Juan."

"What about them? Shouldn't we take them?

"Not without a body bag. We'll send someone back. Let's get moving." Jeffreys checked his compass bearing and led off at a swift pace. Mark needed no encouragement to follow. They made it back to the road and the Jeep in record time and soon Jeffreys was heading for the rendezvous point with Juan at the other side of the karst formation.

"You might want to slow down a little," Mark said as they slid around a turn. "I would hate dying in a car wreck after having survived the cat." Jeffreys only grunted, but Mark noticed that his speed decreased. The sun was setting when they emerged from the Stone Forest. In the distance they could see the main road. Mark was never so glad to see a paved road in his life.

"There's the SUV," Jeffreys exclaimed as they came up to the intersection with the main road and parked behind the SUV. Juan was already standing beside it waiting on them, cell phone in hand.

"Where have you been?" Juan started to say. "I've been calling..." "Where are the others?"

"They're dead," Jeffreys said.

"The cat got them," Mark added.

"What cat?" Juan asked puzzled.

"The alien cat," Jeffreys explained, showing Juan the pictures of the dead men. "Did you see anything? Did you see their ship? A meteor looking thing? Anything?" Jeffreys asked.

Juan stared at the grisly pictures on the cell phone trying to comprehend. "What did this?"

"The cat," Jeffreys repeated. "The alien cat. It attacked. Just like last year on the *Ronald Reagan*. Did you see its ship? Looks like a meteor coming down."

"I saw a red streak, like a meteor," Juan finally answered. "But then it was gone. If I had been looking the other way, I would have missed it. It was quick."

"Do you have a sat phone? We need to report!" Jeffreys asked.

"No," Juan answered, obviously still trying to comprehend what they had told him.

"How do you report?" Jeffreys pressed.

"Bob does, on the laptop. It's encrypted."

"Laptops fried. You must have a back up plan."

"I've got a phone number. It's for the tour company. But it's an open line. Not secure," Juan added for Mark's benefit.

"We'll have to call that then," Jeffreys decided.

"Wait a minute," Mark interrupted when Juan lifted his phone. "I've been thinking about this on the way down the mountain. We are still in China and we have four dead bodies that we have to explain, unless you want to spend the rest of your life here."

"Four?" Juan interrupted.

"Yes," Jeffreys explained. "The cat killed a local also."

"Oh, great!" Juan sighed.

"Right," Mark continued. "So unless you want to be the prime suspect in a quadruple murder investigation, we have to play this just right."

"What do you suggest?" Juan asked.

"How good is your cover story?" Mark asked.

"Pretty good," Juan replied. "I work in China, have for years. Full background. I signed up for this tour because I wanted to see the sights and get out of the city for a vacation. It should hold pretty well."

"Jeffreys? What's yours?" Mark asked.

"Same as yours," Jeffreys replied. "All original. The only thing they added was that I contacted the travel agency to go on this tour during my leave. It should be airtight, it's almost all true."

"Ok," Mark continued. "Here's what I'm thinking. You have to look at this from the Chinese point of view. They have four dead bodies, one local and three Americans. And three American witnesses who saw nothing. We have to stick with our cover story."

"What about the alien?" Juan asked.

"You think that the Chinese will believe a space alien came down and killed them?"

"I'm having trouble believing it," Juan admitted.

"Exactly," Mark continued. "So, we stick with the cover story. We all just met and this was our first outing. Bob is with the tour group and he knows all the details. We are just along for the ride, or the walk. Anyway, we toured the first site and we have the pictures to prove it. Then Bob decided to let us tour this second formation, much less touristy. Juan, you opted out. Had enough for one day, so you agreed to take the other car and meet us here. You can give all the details of what you did and how you were getting frantic or pissed when we were so late. But you didn't see anything, especially not a meteor. Let them get that from someone else, assuming someone else saw it. We don't want to be the only ones who saw it.

"The rest of us went up that mountain and then went for a hike in the karst formation. Jeffreys and I teamed up and Bob, Chin and Hwang teamed up. Ok, here is where it is crucial," Mark addressed Jeffreys. We were just hiking. We got separated from the others only because we took a different route around one of the formations. Then there is a lightning bolt out of nowhere. It knocks us down, but we were not hurt. Then we find Bob, Chin and Hwang and also some Chinese person, all of them apparently hit by lighting. After we overcame our obvious shock, we found Bob's keys and came down here to meet with Juan and then immediately after telling Juan what happened, we called the Chinese authorities. And while waiting for the authorities, we also called the only number we had for the tour group to let them know what happened, particularly since we are alone in China and don't know what to do next." Mark paused while they considered his story.

"We need to explain the wounds," Jeffreys objected. "And the ship. Certainly someone saw it, probably thought it was a meteor."

"No," Mark maintained. "That's where criminal defendants always get in trouble. They try to explain too much and get caught in the details. Unless you want to try to explain the cats to the Chinese, which they will never buy, at least not from us, then you keep it real simple. All we know is that we were hiking and something hit us. We think it must have been lightning. That would certainly explain the burn marks. It makes perfect sense from our perspective."

"But the wounds," Jeffreys continued.

"Let the Chinese figure that out," Mark explained. "The important thing is that there is no weapon that we have that could have caused that, so we couldn't have done it! We are as baffled as everyone else. So unless the Chinese discover the cats, then they will have to accept that it was lightning."

"And if they spotted the cats?" Juan asked.

"Then we are as shocked as they and probably won't believe their explanation. Who believes in space aliens?" Mark finished and waited while they considered his comments. After some more conversation they all agreed. Since Juan spoke Chinese, it was agreed that he would call 110, the Chinese equivalent of 911, and make the frantic report that lightning had killed four people. Mark and Jeffreys held their breaths while they listened to Juan's call, understanding none of it. At one point, he interrupted his conversation and asked them in English, whether they could find the bodies. Jeffreys nodded his head 'yes,' but Mark shook his head 'no.' "Not in the dark." Juan continued his Chinese phone call. When he was done, he explained that they would have to drive back to Naigu, where they would meet with the Chinese authorities.

"You know how to get there?" Mark asked Juan.

"Yes."

"Okay. Then you lead and Jeffreys and I will follow in the Jeep. Give me your phone and the contact number. I'll make the call while we are."

"Remember, it's not a secure line. The Chinese may be listening," Juan warned.

"I'm actually counting on that," Mark replied. Juan gave him the phone and showed him the number on contacts and they started the short drive back to Naigu. "I hope someone answers this number," Mark said to Jeffreys as they pulled onto the main road. Mark dialed the number. After several rings a female voice answered.

"World Wide Tours. How may I help you?"

Mark took a deep breath and then started, trying to sound a bit frantic. "This is Mark Williams. I'm on one of your tours. The one starting at the Stone Forest near Naigu. There's been an accident. Your tour guide, Bob, Bob...." Mark stuttered. "Oh, I can't remember his last name. But he's dead. And Chin and Hwang, too.

Lightning. They were hit by lightning, killed them. It was horrible. And another person. A Chinese man. He was killed too. We were just walking through this karst formation and suddenly it hit, no warning! Oh my God...." Mark trailed off.

"Can you hold a moment?" was the startled reply.

The wait seemed to take forever. When another voice came on the line they were pulling into Naigu and Mark could see blue lights flashing up ahead. He didn't have much time. "This is John Peterson," the voice on the phone was saying.

"I can't talk long," Mark interrupted. "The police are here. We have to talk with them. We'll have to take them to the bodies. It was horrible. Blown apart. Lightning. Had to be lightning. But now it's just the three of us, Jeffreys, Juan and me. And we don't know where to go, no hotel, no money, and no plane tickets. Bob had all of that and he's dead. Juan thought he had all the tour info on his computer, but it got blown to pieces. Oh it was horrible." They had pulled up beside the Chinese police car and Juan was getting out. Mark thought of staying in the car on the phone, but then thought that it would be more natural for him to get out while talking on the phone so he and Jeffreys approached the Chinese officer while Mark was still talking excitedly on the phone.

"We're with the Chinese police now," Mark continued. "Juan knows Chinese so he is talking to them. Oh, the Officer wants me off the phone, I'll have to call you back." With that Mark pulled the phone away from his ear and stood next to Juan and the Officer, listening to them speak back and forth in Chinese. In his excitement he "forgot" to disconnect the phone call, hoping the microphone would pick up enough of the Chinese to keep the folks on the line informed as to what was happening.

CHAPTER 5

It seemed to take the Chinese police forever to decide what to do. Mark wanted to return to the scene in the morning. He had an overwhelming anxiety about going back into the karst formation at night, although he reasoned that the cat was long since gone and would not likely return. However, his anxiety remained. He told the officers that he could not find it in the dark, but they would not be deterred. So, they climbed into three police vehicles and headed back the way they had come. Jeffreys was in the back seat with Mark, while Juan was in the lead car, giving the driver directions.

During the short ride back, Mark kept going over their story, looking for inconsistencies. He found one. He would have to get with Jeffreys alone to correct it. That was not likely now that the police were involved and he was sure they would be questioned separately. He would have to fix the gap in their story in front of the officers. Mark assumed that at least one of the officers spoke English, even though they had not spoken English yet. Probably just listening to see what they would say, Mark thought.

When they got to the dirt road leading into the karst formation, the car with Jeffreys and Mark took the lead, since Juan had never been up there. Juan squeezed into their car to act as translator. Mark wasn't much help as he said that it all looked alike in the dark and he couldn't say where they had been parked. But Jeffreys had an uncanny recall of the terrain. He identified where they had parked and then taking a compass heading, started leading them into the karst formation, with Mark right behind him, followed by eight Chinese officers and Juan.

As they walked down the trail, Mark had an idea. "Do you remember what year you visited Pensacola?" Mark asked Jeffreys casually.

Jeffreys appeared puzzled by the question. But then answered. "2006, I think."

Mark was relieved. He was banking on the fact that Jeffreys probably visited Pensacola at one time since it was such a big training facility and always had a number of Marines there. "Did you ever think when we met at the Seville bar, that years later we would be hiking here in China?"

"Uh, no." Jeffreys replied.

"I know we had always talked about going hiking somewhere exotic, but did you ever think we would actually do it?" Mark continued.

"No," Jeffreys replied, still obviously confused about the point of Mark's remarks.

"That's why I was so surprised to see you at the airport," Mark continued, hoping that Jeffreys realized that part of their cover story had to be that the two of them knew each other, otherwise if the Chinese found the surveillance film from the airport, their cover would be blown. "But I never realized that our journey would end up like this," Mark finished somberly.

They walked on in silence, Jeffreys consulting his compass and map on occasion. "We should be getting close," Jeffreys said and Juan translated into Chinese. "It should be right around here." They walked around another stone outcropping and suddenly emerged in the clearing.

The group's flashlights lit up the Chinese corpse, which still lay in the same tortured position. The group stopped, momentarily stunned. Juan gasped and almost threw up. Even though he had seen the pictures, he was not ready for the reality. The three Americans stayed on the other side of the clearing while the Chinese officers examined the corpse and took photos. Then they asked, through Juan, to be shown the other bodies.

Jeffreys looked around the clearing and then pointed to a side trail. "We left this way," he said, and again Juan translated. Jeffreys led the group out the trail and around the stone works. He slowed as he got to a corner, appearing reluctant to go on. "I think they are around this corner," he said, not offering to be first.

A young officer pushed past and disappeared around the corner, only to return very quickly looking quite green. As he retched off to the side, two other officers went around the corner. There was silence and then a burst of Chinese. The other officers escorted the Americans around the corner and they all saw the bodies. This time Juan did throw up, running back and joining the young Chinese officer. There was a lot of excited chatter in Chinese and talk on the radio.

When asked to show where they had gone and Jeffreys pointed out an area near the rock overhang where they had hidden. "It was somewhere around here that we were knocked down," Jeffreys said, looking at Mark for confirmation.

"This looks like it," Mark agreed. "Of course a lot of this area looks the same, but this looks like it."

The Chinese police studied the scene for hours. Sometimes they asked question, translated by Juan, but most of the time they ignored the Americans. While they waited, Mark paced near the ledge he and Jeffreys had hid under, hoping to disturb any telltale marks they may have made. He felt it would be better if the Chinese did not think they hid under the ledge. That might be hard to explain. Finally they were escorted back to the road and taken to a local police station where their passports were taken and they waited some more. When they were separated Mark thought, 'Now the interrogation begins.' He was ushered into a small room that contained a simple wood table and two chairs. 'This is straight out of all the movies,' Mark thought. He sat alone for over an hour, trying not to fall asleep, before a Chinese officer came in and sat across the table from him.

"You are an American," the Officer said in passable English.

Mark had to suppress a laugh. They had his passport, he was wearing American clothes and spoke English. But instead of being sarcastic, not a good way to start an interview in a death investigation, he simply replied, "Yes, Officer." The questioning lasted over an hour. Mark tried to keep his answers short and as truthful as possible. Despite the officer's initial appearance, he was really quite thorough, reminding Mark of a Chinese Columbo. Fortunately, as long as Mark omitted any mention of the aliens, his story was completely true and easy to recall. The officer had him repeat several parts of his story, especially when it came to the lightning.

"How could lightning come on a clear day?" the officer asked.

Mark had been waiting for this question. "I don't know?" he answered simply.

"Then why do you say it was lightning?" the officer repeated.

"It felt like electricity when we got knocked over," Mark answered easily. "And what else could cause those burn marks on..." Mark hesitated, partly for dramatic effect. "...on the bodies?" he finished quietly.

"Did you hear it?" the officer asked.

Mark had not thought of that question. "No," he answered, remembering a case he had handled where the people in the strike area never heard anything and wondering how Jeffreys answered that question.

"So how do you explain it hitting four people the same way in different locations?" the officer challenged.

"I can't," Mark answered simply.

The officer continued to question Mark on different aspects. When it was apparent that he was not going to get anything new, he asked, "Did you see the meteor?"

Mark had wondered whether anyone else saw the ship. "The what?" Mark asked, puzzled.

"The meteor," the officer repeated.

"Meteor?" Mark repeated.

"Yes, meteor. We have reports that several people saw a meteor heading into that area," the officer explained.

Mark paused, trying to look puzzled. "How could a meteor kill four people like that?" Mark asked.

"That is what I'm asking you," the officer stated accusingly.

"I have no idea," Mark replied. "I never saw a meteor." The officer was clearly disappointed by Mark's response and kept insisting that Mark make a confession. "But there is nothing to confess," Mark kept responding. When it became apparent that Mark had nothing further to add, the questioning finally ended. Mark was left in the room for a period of time before being escorted to another room where he joined Juan and Jeffreys. They all assumed the room was bugged, so they kept their conversation neutral. "So what happens now?" Mark asked as the three sat together.

"I don't know," Juan replied. "I guess we just wait till they let us go."

"And then what?" Mark continued, hoping that the jailers were listening. "Has the tour company called back? We don't have rooms, money or even plane tickets back home. And I really need to get something to eat and get some sleep!"

"But first we have to get out of here," Jeffreys replied. "I don't know what's taking so long, we've been here forever."

"True, but four people have died," Mark explained. "Even back home it takes time to do an investigation. They are being polite." A little while later Mark asked Jeffreys, "Hey, did they tell you someone saw a meteor?"

"Yea, they told me that."

"Weird," Mark noted. "Do you think a meteor could cause those injuries?" Mark asked.

"I don't think so," Jeffreys answered. "It looked like burn marks to me. I still say it was lightning."

"Can meteors cause lightning?" Mark asked.

"Do I look like an astro-physicist?" Jeffreys replied sarcastically.

They talked for a while longer until Juan asked, "Do you suppose we should call the American embassy?"

"Why?" Mark asked. "We shouldn't be here much longer. We need to call the tour company and find out what to do next. It certainly looks like this tour is over." They lapsed into silence as time slowly passed. When Mark's stomach started growling he asked Juan to ask the Chinese whether they could get something to eat. After a delay, some food was brought in to them. They ended up spending the rest of the night at the police station, sleeping on the benches or sprawled on the floor. The next day another English speaking officer told them that they could leave the station, but they had to stay at the hotel in town.

"Hotel?" Mark asked puzzled. "What hotel?"

"There is one here," the Officer answered. "We talked with your tour company. They are sending someone to make arrangements to take care of you and the bodies. Until he arrives, you stay at the hotel."

"Can we have our phone and passports back?" Juan asked.

"When he arrives," the Officer stated. "Now you will be escorted to your hotel." With that he spoke to another officer rapidly in Chinese and left. The new officer escorted them to their hotel. Although it was morning, the three were exhausted from staying up most of the night. They grabbed a quick breakfast and went to bed.

Despite his exhaustion, Mark had trouble falling asleep. He had been so concerned about getting out of China, he had not analyzed what happened. Could the blue-grays have sent down a control cube, only to have it intercepted by the cats? Which meant the cats survived the collapsing wormhole? He felt sure that the cats had killed all the blue-grays on the *Ronald Reagan*. So there had to be a blue-gray mothership out there.

And how would their war affect the Earth? The cats had the ability to destroy the Earth by hurling asteroids at it. Would they do that again? The last time the cats attacked Earth was 65 million years ago and the impact of the two asteroids killed off the dinosaurs and fifty percent of life on Earth. Mark had seen that event from the eyes of an escaping blue-gray in one of the visions from the memory cube last year. The spectacle had been horrifying as he watched the Earth being engulfed by two giant explosions that raced across the horizon. These thoughts lingered as Mark fell asleep, filling his dreams with eerie visions of aliens and dinosaurs and an approaching apocalypse.

CHAPTER 6

It actually took three days for a representative from the tour company to arrive. During that time, Mark felt like they were under house arrest. The Chinese officer talked with him a few times and each time Mark felt he was testing their story. They were careful to always stay in character. Whether it was paranoia or not, they all felt it wiser to do so. When the tour company representative, a Charles Meader, finally arrived, Mark, Juan and Jeffreys told him the same thing they had told the Chinese. Mark assumed he was a CIA agent, but until Mark was safely out of China, he wasn't going to let his guard down.

"What a horrible tragedy," Charles was saying. "So, is there any reason to continue this tour, or do you feel that you have had enough for one trip?"

They all looked at Mark for the answer. After all, he was the one who had felt the alien contact. "No, I don't think so," Mark answered carefully. "With all that's gone on, I really don't feel the same about the trip anymore. There's nothing more here that I care to look at."

"I agree," Jeffreys piped in.

"Me, too," Juan quickly agreed.

"Okay, then it's agreed. I will arrange your flights home. Since there has been a death of American nationals, we will have to stop and report at the U.S.

Consulate. The Consulate in Kunming is virtual, so we will report to the Consulate in Shanghai. We will fly to Shanghai, where you will have to fill out a report, then we will arrange your flights home. World Wide Tours will work out a refund for you. But the home office will take care of that, if that's agreeable." They agreed and the rest of the day was spent making the necessary arrangements. That afternoon they traveled back to Kunming where they booked a hotel for the night. Their flight was scheduled for 8:00 the next morning. That evening they went out to eat in a crowded restaurant. Wondering if it was safe to talk, Mark tried to discreetly ask Charles.

"You know, I visited Moscow once, back when it was still the Soviet Union," Mark started. "It was pretty creepy. We clearly stood out as foreigners and actually had a KGB agent following us, keeping an eye on us. We had been forewarned, so we were watching for them. Now that I'm visiting China, I didn't know what to expect. You hear so many different things on the news, you don't know what to believe. But although we certainly stand out, I haven't noticed any KGB agents following us."

"KGB is Russian," Jeffreys interrupted.

"I know," Mark retorted. "I mean what ever the Chinese equivalent is."

"It's not as bad as that," Charles said. "But you never know," he added cautiously. "You three certainly gained more attention here than most tourists do."

Mark took that as a warning and decided that he wouldn't say anything else until he was safely out of China. Mark did not sleep well that night, which made getting up the next morning much more difficult. Fortunately, it was a three and a half hour non-stop flight. After clouds obscured the ground beneath him, Mark leaned his head against the window and fell asleep.

Mark awoke with a start, covered with sweat. He looked around. Jeffreys was dozing in the seat next to him, while Juan and Charles were across the aisle. Still concerned that they may be under some type of covert surveillance, he reached over and tapped Jeffreys on the leg. Jeffreys opened one eye and then came fully awake. "You okay?" he whispered. "You're white as a ghost."

"I just had a bad dream," Mark explained quietly.

Jeffreys looked at him quizzically. "What type of dream?"

"It seems to be a reoccurring nightmare," Mark explained. "I've had it before."

"Really? How recently?" Jeffreys asked.

"About a week ago."

"And you had it again, just now," Jeffreys asked, straightening up a little.

"Yes." They were silent for a few moments, then Mark added. "It might be better if we stay here on vacation. You know, maybe tour a different part of the country. It's not like we'll ever get back to China again."

"You think you are up for that?" Jeffreys asked. "After what happened?"

"Especially after what happened," Mark said. "I think we need to finish this vacation and not just quit."

"You certain about this?" Jeffreys asked.

"Yes."

"I think we better tell our new tour guide, then. He will need to make some new arrangements. Do you know where you want to go?"

"I'll have to see a map. I think there are multiple places we need to visit."

"Multiple?" Jeffreys asked, surprised.

"Yes. We may have to plan a whirl-wind tour to see them all."

"We are definitely going to have to talk to the tour guide about this." The fasten seat belt sign came on before Jeffreys could get up, so they had to wait until they landed to talk with Charles. After disembarking, Mark told Charles that they needed to talk. The group found an unoccupied waiting area where they could sit and talk without too much concern of being overheard. "What do you know about the tour we were scheduled to go on?" Mark asked Charles.

Charles glanced around before answering. "Not much really. Only that you had run into some trouble with the locals and that I had to either help you finish your tour or, preferably, get you out. The choice was yours. And arrange to have the bodies and all the personal effects shipped home, of course," he added.

At first Mark was irritated that Charles didn't know more, but then he realized that it probably made sense not to send someone with too much information in case things continued to go wrong. Still, it made it more difficult for him to explain, especially since he was not willing to break his personal vow of not speaking in public while still in China.

"It was our choice whether we stayed?" Mark asked.

"They said to ask you, that you would know," Charles responded, indicating Mark.

"Well, I've been thinking about that," Mark said. "I think we've had a change of heart. I think we're leaving too soon. We still can accomplish more here."

Juan looked at Mark intently. "Something has changed?" he asked.

"Yes," Mark said.

"Just now?" Juan asked quizzically.

"It came to me on the plane," Mark said. "I have a very strong feeling that we need to continue our plans. We shouldn't just give up on our... vacation plans."

"Even in light of what has happened?" Juan asked.

"Especially in light of what has happened!" Mark answered emphatically, feeling a sense of deja-vu.

Charles realized that he was clearly missing what was really being said. "So you want to continue the trip?" he asked tentatively.

"Yes," Mark said. "Can you set it up, the travel arrangements?"

"Yes. But first we have to report to the Consulate. They were rather insistent that they get a chance to hear what happened."

"That's the problem," Mark tried to explain. "I'm concerned about the timeframe. Filling out reports takes a lot of time, time that we might not have. There are a couple of places that I would like to visit and the sooner we get there, the better. In fact, since we are in an airport, I think it would be a good idea to book a flight right now, rather than waiting for tomorrow."

"Time is that critical?" Charles asked.

Mark wanted to scream, YES, YOU IDIOT! But of course Charles knew nothing about what was going on and Mark was afraid to tell him in public. So instead he tried to figure out how to carefully get his point across.

"Yes," Mark said. "The trouble with sightseeing, as we recently discovered, is that everyone wants to see the same thing. I think if we leave immediately, we can probably get there before anyone else, before our competition, so to speak. That would be very... " Mark paused, trying to decide upon the right word. "...beneficial for all of us," he finally concluded.

"Where do you want to go?" Charles asked.

Mark paused. That was tough, because he didn't know. He thought for a moment before replying. "I assume that you can contact the tour agency."

"Yes, I can call them."

"On a regular phone?" Mark asked disappointedly.

"Yes."

"You don't have a better way to contact them?"

"Not at this time."

That made things more complicated, Mark thought. He paused to consider. "Okay," he said at last. "Tell them this. Tell them that I have this hobby. I like to stargaze." Charles looked at him completely puzzled. "I particularly like to watch meteor showers. You know, like the *Pleidies*. Find out if there have been any recent, very recent, meteor showers. That would probably narrow down where we should travel next."

"You want me to ask them that now?" Charles asked.

"Yes. The sooner, the better. Meteor showers don't usually last very long. Just a couple of days. We don't want to miss any."

Totally confused, Charles said he would make the call. He walked over to the windows overlooking the tarmac as he made the call on his cell phone. When he had left, Jeffreys turned to Mark. "You think there have been several meteor showers lately?" Mark shook his head affirmatively. They waited in silence. A few minutes later Charles returned, saying that he had made the call and the tour group would check and call him back. Fifteen long minutes later, Charles' cell phone rang. He listened for a moment and then pulled out a pen and paper and started writing. When he finished, he turned to the group, who were watching him intently. Still not understanding, he relayed the message. "They tell me that there have been four meteors reported in China in the last couple hours!" Jeffreys and Juan looked up in surprise, while Mark only nodded. "And one three days ago."

"Did they give you locations?" Mark asked.

"Yes, they told me the towns they thought they were near." With that he showed them the sheet of paper he had written on. They all looked at the names.

"Anyone have a map?" Mark asked. Juan pulled out a map and after some searching, they located the four new locations. "These two are fairly close to each other and the closest to us," Mark said, pointing to the map. "We need to go there."

"When?" Charles asked.

"As soon as possible, like right now!" Mark said. "If we can get there before any one else..."

"And before our other friends," Jeffreys added pointedly.

"Definitely before our other friends," Mark agreed. "Then maybe we can figure out what is going on."

Charles hesitated at first, and then said, "Okay, let me work on it. With that he stepped away to make another call without interruption.

While he was gone, Jeffreys turned to Juan. "You live here in China, right?"

"Yes," Juan replied.

"I like to hunt. Any chance I can get a hunting rifle here in China? In case I want to do some hunting?"

"Not in China," Juan replied. "They closed hunting to international visitors back in 2006. Big political thing."

"Too bad," Jeffreys replied. "I would love to go hunting the next time we go out in the woods."

"I know what you mean," Mark agreed wholeheartedly. What were they going to do the next time they came across a cat. They were lucky last time. But Bob, Chin, Hwang and that Chinese local were not. Mark certainly did not want to add any more names to that list.

CHAPTER 7

Forty-five minutes later Charles announced that World Wide Tours was now back in business. "We need to go to the ticket desk," he said. "There is a China Eastern flight leaving at 4:05 p.m. for Huangshan, which is very near your..." Charles paused, "...one of your requested destinations. We have a layover, so we will arrive at Tunxi International Airport at 9:40 p.m. It is a small airport that caters to tourists coming to see the Huangshau mountains. You will fit right in."

"The what mountains?" Jeffreys asked.

"Huangshau or Yellow Mountains. They are really quite famous," Charles explained. "You probably have seen pictures of them and never knew it. Much of traditional Chinese art is based upon this area. Mount Huang is the most famous and the area has been designated as a UNESCO World Heritage Site."

"Our friends seem to like exotic locations," Jeffreys joked.

"Is that our destination?" Mark asked.

"One of your sightings is in that region," Charles answered.

"Great. Mountains." Mark muttered sarcastically.

"The other is southeast of it, in the area of Qiando Lake," Charles continued.

"A lake, you should like that a lot more," Jeffreys jibed Mark. "Should be easy to find on a lake."

"Qiando lake means thousand island lake," Charles explained. "It is a man-made lake built back in the late fifties, when they built a huge dam on the Xin'an River for a hydroelectric station. The lake covers an area of over five hundred square kilometers and has over a thousand large islands and thousands of smaller ones."

"So much for easy," Jeffreys muttered. "You better have that internal compass of yours working," he added to Mark.

"You get me there," Mark answered. "I'll find it."

It was a five and a half hour flight to Tunxi, including the forty-minute layover, but the plane was a Boeing 737 so it was relatively comfortable, for airline travel. To a casual observer, Mark appeared to sleep through most of it. But he wasn't asleep, he was trying to plan for the unknown. He knew he could find what ever it was the blue-grays had sent. He could 'hear' it and his earlier experience in the karst formation had confirmed it for him.

The question was, what to do once he found it? What if Jeffreys was right and it was a cube, a control cube? What should he do then? He couldn't touch it, that was certain: it would control him. But if it was a control cube, how could he find out what they wanted if he didn't touch it? But what if it was something else? Since he didn't know what 'something else' could be, he decided he would just have to worry about that if and when the time came. It could be a memory cube, Mark thought. Maybe they would start by sending a memory cube, like last time, then move up to the control cube. Unlikely, Mark thought. The blue-grays had tried a memory cube last year and it had taken Mark several days to view the memories and even then he wasn't prepared when they tried the control cube on him. The blue-grays had almost a year to prepare since then and now that they had made their move, the cats were hot on their trail. No, whatever it was, Mark decided, it would demand immediate action. Nothing long or drawn out. But then the question remained: What action?

Mark still did not have an answer when they finally arrived at Tunxi airport. He looked out the window as they taxied to the terminal. Charles had been right, it was a small, one runway airport. They even had to walk across the tarmac to the terminal. As predicted, it was filled with tourists, so the four Americans did not stand out too much. Wait here a minute, Charles said before disappearing into the crowd. A few minutes later he returned and led them to a taxi stand where he hailed a taxi. They piled in and gave the driver some instructions in Chinese. "We have reservations at Motel one-six-eight in the Tunxi district," Charles told the group in his best tour guide voice. "You will be able to get something to eat and then get a good night's sleep before we go exploring. You are probably exhausted from all your traveling today."

Mark wanted to object to the delay, but it was almost 11:00 at night and he was tired and hungry. Mark watched the sights of the city flash by as they drove downtown. They arrived at Motel 168, a nondescript six-story motel that reminded Mark of a Motel 6. Charles escorted them in and booked them into two rooms, Mark and Jeffreys in one and Juan and Charles in the other. "Since it is late, I'm having some food delivered," Charles told them. "Just stay here and relax. It should be here shortly." With that, he and Juan left the room. Mark flopped down on one of the two beds, exhausted, but at the same time anxious to get moving. He could feel the call.

"We're wasting time," Mark complained to Jeffreys.

"Is it close?" Jeffreys asked.

"Relatively," Mark responded. "Certainly within several miles. We need to start looking for it."

"We need to eat and come up with a plan first," Jeffreys cautioned. "We can't just run off half cocked. That will only get us all killed."

Mark had to concede the point. Fortunately, there was a knock at the door before Mark's impatience got the better of him. He opened it to find Juan, Charles and a delivery person in the hall. The three came in and the delivery person placed a huge spread of food on the little motel table. Mark started to chuckle and Jeffreys glanced at him.

"I never thought I would be ordering Chinese take-out in China!" Mark said, with a laugh.

"His humor gets really bad when he's tired," Jeffreys explained.

When the delivery person finished spreading out the plates, he took out a pen and slowly walked around the room, waving it up and down. When he finished, he turned to Charles and gave him a thumbs-up and then left as Mark and Jeffreys simply stared.

"He's one of ours," Charles explained. "The room is clean, so we can talk. So, tell me what happened."

"At the airport you said you didn't know anything about the mission. What do you know?" Mark asked.

"Really not much," Charles admitted. "I don't know what your mission is. Only that you lost three people in the process and the Chinese were investigating. I was told your cover stories and that Washington thought that you weren't compromised. I was to make contact and get you to the Consulate. When that plan changed at the airport, they told me to assist you and that you would brief me."

"Sit down and eat," Mark said. "This is going to be a long story." Mark dug into the food as he told Charles the same story he had provided to Bob, Chin and Hwang, with Jeffreys and Juan adding details as the story turned to the last several days. When they got to the recent details, Charles started typing notes into a small laptop computer. "Is that the same type of computer Bob had?" Mark asked in the middle of his narration.

"Yes," Charles answered. "It will give us a secure link to the Agency."

"Where did you get that?" Jeffreys asked.

"It came with room service," Charles answered.

"That's handy," Mark said as he continued his narrative.

When Mark had finished his narrative, Charles stopped typing and leaned back. "That's hard to believe," he said. "I mean aliens?" Mark started to bristle. He was too tired to put up with this all over again. But Charles held up his hand, "I didn't say I don't believe you," he quickly added. "After all, a lot of assets have been mobilized to assist in this mission. But it still is hard to comprehend."

"I agree with that," Mark admitted. "So how come you didn't know about this when you came and got us?" Mark asked.

"They didn't know if you were compromised so they didn't want to brief me in case I got caught as well."

'That's a brave man,' Mark thought.

"So what do we do now?" Charles continued. "Do you know where these things are? We need to come up with a plan."

Juan spread a map out on the bed and they gathered around it. Jeffreys quickly orientated it with a compass. Mark closed his eyes for a moment and concentrated on the call. "Ok," he started. "There are two of them. One is in this direction," he ran his finger across the map. "It's the closer one. The other is in this direction." He ran his finger the opposite direction on the map. "It's much farther away." Having eaten, Mark's sense of impatience returned. "We need to find this one right now!" Mark instructed. "It's not very far. Perhaps within five miles or so."

"You want to go looking for it at midnight?" Juan asked.

"I want to find it before the cat does," Mark answered.

Charles pulled down a satellite view on his laptop. "I'm afraid that we will have to wait for morning before we can begin our search." Mark's objection stopped when Charles spun the laptop to face Mark. "This," Charles said, pointing to the screen, "is what is within five miles of us." Mark studied the screen. They were located at the base of a very large mountain. "This is Mount Huang. It is steep and treacherous," Charles explained. "It is a huge tourist attraction, so there are stairs and a cable car, *if* what we are looking for is on the path. But even then, it is not something you want to do at night. This is not the U.S. They are not big into railings in China and I doubt they ever heard of OSHA."

Mark swallowed his frustration. "Point well taken," he conceded. "In that case, how about we get some sleep and start first thing in the morning?"

"Done," Charles agreed. "I need to upload this report. The folks at home are quite eager to hear what is going on." They discussed some further details before Juan and Charles left for their room.

"I could sleep for a week," Mark complained as he fell onto the bed. Jeffreys only chuckled as he turned off the light.

The next morning Charles cheerfully woke them up bright and early. Mark could have killed him, as he hated cheerful people first thing in the morning. He felt like a truck had run over him as he had trouble sleeping this close to the call. They went downstairs to get breakfast in the hotel. It was not fancy, but Mark was too preoccupied to notice or care. After breakfast they went back up to the room to pack a light daypack and make last minute preparations. As usual, Jeffreys was studying the map.

"Do you think we can narrow down the search," Jeffreys asked Mark. "Last time we went through the first karst formation, only to find that our target was actually past it. As nice as this tourist attraction is, in the interest of time, we may want to check around it first. Besides," Jeffreys couldn't resist adding with a chuckle, "I know how much you like to exercise and this mountain hike looks like a lot of exercise."

Mark looked at the map. They were in a valley next to a large mountain. The call was, of course, coming straight from the mountain. "Any chance it could have landed in this valley on the other side of the mountain?" Jeffreys asked, pointing to the other valley. "Have you been able to see anything? Last time you had visual also."

"No," Mark answered. "I haven't received any visuals this time. I hear the call from them, but no visuals."

"I wonder why not?" Jeffreys asked.

"I don't know," Mark said. "Maybe to cut down on the chance of the cats picking up the signal."

"I'm wondering if we should drive around to the other valley first before we commit to going up the mountain," Jeffreys continued.

Mark stared at the map some more. "Where's the airport?" he asked. They showed him on the map. "Can you pull up a satellite view for me on your computer?" Mark asked Charles.

"Sure." Charles booted up the computer and in a few minutes had the requested screen up.

"Now orientate this with the map," Mark requested. They placed the laptop next to the map and spun it around so that it mirrored the map. "Now zoom into the airport, specifically the exit road." They complied and Mark studied the screen and the map. "Here's your answer," Mark finally said to Jeffreys. "When we were leaving the airport last night I remember the call was coming from straight ahead, which would be this direction on the map." Mark ran his finger across the map. "And now it is coming from this direction." He indicated again. "The intersection of these two lines is, unfortunately, right on that mountain." The group gazed at the map.

"How precise are these coordinates?" Jeffreys asked.

"I can be pretty precise on the one from here," Mark answered. "The one from the airport is rough, although it still places our target on the mountain."

"That's still not very helpful," Jeffreys said.

"So we go up the mountain and as we get closer, I'll let you know," Mark said a bit exasperated.

"You haven't looked at the travel brochure for this mountain, have you?" Jeffreys stated. Mark shook his head no. "This is not a mountain like at home or the Alps, where you climb 'a mountain.' This mountain consists of 36 separate jagged granite peaks. It's 1,800 meters tall and is serviced by miles of paths and four separate telphers or cable cars. You don't just walk up it. Have you seen *Avatar*?"

"Of course I have."

"Well, the flying dragon scene among the floating mountains, they got that idea from this mountain."

"Oh."

Jeffreys analyzed the map and then summarized the situation. "Taking these points as rough estimates, our target will be in this area," he pointed to a spot on the map. "It is unlikely that it will be on a trail, or it would have been found already and Mark would sense its movement, like he did last time. So we can assume it is off the trail. For now we will have to assume that we don't need mountain climbing gear to find it. If I'm wrong... Well, we'll cross that bridge if we come to it. For now, Mark roughly describes the southwestern part of this range. So I would suggest taking the Jade Screen Telpher from Merciful Light Temple near the south entrance. It takes us up to Jade Screen Pavilion. The cable car trip takes about 10 minutes and saves us a three-hour hike. Once we get there, we can get a new bearing from Mark. There are two different hiking trails up there. If we are too far away, then we come back down and drive over to the Cloud Valley New Telpher, which will put us up on another peak. How does that sound to you?"

"That sounds good to me," Mark said.

"As good as anything else," Juan agreed.

"Ok," Charles said.

"Do you know how to get to this telpher station?" Jeffreys asked.

"I can get us there," Charles answered.

"Okay," Jeffreys continued. "Let's pack our daypacks. Charles, you are in charge of communication since you have the computer. I assume that you are going to take it and a phone with you."

"Yes."

"Good. Pack standard hiking clothes: waterproof jacket, hat, sunglasses, water, binoculars, compasses and cameras. We have fifty feet of rope and we each have carabineers on our packs. Hopefully, we don't have to use any of that, but just in case. Anything I missed?"

"I thought you were going to add an M-60 and a thousand rounds of ammunition," Mark said.

"I would if I could," Jeffreys remarked wistfully.

They packed their daypacks and headed out to the Merciful Light Temple where they would pick up the first telpher or cable car. Although they arrived early, the crowds were already assembled and they had to wait over an hour in line before they could board the 6-person cable car. By the time they got to the cable car, Mark was pacing with frustration. But it evaporated when the car started its assent as the ten-minute ride provided a stunning view as they ascended between steep pinnacles and a sheer drop.

Arriving at the top, only Jeffreys seemed unmoved by the spectacular view. "We can sightsee later," he whispered to Mark. "Which way?" Mark closed his eyes and pointed. Jeffreys took a compass bearing. "That's towards Ladder in Clouds," Jeffreys said, consulting the map. "The trail should be this way," he added, leading the way.

The trail was filled with tourists strolling and stopping for scenic pictures. In contrast, Mark's group was moving quickly, weaving between the tourists as they headed down the trail towards Ladder on Clouds. It took them almost an hour, but when they arrived even Jeffreys was impressed by the view, although his take on the view was very different from the others.

"Tactical visibility is going to drop tremendously if we have to go down there," Jeffreys remarked as they gazed at a cloud bank beneath them that made the mountain peaks look like islands in a fluffy white sea.

"You're right, this is straight out of *Avatar*," Mark remarked.

"I think you mean *Avatar* is straight out of this," Juan corrected.

"Oh, yeah."

"Which direction is it now?" Jeffreys interrupted, not to be deterred from the mission at hand. Mark pointed at a jagged peak rising out of the clouds.

"That's not good," Juan remarked. "We would need full climbing gear to get over there. And that's just assuming that the locals would allow it, which I doubt."

They continued on the trail, Juan and Charles mesmerized by the view, while Mark was torn between the incredible sights and the call getting louder and louder in his head. Only Jeffreys seemed immune to the view. "How can you ignore this?" Mark asked as he walked next to Jeffreys.

"Training," Jeffreys replied. "Yes, the view is incredible. But the mission is paramount and the view, or what it represents, only complicates matters. We are walking on the edge of a mountain with a sheer drop on one side and steep incline on the other. Visibility will drop once we get into that cloudbank and we are facing an enemy that has air superiority and we are unarmed. The only tactical advantage we have, if you can call it that, is for now we are four among hundreds of tourists. There is nothing to stand us apart from the others, so we are not a special target. Of course, once we find what ever the blue-grays dropped here, then that will probably be a different story."

"You have a wonderful way of spoiling a vacation," Mark said ruefully.

"Hoo-rah," Jeffreys gave the Marine response.

They continued in silence, their pace slowed by the number of tourists they had to weave between. At times the trail was so narrow they could not pass, but had to walk behind a slow moving person until the trail widened. As they followed the winding trail, Ladder on Clouds moved to their left and then slowly behind them. "You were right," Mark said to Jeffreys. "The call is still coming from ahead of us."

"Thank heavens for that," Juan said from behind Mark. "This is as much mountain climbing as I can do." Mark noted that even on the stairs Juan was winded.

"We are coming up to Yunji Peak, for you sight-seeing folks," Jeffreys stated after they had traveled farther down the trail.

"I thought you weren't into sight-seeing," Juan remarked, now clearly out of breath.

"I'm just noting our location," Jeffreys said, not winded at all. "I think it is import..." he cut off in mid word. Juan and Charles came to a stop, which caused a mild commotion until they moved to the side of the trial so the other tourists could pass. They all watched Mark, who was standing still, eyes closed while turning his head slowly back and forth.

Finally opening his eyes, Mark whispered, "It's here. Just above us. And not very far."

They gazed up. The stone stair trail that they were on had a sheer drop a thousand feet on one side, while the other side, the side Mark was looking up, had a five foot rock face and then steep woods above them. They could see about 10 feet before the vegetation blocked their vision.

"At least it's up and not down," Juan commented.

Jeffreys moved next to Mark as Juan and Charles played tourist, taking pictures of the surroundings. "Can you tell what it is?" Jeffreys asked.

"No," Mark replied. "Still just the call. But louder now."

"How far?"

"Judging by our last... adventure, I would guess fifty, one hundred feet?"

"You realize that once we commit to it, we may be opening ourselves up to the cats," Jeffreys stated evenly.

"Yes, I know. But I can't think of anything else to do. We need to find out what it is, and the sooner, the better."

"Let's just hope that the blue-grays' trick has worked and the cats are busy with the other sites and not this one," Jeffreys reasoned.

"I'm with you on that," Mark agreed. "Now what do you propose?"

Jeffreys thought for a moment, trying to scan the area above them without being too obvious as a constant stream of tourists passed them. "Okay. There's no way to be inconspicuous, so we will just have to climb up quickly and hope no one objects. I'll climb up first. Then Juan will boost Mark up. Then Charles, you boost up Juan. Charles, you stay here. You speak Chinese, so you run interference if any of the locals make a scene. We'll tie a rope off on that tree trunk there and use that as a guide so we can come back to this point. I don't want to lose this trail and end up on a ledge a thousand feet above ground. Any questions?"

"What do we do when we find it?" Juan asked.

"Depends what it is," Jeffreys replied. He waited for a lull in the seemingly endless stream of tourists before effortlessly climbing up the rock face to the woods above. Turning, he put a hand down and helped hoist Mark up and then repeated the move for Juan, while Mark climbed up into the trees. They were up into the tree line in under a minute. Jeffreys quickly tied the end of his climbing rope around the base of a small pine tree and scrambled up after the other two. He traveled about 15 feet before catching up with them. The incline was steep, so they had to hold on to the base of the small native pine trees to make their climb. But fortunately not so steep that climbing gear was required. They traveled about 50 feet up before the slope leveled out some so they could walk without having to hold on.

"Give me your line," Jeffreys said to Juan. Juan pulled his rope out of his daypack and handed it to Jeffreys, who quickly tied it to the end of his line and continued to pay it out as they moved up the hill. Jeffreys glanced up and saw Mark staring at the ground. He moved up next to Mark. On the ground was a patch of fresh dirt about three feet in diameter with scorch marks around the perimeter.

"That's it, isn't it?" Jeffreys asked unnecessarily. Mark merely nodded. "I suppose we need to dig this up." Mark nodded again. Jeffreys looked around. "Juan, grab a couple of those sticks. Mark, move over there, beside that tree. You can watch. In fact, you probably should, but stay somewhat covered."

"What are you expecting?" Juan asked concerned.

"I have no idea," Jeffreys admitted. "That's why I'm trying to be cautious." Juan retrieved inch thick branches that they broke into foot long sections. "Use the stick to dig," Jeffreys instructed. "Lets not touch anything with our hands till we know what we're dealing with." They started digging the dirt away with the sticks while Mark watched from six feet away. The dirt was soft and easy to move, having recently been disrupted.

They worked diligently, quickly digging down a foot in the loose dirt before Juan said, "I hit something!" They worked together and unearthed a small clump of dirt. "Oh, it's just a rock," Juan said disappointed as he flicked the dirt clod away with his stick and turned his attention back to the deepening hole. Jeffreys looked up when Mark gasped and saw him staring at the ground next to him. Shifting his position, he saw that Mark was staring at the clod of dirt that Juan had hit away. It had broken apart and a flat red surface gleamed in the light.

"It's a cube," Jeffreys exclaimed, jumping to his feet. "This is it, isn't it? There's no need to keep digging, do you think?"

Mark stepped between the cube and the hole in the ground and looked back and forth. "No. The call is coming from the cube. There's nothing else in the ground. Nothing I can feel anyway."

"So they sent another cube," Jeffreys said, puzzled.

"What's a cube?" Juan asked, reaching for the dirt clump.

Jeffreys stopped Juan's hand, and then tapped the rest of the dirt off the cube with the stick until he could see a red cube about two inches in diameter. "It's a different shape than the memory cube," Jeffreys noted. "It looks more like the one the blue-gray had in his hand."

"It is," Mark finally said, his voice stressed. Jeffreys looked up at Mark concerned. "Its call is almost irresistible," Mark answered the unasked question. "It wants me to pick it up."

"That would probably be a bad idea," Jeffreys remarked.

"A very bad idea," Mark agreed.

"We probably shouldn't stay here too much longer either, now that we found it," Jeffreys noted. "I suppose we take it with us?"

"I think we have to," Mark answered.

"Do you think the cats can hear this thing calling?"

"I've been thinking about that," Mark said. "I would have to guess no. I think the cats probably track it the same way NORAD does. I have to assume the blue-grays would not program it in a way the cats could follow it."

"But the cats found that Chinese guy when he had it," Jeffreys objected.

"They did," Mark conceded.

If we take it with us and the cats can follow it, we're dead," Jeffreys remarked.

"And if we stay here long enough, we are certainly dead," Mark stated.

"Nice choices," Jeffreys said sarcastically. "Okay, we take it with us. Any suggestions on how?"

"I can't touch it, we know that," Mark stated quickly.

"The memory cube didn't work on me, I'll carry it," Jeffreys said, reaching for the cube.

"Wait!" Mark commanded. "That's not a memory cube!"

"What is it then?"

"Later," Mark answered. "I don't think any of us should touch it."

Jeffreys pulled off his cloth hat. "Can I wrap it in this?" he asked. Mark nodded his agreement. Carefully Jeffreys wrapped his hat around the cube and gently picked it up.

"Feel anything?" Mark asked worriedly.

"No."

"Okay, good. If you even think you feel anything, drop it immediately."

"All right," Jeffreys agreed as he wrapped his poncho around his hat and stuffed it into his daypack. "Now let's get out of here!" With that the three followed the rope back down. When they got down to the ledge they called down to Charles, who helped them down. They got a couple strange looks from passing tourists, but no one stopped or said anything. They let those tourists pass by and soon were surrounded by new tourists, who never saw them climb down.

"Did you find it?" Charles asked as they quickly brushed themselves off and melted in with the stream of people as they continued their descent.

"Yes," Jeffreys said as he deftly coiled the rope and stored it in Juan's backpack.

"What is it?" Charles whispered as they walked down the trail.

"It's a cube," Jeffreys replied, also in a whisper.

"What's that?"

"I'll explain later," Jeffreys said. "We might as well keep going this way," he added. "It will take us back where we started, but we have a bit of a hike ahead of us," he warned.

"Can we go back the way we came?" Juan asked.

"We would be going uphill and against the flow of traffic," Jeffreys explained. "This way will probably be easier."

They hadn't traveled far before Jeffreys noticed Mark's tension. "You're not all right," he stated, rather than asked.

"I can't stay near that thing too much longer," Mark admitted. "Its call is numbing. Do any of you feel it?" A chorus of "No's" confirmed that Mark was the only one affected. They traveled less than five minutes more before Mark said, "We have to separate. I can't stay near it any longer."

"You take my pack," Jeffreys said to Juan. "You and Charles stay together. We'll fall back a bit. I need to see what's wrong with Mark. And Juan," Jeffreys added quietly. "If you see another meteor or a red light in the sky or anything unnatural, drop the pack and run. We don't want any more casualties." They agreed and Mark and Jeffreys stopped while the other two continued down the trail. When they had disappeared, Jeffreys asked. "You okay?"

Mark nodded. "It's easier here. I can't stay near it for long."

"What is it?" Jeffreys asked quietly as tourists passed them without paying any attention. When Mark hesitated, Jeffreys added, "You promised no secrets."

"No, you're right. I'm just recovering," Mark agreed. After resting a few moments longer, he continued. "It's not a memory cube, it's a control cube."

"A control cube?"

"Yes, they use it to control their subjects."

"So if you touch that..."

"I will do whatever the blue-grays want," Mark finished.

"But you touched one before and it didn't control you," Jeffreys stated.

"When?"

"The cube the blue-gray handed you on the aircraft carrier, it was a control cube, wasn't it?"

"How do you know?" Mark asked.

"I could see it in the rifle scope. It was the same design as this one," Jeffreys answered simply.

"Yes," Mark admitted. "But they had not programed it properly, it kept knocking me back before I could make the connection."

"So how do you know this is a control cube?" Jeffreys asked.

"When you gave me the dead blue-grays' cube as you dragged me to safety. I accessed his memories and one of them was about the control cubes."

"You neglected to mention that part in your debriefings also," Jeffreys noted. "Unless you told them later in Guam."

"No. You're right. I didn't mention it. You remember that a number of people wanted my head for shooting at the cat ship, thought I was trying to drag us into the war between the cats and the blue-grays. Since both the cats and blue-grays were dead, or I thought they were, and since the control cube was destroyed by the cat, I figured that I didn't need to volunteer any information they could use to attack my account of what happened. If I told them about the control cube, someone would have accused me of being under the blue-grays' control and biased."

Jeffreys thought about it for a minute. "Anything else you haven't told me?"

Mark considered. "You know about the cat visions and how the emotions from them overwhelmed me and caused me to strike out at people."

"They gave you power," Jeffreys interrupted. "I always wondered how you could suddenly disable so many people so quickly. The three orderlies. Those guys in the weight room. And probably those two officers, if I had not stopped you."

"Yes," Mark agreed. "That was close."

"No offense," Jeffreys continued. "But I never completely bought your explanation that you had taken karate in your youth."

"I did take karate in my youth." Mark held up his hand when Jeffreys started to respond. "But you're right. That did not explain it. I was using the same type of power I felt the cats use in the vision, but I have no idea how I did it. Maybe I was still the cat. It was just reflex. Really nothing I had any control over. And I have never been able to reproduce it, although I have tried several times in the last year, just out of curiosity, but to no avail."

"Too bad. That could come in handy if you could control it."

"But I couldn't control it," Mark stated. "And now you know about the control cube," Mark continued. "That's really about it. Oh yes," Mark added after a moment's consideration. "I did fudge a bit when I reported on the effects of the psychotropic drugs those two so-called doctors gave me when I was having a vision from the memory cube."

"You lied to the President of the United States?" Jeffreys stated, shocked.

"The drugs did have the effect I reported," Mark said defensively. "They did adversely affect the vision. I just got a little more of the vision than I let on. But I needed those guys gone before they administered any more drugs to me."

"Remind me not to be your enemy," Jeffreys said with a smile.

"You're not," Mark said meaningfully. "And I would be greatly indebted if you didn't tell anyone what I just told you."

"Don't worry. I won't," Jeffreys agreed. "So what do we do with this control cube?"

"I can't get near it again," Mark said. "It's all I can do not to grab it and once I do, the blue-grays will control me."

"You sure about that?" Jeffreys asked.

"Absolutely." Mark stated emphatically. "I've been in the blue-grays' memories. This is what they do. They control alien species through the use of these cubes and command them to fight the cats. The only reason they didn't get me last time was because they were rushed and the programming wasn't right. It was too strong. And then the cat showed up before they could fix it. They have had a year to perfect it and I think they have. I could hear this cube calling me from thousands of miles away and I can barely resist its command to touch it. Probably the only reason I can resist it now is because I have accessed the blue-grays memories and know what it is. But even now it's difficult. Like giving an alcoholic an open bottle and telling him to hold it, but not drink it. Sooner or later he is going to drink. So to answer your question, I think we have to destroy it. Right here, right now."

Jeffreys considered Mark's comments. "That will probably piss off Washington. They probably want the cube to study."

"It's too dangerous," Mark objected. "Remember. I'm not the only one who hears it. That poor farmer in the karst formation heard it. We can't hide it. It's still calling. Someone will find it. Maybe someone on this trail. What do we do then? And what are the odds of getting it out of China without coming across other people who can hear it? And once you get it out, you're still not safe. Anyone with the right genetic make-up will be affected. Anyone. What if one of the scientists studying it hears the call? Or a general? Or the

President? And we don't know if it is safe for you to touch it. We know touching the memory cube did not work on you and we know that you can't hear this cube. But we don't know what will happen if you touch it. They have spent a year reprogramming, refining it. And I can tell you that it works a lot better now!"

Jeffreys thought for several minutes. "I can't fault your logic," he admitted. "You don't think you can get close to it again?" he asked.

"It's all I can do just standing this far away from it," Mark said.

"All right, we destroy it. Any suggestions on how?"

"The scientists said the memory cube was some type of crystal. I would hit it with a hammer. See if you can break it."

"Except we don't have a hammer," Jeffreys said. "But we can probably find a loose rock, that might do. So what do we tell the others," Jeffreys asked. "They will report to Washington."

Now it was Mark's turn to consider. "We tell them it is a control cube. We know… I know," Mark corrected, "because I can feel it trying to control me right now. And that is true. We need to destroy it before another local finds it and us. We don't have to tell them about the other control cube. And we can say we are concerned that its call could still be heard by the cats, which is also true."

"That will work," Jeffreys said.

"Make sure not to touch it with your bare hands, just in case," Mark warned.

"Okay. Now let's catch up with the others."

"They are not that far ahead," Mark said.

"How do you…" Jeffreys started to say. "Oh yea, you can still feel the cube."

"Right," Mark answered. They picked up their pace and within minutes caught up with the others who were walking slowly, nervously, down the trail. Mark held back as they neared and watched as Jeffreys approached the others. After trading day packs, he sent Juan back to be with Mark and then had a conversation with Charles as they stood off to the side of the trail, a steady stream of tourists passing them by. After a short conversation, Mark saw Jeffreys find a fist size rock. Kneeling at the side of the trail, Jeffreys carefully removed the cube from his daypack, raised the rock over his head and brought it down with a whack on the cube. Three times he struck it as passing tourists glanced over. On the third strike the cube shattered and Mark felt an overwhelming sense of relief as the call evaporated. Mark walked over to the shattered crystal. "Did that work?" Jeffreys asked.

"Yes," Mark replied. "I can't hear it anymore.

"What should we do with the pieces?" Jeffreys asked, eying the hundreds of fragments that littered the path.

"I don't care," Mark replied. "But we will have to lose them at some point. Hard to explain how we have all these pieces of broken glass when we go though security."

"Security?" Charles asked.

"Yes," Mark replied. "There are three more of these. Now that we know what they are, it is even more imperative that we find them and destroy them before someone else comes under their control. I don't know what the blue-grays want, but you can bet it's not good for us."

Charles scooped up the fragments and put them in his daypack. "Someone may want to collect these from us later," he said.

"Now," Mark said to Jeffreys as they started walking down the trail, "lets find the other ones."

CHAPTER 8

They reached the bottom of the mountain several hours later, tired and hungry, Jeffreys having set a pretty brisk pace down the mountain. Mark had even been tempted to rent one of the pole chairs that you sat in while two locals carried you down the mountain by resting the poles on their shoulders. Only stubborn pride kept him from doing so. Jeffreys didn't look worn out at all and Mark suspected he could jog the whole trail again if needed. 'Marines!' he thought, with a mixture of disgust and envy. Juan and Charles, particularly Juan, were clearly exhausted.

When they finally arrived at their motel, Mark dropped wearily onto his bed. "I am never going to sign up for another tour with you as the tour guide," he said half jokingly to Jeffreys.

"Now you know why they say the Marines lead the way," Jeffreys joked back. Mark only grunted in response. Juan was sent for some food while Jeffreys and Charles poured over the maps and the computer, Mark half listening from the bed. Mark was feeling his body sink into the bed when Jeffreys interrupted. "Mark, is the bearing the same on your second contact?"

It took a moment for Mark to register the question. With a loud, complaining sigh, he rolled off the bed and walked slowly over to the table, thinking that he would probably be really sore in the morning. Mark closed his eyes and felt for the contact. It was easy to find. He turned slightly and then opened his eyes and pointed. "This direction," he confirmed. Jeffreys took a quick compass bearing on Mark's outstretched hand and then transferred it to the map. No longer needed, Mark flopped back on the bed, while Jeffreys and Charles continued their conversation. Mark was surprised when Jeffreys called out his name. Opening his eyes he noted that Juan was back and food was spread across the table. "Tell me I've slept for seventy-two hours," he said groggily as he staggered over to the table.

"How about fifteen minutes," Jeffreys answered.

"That's what I love, a power nap," Mark complained as he fell into a chair.

"Jeffreys said that you didn't like to miss your meals," Juan said with a surprising straight face.

"Yep, sleep and eat, that's all I live for," Mark agreed good naturedly, despite his exhaustion. He picked up his chopsticks and placed some unrecognizable food on his paper plate. He took a tentative bite of some whitish looking glop and almost retched. "What is this?" his last word was cut off by another cough.

"It's tofu," Juan answered brightly. "Very popular here."

"Ugh," Mark responded as he pushed his plate away. "I'm sorry, I can't eat American tofu, and I certainly can't eat this.... stuff." They managed to find enough rice and noodles so that Mark got something to eat. "I certainly miss the fine dining that we had on that cruise liner I was on last year," Mark said to Jeffreys, referring to Officer's Mess on board the *USS Ronald Reagan*.

"They certainly could prepare good food," Jeffreys agreed.

"Well," Mark responded, trying to make the best of things, "My wife always said I needed to go on a diet. "Hiking a mountain and eating rice and noodles every day ought to do it." After Mark ate some more, he asked, "So what is the game plan now?"

Charles responded. "It's kind of up to you. Jeffreys said that you would want to leave immediately for the next site, the lake, and we should leave within the hour. I wanted to report to the tour company and get some input from them before we moved on. That way we could spend the night here and get some rest before we set out again."

Mark saw all eyes were upon him. "How far away is the next site?"

"It's a little over a three and a half hour drive," Charles answered. "As the crow flies, its a lot closer. But, because of the mountains, we take a very circuitous route to get there. We have to go down G fifty-six, across on G sixty and then back up G twenty-five to S three-o-three," he explained as he pointed out the roads on the map. Assuming this is the location you are looking for," he added, "we will arrive well after dark."

Mark sighed before responding. "As good as spending the night here sounds, we really need to get going. We were lucky today, our... friends... did not arrive. If giving up a night's sleep means we can get to our next target before their arrival, I'd choose that any day."

"You think they would have shown up with all those tourists there?" Charles asked surprised.

Mark snorted. "You still don't get it," he said to Charles. "We are insignificant to them. Nothing more than cavemen, if that. These creatures can ...," he paused. "Is this room secure?"

"Yes, it was scanned right before we came back," Charles responded.

"These creatures are literally light years ahead of us," Mark continued.

"Then why are they hiding from us? Why these drops all over the countryside?"

"No," Mark shook his head. "The blue-grays are hiding from the cats! Not from us. If the blue-grays landed in the open, the cats would swoop down and kill them like they did before. And the cats don't care about us at all. One cat ship not much bigger than a couple of these rooms, swooped down on a carrier battle group and with one shot completely disabled the *USS Ronald Reagan*. One shot! You think they care at all about a couple hundred unarmed tourists walking on a mountain? It would be like you stepping on an ant trail, you wouldn't even notice. The only reason we got away with it today is that the cats hadn't located this site yet. So, to answer your question, yes, I want to get to the next site as soon as possible so we have a chance of getting there before the cats."

After Mark's little speech, it didn't take long for the group to pack up and head out in the car. Juan drove so that Charles could send a report on the computer once they were on their way. Jeffreys sat in the back with Mark, studying the map. "We will be heading south for about an hour, then southeast for a while, then due east and then northeast," Jeffreys explained, while he pointed out the intersections to Mark. "If we stop somewhere along each of these legs and get a bearing, by the time we get to the target area, we should have at least five different points from which to triangulate its location."

"You're not plotting an artillery strike," Mark noted.

"No, but I would like to narrow down the possibilities before we start walking around aimlessly in the dark."

"Point taken," Mark admitted, before leaning against the back window and closing his eyes. If it was a three and a half hour trip, surely he could get a couple hours of sleep in.

It seemed like only seconds later when Mark was awakened. The car was stopped on the side of the road and the sun was setting. "Thought we should take a bearing," Jeffreys explained apologetically. "Then you can get back to your beauty rest."

Mark stepped out of the car, closed his eyes, and pointed to the direction of the call. Once again Jeffreys took a compass bearing on it and traced a grease pencil line on the map. "I wish this were a military grade map," Jeffreys complained for the hundredth time. But this gives us almost a ninety degree angle, which puts our target about here, south of Chun'an," he pronounced the name hesitantly.

"I can upload our position to the agency," Charles suddenly said. "They should be able to help us triangulate!"

"Now you tell me," Jeffreys muttered as they climbed back into the car. "How secure is that," Jeffreys asked as Juan pulled back onto the road and Charles fired up his laptop.

"The cryptology is solid," Charles explained. "The signal goes straight to the satellite. It's pretty tight, but it could be picked up. It's burst transmission, so it's pretty quick, though."

"Would it be more noticeable coming from a deserted area like this, than from a crowded area?" Jeffreys asked.

"I really don't know," Charles admitted. "We are told to use the satellite connection sparingly. Usually we jump onto a modem and have the encrypted message ride along with the normal traffic. Blends in that way. It may be pretty rural here," Charles continued. "But once we get past Quzhou city, which is about three quarters of the way, then we get back into cities. Qiandau Lake is a huge resort area.

"Where are you going with this?" Mark asked Jeffreys.

"We can't forget that we are in a police state," Jeffreys explained. "It would not do to avoid the cats and then get picked up by the locals on an espionage charge."

"That could ruin your whole day," Juan interjected from the driver's seat.

"Great," Mark muttered from the back seat. "I'm going back to sleep. Wake me up when it's all over." With that he curled up against the window again, trying to get comfortable as they drove in the gathering dusk. They stopped two more times for Mark to give them new headings to the target. Each time Jeffreys marked the direction on the map and Charles uploaded it to the satellite since they were back in heavily populated areas.

"I hope the agency has a better plotter than we do," Jeffreys complained as he looked at the lines on his map. They converge, but not exactly at the same point."

"I told you this was not artillery precision," Mark said as he looked at the map.

"Tell that to the poor smuck who has an eight inch round land on his head," Jeffreys remarked.

A short time later, Charles' computer beeped and he downloaded a file from the satellite. "Don't feel bad," Charles said to Jeffreys as he held the computer so they could see the screen. The agency's plotting is not much better than yours. Although they do narrow it down to about a mile or two."

"You get me there and I'll get you the rest of the way," Mark interjected.

The computer beeped again and Charles downloaded another file. "This is interesting," he said as he read the file. "I gave them the report on the control cube and they came up with a theory that they wanted to run by Mark.

Of the five recent meteor sightings, four of them, five if you count the one we are headed towards, are near known nuclear sites."

"Nuclear?" Juan exclaimed.

"Yes," Charles continued.

"There was a nuke site on the mountain?" Mark asked.

"No, but there is a missile silo in a restricted area northwest of it. So both the mountain site and the lake site that we are heading to are relatively near a nuclear site."

"Isn't that stretching it a bit," Juan asked.

"China has nukes all over it," Jeffreys added.

"Not when you look at these two," Charles continued. "The two sites in the northwest of the country are near Malan and Delingha. Malan is in Xinjiang Autonomous Region and is known for having the largest nuclear weapons test site in the world. Delingha is in Qinghai Province and recently there have been reports of a large number of nuclear missiles located there."

What about the fifth area, the one west of us?" Juan asked.

"That's in Sichuan province," Charles continued to read. "That houses the Chinese Second Artillery. They protect China's mobile nukes."

"I've heard about them," Jeffreys interjected. "They are part of the Underground Great Wall of China."

"The what?" Mark asked.

"The Underground Great Wall," Jeffreys explained. "China is reported to have over 3,000 miles of underground tunnels housing their mobile nuclear launchers. They first came to light after an earthquake several years ago. I think around 2007 or 2008. The satellite images showed a number of hills had collapsed inward and there were reports of hundreds of inspectors in the region with radiation monitors. The cat was out of the bag, so to speak, so China did this big media campaign, heralding it as the Underground Great Wall that would protect China from nuclear attack. And then recently, a bunch of students from Georgetown University presented a paper on the Underground Great Wall, claiming that Washington's analyses of China's nuclear capability was wrong and that China had thousands more missiles than originally believed. They based their findings on Internet research and analyses of civilian satellite images such as Google Earth. It caused quite a stir, particularly since their supervising professor was some prominent ex-defense strategist who used to work for State or the Pentagon. The government downplayed it, but my guess is that they were embarrassed they had missed it."

"What about the karst formation area?" Mark asked.

"Nothing on that here," Charles responded.

"It was in Yunnan Province," Juan noted. "That's south of Sichuan Province."

"They want your thoughts about whether the blue-grays are trying to get nukes," Charles finished, reading the file.

Mark thought for a moment. "It's possible," he said finally. "Last year they landed almost on top of a carrier task force. A nuclear carrier task force and were trying to get us to fight the cats. Now they are sending control cubes near Chinese nuke sights."

"They didn't say anything about nukes last year," Jeffreys noted.

"They didn't 'say' anything," Mark corrected. "But you're right, the images they sent showed aircraft and ships fighting. But the images were pretty basic, cobbled together images."

"They could have showed a picture of a nuclear explosion," Jeffreys pointed out.

"Yes, but the classic nuke picture was the first test on that atoll with all the Navy ships being blasted. Probably not something you want to send to the Navy," Mark countered.

"There are lots of nuclear images on the net they could have used other than that one," Jeffreys said.

"Why would they want nukes?" Juan asked from the driver's seat. "An advanced race like that?"

"The blue-grays are in a science vessel," Mark explained, realizing that Juan did not know the details of last year's events. "The cats are in a warship and were attacking them when they escaped to Earth." Mark omitted the fact that the attack occurred 65 million years ago and that both ships were caught in a wormhole that whisked them through time to deposit them in Earth's solar system in the current time. The story was unbelievable enough as it was. "The ships were damaged," Mark continued his abbreviated explanation, "and the blue-gray ship fled to the Earth and tried to enlist our aid in their fight against the cats. Unfortunately, or perhaps fortunately, we'll never know, the cats attacked and killed the blue-grays before they had successfully communicated with us. Then both ships were caught in a collapsing wormhole and disappeared."

"What's with all the wormholes?" Juan asked.

"That's how they travel," Mark explained. "They create a wormhole and travel through it. The problem arises when something goes wrong with the wormhole and it collapses."

"So, if the cats killed the blue-grays, who is sending these control cubes?" Juan continued.

"That's a good question," Mark agreed. "We thought they were killed. We know one certainly was because we saw that."

"And any blue-grays on board their ship would have been killed when that cat boarded it," Jeffreys added.

"But the control cubes are blue-gray technology," Mark continued. "So I am assuming there are more blue-grays out there, perhaps on a mothership. And either the same cat that attacked us last year survived the wormhole collapse or some new cats are also out there continuing the war. Either way, we, I mean Earth, is their current battleground and that is bad news for us." Mark paused while Juan and Charles digested what he told them. "Obviously, there are very few people who know what I just told you. But that is why we need to stop them. Before things get really out of hand."

"You still have targeting problems," Jeffreys said.

"What?" Mark asked confused.

"Targeting problems," Jeffreys explained. "Let's say the blue-grays controlled the Chinese and told them to nuke the cats. How could they do that? The cats' ship does not register on our radar and it might even be able to out-run one of our missiles, even if we somehow got a lock on it. And if it is in space, we don't have anything that could hit it anyway, certainly nothing fast enough to hit a cat ship in space."

"I don't have a clue," Mark admitted. "But if I was fighting the cats I would want the biggest gun I could find and a nuke is our biggest gun."

"So what should I tell Washington?" Charles asked.

"Tell them I don't know," Mark said. "But it is possible, maybe even probable."

They pondered these thoughts in silence while Juan continued to drive and Charles typed in the computer. Traffic was light to nonexistent. "We should be getting to the turn-off for S three-o-three pretty soon," Juan stated. As if on cue, a sign appeared noting the approaching intersection.

They made the turn and Charles pulled out the map. "According to these coordinates, we don't actually get to Chun'an," Charles announced. "The predicted impact point is actually south of it, around here," he pointed to the area on the map where multiple lines crossed.

"We're getting closer," Mark assured him. "I can feel it much stronger now. I'll let you know." Mark sat back, eyes closed, following the call in his head.

Some time later Mark opened his eyes and straightened up as the direction of the call started to move to his right. Mark closed his eyes again and concentrated. The call was starting to fall behind them. "We're passing it," Mark called out. Juan traveled a couple miles further before he found an exit off the highway. "Let me see the map." They handed Mark the map and Jeffreys pointed out where they were. They were in the area of most of the converging lines. "We passed it," Mark said. "Go back."

Juan turned the car around and started driving back along a secondary road that paralleled the highway they had been on. They traveled a couple miles before the call came from a point ninety degrees to Mark's left. "Stop," Mark commanded. They were out in the countryside, between two towns. "It's over there," he pointed across a dark field towards the woods.

"At least it's out in the country," Charles commented. "Don't have to worry too much about the locals."

As they got out of the car, Jeffreys turned to Mark. "Are we close?"

"Yes, very close," Mark replied. "I'd guess right inside the wood line.

"What do we do if the cats show up?"

Mark paused and considered. "On a clear night like this, we should get some more warning. Certainly more than we did last time."

Jeffreys studied the clear night sky. "Some," he conceded. "But not much. Maybe fifteen or twenty seconds. Certainly not much more."

"Can we get the agency to warn us if NORAD makes a sighting," Charles asked, pointing to his computer.

"They wouldn't be able to get the warning to us any sooner," Jeffreys answered. "So what do we do if we see them?" he repeated to Mark.

"We run like hell," Mark said.

"Great plan," Jeffreys grunted.

"Have a better one?" Mark asked.

"Unfortunately, no." Jeffreys considered for a moment. "Okay folks. Here's the way we'll play it. Mark and I will take point. Charles and Juan, you follow on the flanks. While we're in the open, fall back a hundred feet or so and off to the sides. If we get into the woods, you'll have to close in accordingly, but still try to keep some distance. We don't want to bunch up. Now, Charles and Juan, keep an eye on the sky. Watch it for your life. If you see anything, call out. If it looks like a meteor, we have seconds. So yell and then run for your lives. Each run in a different direction, don't clump up. And don't run toward our target. A cat is fast and deadly. If it wants to kill you, it will. So don't do anything to attract it. Just scatter."

"Aren't cats attracted by movement?" Charles asked.

"Earth cats are," Jeffreys agreed. "But this one is intelligent. You stay, you die. We know that's true. So I opt for running." They all agreed and took their positions with Mark and Jeffreys in the lead. "I should have shot that cat on the carrier when I had the chance," Jeffreys whispered to Mark as they started hiking across the field.

"You were under orders not to," Mark objected.

"I don't recall you following those orders."

"I'm a civilian," Mark chuckled. "Besides, I only started firing when the cat was trying to kill us." They walked on in silence, Mark concentrating on the call.

"Can you tell if it is much further?" Jeffreys asked. "If we get caught in the open like this we're dead."

"Not much farther," Mark responded. "I think it's somewhere in those trees up ahead." Their pace slowed when they got to the tree line and Charles and Juan moved in closer. They all turned on their flashlights, which they had kept off for fear of attracting unwanted attention in the open field. But in the forest, the wan moon did not provide enough light. They traveled about 300 hundred yards in the woods before Mark came to an abrupt stop. Jeffreys watched Mark expectantly. "We are close, very close," Mark whispered. "It's right around here."

Jeffreys glanced around nervously and flexed his arms. He didn't like being unarmed. Since they had been on airline flights, he didn't have so much as a jackknife. He promised himself that he would remedy that condition next time. Assuming they lived through this night, he thought pessimistically. Mark stepped forward slowly, shining his light around. Jeffreys followed, scanning the ground with his light, while also casting worried looks through the treetops to the sky above. On one such glance he thought he saw something unusual. Shining his light up, he noticed a broken branch. Searching more, he saw several broken branches.

"Look here," he said to Mark. Mark looked up and together they discovered a line of broken branches, starting high up and angling down. They followed the path until it angled to the ground. "This branch is burned," Jeffreys noted. When Mark didn't respond, Jeffreys glanced over and saw Mark staring at the ground. Jeffreys stepped past Mark and looked down. On the ground was the now familiar patch of fresh dirt about three feet in diameter with scorch marks around the perimeter. "Same as before," Jeffreys stated unnecessarily. Mark merely nodded. "We found it," Jeffreys called out and Juan and Charles converged on their location. "Juan, you and I will dig it up, just like before. Charles, you move away and find as clear a spot as possible and watch the sky. If you see so much as a firefly, let us know immediately.

Like before, Jeffreys and Juan dug with broken sticks while Mark held their flashlights. They dug about a foot before a red cube was revealed in the light. Jeffreys knocked the dirt off it and looked up at Mark, who was clearly in distress. "It's not getting any easier to ignore these things," Mark said through clenched teeth.

Jeffreys wrapped the cube in his hat and stuffed it into his daypack. "Let's get out of here," he commanded and they set off back through the woods towards the car. When they got to the field, they broke into a run, wanting to put as much distance between them and the landing site as possible. Jeffreys got to the car first. When the others arrived, he had the cube out, lying on the asphalt and was holding a tire iron.

"The agency wants you to keep it intact," Charles said when he realized Jeffreys' intent.

"Can you ride in the car with this thing?" Jeffreys asked Mark.

"Not a chance," Mark answered through clenched teeth.

With a resounding whack, Jeffreys brought the tire iron down on the cube, shattering it with the first strike. He looked up at Mark, who was now visibly relaxed. "I guess I don't have to hit it again," Jeffreys commented.

"No, that did the trick," Mark stated.

"We still need to get out of here," Jeffreys said. They paused long enough for Charles to scoop the broken crystal pieces into a container before Juan pulled out, spraying dirt with the tires.

"Don't get too crazy with the driving," Jeffreys warned. "We don't want to draw any unwanted attention, and that includes the local police." Juan slowed slightly.

"Get back on the highway, heading north," Charles instructed. "We'll spend the night in Chun'an. Then we'll decide what to do next. It's almost midnight and we need to get some sleep," he added the last part looking at Mark.

"No objection from me," Mark stated as he relaxed in the back seat.

Mark actually dozed off. When he awoke he stared out at the lights of a bustling city. "Where are we?"

"Chun'an," Juan answered. "We're almost at the hotel."

"Look at the size of this hotel," Mark remarked as they pulled into the Sheraton Qiandao Lake Resort. "I can't believe I'm staying in a Sheraton in China," Mark exclaimed. It was a huge, modern, luxury hotel that would have fit in anywhere in the world. "I hope the tour agency is paying for the room."

"I told you this was a resort community," Charles said.

"You did," Mark agreed. "It just seems weird to be in this bustling city with luxury, hi-rise hotels after traveling through some of the rural country we were just in."

"Welcome to China," Charles said.

They quickly checked in, Mark too tired to care about any of the details. Once again Mark and Jeffreys shared a room. When they walked into their room, Mark collapsed on the bed, too tired to even take a shower. "Don't wake me until sometime next month," he said as Jeffreys headed for the shower. A nagging feeling that something was amiss lingered in Mark's consciousness, but he was too tired to care and soon fell asleep.

CHAPTER 9

Charles awakened Mark the next morning at 8:00 a.m. Even with almost seven hours of sleep, Mark still felt drugged.

"Are you a clean freak?" Mark asked as he noticed Jeffreys coming out of the bathroom, clearly having taken a shower. "Didn't you take a shower last night before we went to bed?"

"Yes. But I just finished a 5 mile run, so I thought I needed another shower."

"How do you do it?"

"It's my line of work," Jeffreys responded, much too chipper for this early in the morning.

"I said not to wake me up this month," Mark grumbled.

"Army!" Jeffreys said with mock scorn. "You slept almost eight hours."

"Not even seven," Mark interrupted.

"Almost seven hours in a wonderful bed in a luxury hotel and you still complain!"

"I keep telling you, I'm a civilian," Mark responded. "My days sleeping for an hour or two in snow banks are over and have been for a long time."

"Ignore my friend here," Jeffreys said to Charles. "He's not happy if he doesn't have something to complain about."

"I'm going to ring room service so we can plan our next move undisturbed," Charles commented as Mark got up and staggered to the bathroom. "What do you want for breakfast?"

"Anything," Mark muttered. "As long as there is a lot of it and it's American. And orange juice, lots of orange juice," he added as he slammed the bathroom door. Thirty minutes later he emerged, wrapped in a hotel robe and almost feeling human after having taken a long, luxurious bath, shaved and brushed his teeth. He found some fresh clothes and went back into the bathroom to change. When he emerged, breakfast was spread across the table and the three others were looking over the maps that were spread across one of the beds. Juan was chewing on a biscuit.

"Mind if I eat?" Mark asked.

"Help yourself," Charles said.

"We need to be a little more prepared this time," Jeffreys was saying as Mark sat down at the table and started choosing what to eat. "We were lucky yesterday. But we can't count on that every time."

"What do you suggest?" Charles asked.

"For starters, we need some tools. A shovel would be nice. We can get a small collapsible entrenching tool. That goes with the backpacks and the camping theme. We need a container for the cube. Say a small camping pot and pan set, along with a set of tongs. Again, all consistent with camping and easily purchased at a camping store. And a hammer. That's the easy part. Now the hard part, we need some weapons."

"That's out of the question," Charles interrupted. "We can't be carrying weapons in China!"

Jeffreys was quiet for a moment. "Okay, how close to a weapon can I get? A sheath knife? A machete? An ax? How about a samurai sword? We need something to protect us."

"You won't get close to a cat with anything like that, not even the samurai sword," Mark pointed out from the table where he was eating.

"I know," Jeffreys agreed. "I don't think anything short of an assault rifle would have a chance against a cat. But we need something against humans as well," Jeffreys continued. "We can't assume that we will always find the cube first. That poor Chinese in the karst formation. He seemed reluctant to give it up."

"But there are four of us," Charles objected.

"Who says next time there will only be one of them," Jeffreys responded. "I want something to increase the odds."

"You mean even the odds," Juan corrected.

"No, I mean increase the odds," Jeffreys maintained. "I never want even odds when it comes to a fight. I intend them to be very uneven and against the other side."

"I will see what I can do," Charles said hesitantly. "But we can't go in looking like a Marine combat patrol."

"Too bad," Jeffreys said. "But lets do something. Even an entrenching tool would help. There was a Medal of Honor recipient who took out a score of enemy soldiers in Vietnam, armed only with an entrenching tool."

"We don't want to be taking out a score of people," Charles objected.

"No, we don't," Jeffreys agreed. "But we want the capability to take them out."

Mark zoned out while Jeffreys and Charles debated. He had finished a helping of scrambled eggs and biscuits and was working on some bacon as his mind wandered.

'Where were the aliens coming from?' he wondered. 'The blue-grays had been killed by the cats on the *USS Ronald Reagan*. Everyone had seen that. The blue-gray on the flight deck was blown apart by the cat. And then the cat boarded the blue-grays' ship. Any blue-gray on that ship would have been killed by the cat during that attack. So where were the blue-grays coming from? And the cat had been lost when the wormhole collapsed. So there must be a blue-gray mothership. That had to be the answer. But what about the cats? Another mothership? No, that wasn't the answer,' Mark thought. 'It must be something else.'

"What do you think, Mark?" Charles' question broke Mark out of his reverie.

"We're trying to figure out the next leg of this trip," Charles repeated. "We have three sites, two up in the northwestern part of China and one due west of us. The agency is recommending the northwest and is divided between Malan and Delingha. Jeffreys is recommending focusing on Sichuan province, where the Second Artillery is located. What do you think?"

"It's closer," Jeffreys added. "And as for Malan, I don't see how four Americans are going to get anywhere near a nuclear testing ground. If the blue-grays dropped a control cube in there, we are going to have to get the State Department involved and do it diplomatically. I don't know about you two," he referred to Juan and Charles, "but I don't think either Mark or I qualify for that type of James Bond work."

"He has a point there," Juan agreed.

Mark closed his eyes and concentrated on the call. There was something odd about it. He had noticed it last night, but was too tired to pay any attention. Now that he was rested and fed, the difference was very noticeable. "Let me see a map," Mark asked. They pulled over a large map of China and pointed out where they were and where the other three targets were located, one due west and the other two northwest. "How far are we from the site due west of us?"

"The Sichuan site is over six-hundred miles away," Charles answered.

Mark frowned. "Let me see the local map, the one we used last night." They pulled over that map and Mark had them orientate the two maps with a compass, before closing his eyes and concentrating on the calls. He could feel the calls and with his eyes closed he pointed to each one, holding the position while Jeffreys took a compass bearing for each and at Mark's request marking the bearings on the map. Mark started on the northwest calls and then moved down to the western. He did the western one twice, telling Jeffreys to mark the second western bearing darker. He opened his eyes and looked at the map of China. Four lines radiated out from their town of Chun'an with degree notations on them. Three lines either passed through or near the circles that had been placed on the map showing the estimated impact points, the fourth missed.

"You can't expect your heading to be dead on over several thousand miles," Jeffreys explained the apparent discrepancy. Just a degree or two off will result in a huge difference at these distances. For instance, your last two headings for the western target are a few degrees apart, and you can see the distance change," he traced out one that passed by Chengdu in Sichuan Province and the second which passed substantially south of Chengdu.

"That's not what I am worried about," Mark said and then instructed Jeffreys to place the last two headings on the local map. Confused, Jeffreys complied nonetheless.

"See, we had the same problem last night," Jeffreys noted as he drew the lines on the local map. Mark studied the local map. It still had the markings from the four bearings that were taken during their late drive.

Three of the lines crossed near where the cube was ultimately found, but one set crossed out in the lake. The second bearing he had taken just now, the one he had Jeffreys mark in bold, went directly through the crossed lines in the lake.

"How far do you think we are from this point?" Mark asked, pointing to the crossed lines in the lake.

Jeffreys looked at the scale. "About two and a half miles. I could narrow it down."

"In a minute," Mark said. "Gentlemen, we have a problem. I think two cubes landed here, not one." They all looked up surprised. "From a distance, they were so close, I thought they were one," Mark explained. "And then when we got closer, the closer cube pulled my attention. But obviously, while we were traveling down the road, I mixed up one for the other."

"That could just be a small heading error," Jeffreys pointed out.

"I would agree," said Mark. "Except that I still hear four cubes calling. And this one, the one I had you mark in bold is close. Not six-hundred miles away. I was too tired to appreciate it last night. But now it is clear. We have another cube nearby and it just happens to intersect with two of the headings I gave yesterday. That's why we were having some trouble pinning it down last night. There were always two cubes here, not one."

Jeffreys was the first to respond. "Then we need a boat."

"Yes," Mark agreed. "We need a boat."

"This is just getting better all the time," Jeffreys complained as Charles left to make arrangements for a boat.

"What do you mean?" Mark asked.

"It's hard enough to hide in the woods or a field, but hiding in a boat, particularly in the daytime is impossible. It took the cat what, three, four days to find the first cube. These cubes have been on the ground for, say forty-eight hours now."

"So we still have a two day buffer," Juan said optimistically.

"Except that now we know the cats are looking for them."

"So much for my buffer."

"Exactly," Jeffreys said.

"So we need to get out there immediately," Mark said impatiently.

"I still would like to have an M-60," Jeffreys muttered as he sat down to study the map. "Can you handle a boat," Jeffreys asked Juan.

"I'm okay," Juan answered tentatively.

"Swim?"

"Yes," Juan answered with more confidence.

Jeffreys looked at Mark. "Hey, I live in Pensacola. I am very confident in a boat," Mark answered the unasked question. "I just didn't like being in the middle of the Pacific, particularly when they were dangling me from a helicopter, trying to drop me on a moving submarine. And yes, I can swim."

"Submarine?" Juan asked.

"Yea," Mark answered. "The blue-grays played cat and mouse with an attack submarine down in the Mariana Trench and I got invited to come along."

"Cool."

"Not when you are actually doing it," Mark responded.

Charles returned a few minutes later with reservations for a boat. "While you pack for the trip, I want to send a quick message to the tour company, letting them know about these new developments. It will only take a couple minutes."

Instead of objecting over the short delay, Mark asked, "Can you ask them to notify us immediately if they spot another meteor in China?"

"That won't do us any good," Jeffreys interjected. "By the time we get the call it will be on top of us."

"That's true," Mark agreed, "if we are at the landing site. But if we are approaching it or if the cat chooses one of the other sites instead, it would be good information for us to have."

"Good point," Jeffreys conceded. They packed their daypacks while Charles booted up his laptop and sent off a quick message. "Are you going to take the laptop on the boat?" Jeffreys asked when he had finished packing.

Charles looked at his watch and did a rough calculation. "We're going to have a satellite overhead for at least part of our trip. I think I'll take the laptop. Maybe we can have some useful real time images." With that he closed up his laptop, stowed it in his daypack and led the group down to the dock where their boat was waiting. Much to Mark's surprise, the Marina manager gave them detailed instructions on the boats operation in fluent English. It was a 20' center console Boston Whaler looking boat with a 100hp engine, just right for four people in a lake. 'As long as the wind doesn't whip up too much,' Mark told himself. After all, this lake was huge, and a good wind could create some nasty waves. But the day was clear and calm and their destination was probably under two or three miles. They would have to figure out which island it was on. Island? Mark suddenly realized that he had always assumed that it would be on an island. What if it wasn't? Could they rent Scuba gear here? And how deep was this lake?

As the boating instructions were winding down, Mark asked the manager if Scuba diving was possible, should they be so inclined. "Oh, yes," he replied enthusiastically. We have divers all the time. Do you want to dive Shi Cheng?"

"Shi Cheng?" Mark struggled with the pronunciation.

"Yes. The Lion city. It was built in the Dong Han period, which was twenty-five to two-hundred A.D. It was flooded when the dam was built and now sits around twenty-six to forty meters. It is a very popular dive site."

Mark told him that they would consider it. They pulled away from the dock, Jeffreys driving, while Mark listened for the call and pointed out the way. Juan and Charles acted as look-outs.

"You think it's underwater?" Juan asked.

"I hope not," Mark answered. "It just came to me that I was assuming it was on land and wondered what we would do if it wasn't.

"It would be damned inconvenient of them to drop it into the water," Jeffreys joked, lightening the mood.

As they set off on their course, Mark scanned the surroundings with his binoculars. "What's that?" he asked, pointing off to the right. "The white thing in that inlet at...," he read the degrees off his built in compass.

Juan swung his binoculars in the indicated direction. "Oh. That's a fish farm."

"A fish farm?" Mark asked incredulously.

"Yes. The fishermen build large cages and grow their fish in there. They feed them and of course there is always a supply of fresh water. At harvest time, they are easy to catch."

"Not very sporting," Jeffreys remarked.

"When you have to feed as many people as they feed in China, you don't care much about sport," Juan explained.

They continued on, Jeffreys altering their course on occasion to avoid small islands or other boats. The lake was not round like many of the lakes Mark was used to. It sprawled out like a many-legged hydra, with nooks and crannies everywhere. That made sense, Mark reasoned, since it was originally a valley, perhaps several valleys, which had been flooded when they dammed up the river. The islands he was seeing were actually mountain peaks before the flood.

As they approached one of the larger islands Mark noted that the call appeared to be coming from it. "From it, or from past it?" Jeffreys asked, when Mark pointed out the island.

"I don't know," Mark admitted.

"Okay," Jeffreys said, "We'll go around it. Tell me if the direction changes. With that Jeffreys piloted the boat around the island, which was about a quarter mile long and covered with some type of pine tree.

"From it," Mark confirmed as Jeffreys piloted the boat around the island, looking for a safe approach.

"We're not landing on this side," Jeffreys remarked as they motored past a sheer rock wall about fifty feet high. "One hundred feet down," Jeffreys called out, reading from the depth finder.

"That was one heck of a cliff before the lake was made," Mark said as they passed it. They continued around and saw a beach area with a couple boats pulled up on it.

"Let's go all the way around and check it out first," Jeffreys said. "Then we can come back if we need to." They continued around until they found an unoccupied landing site and decided to dock there rather than join the other boats they had passed. "Just in case we don't like the company," Jeffreys explained.

"What's the plan?" Charles asked, relying on Jeffreys for the tactical decisions.

Jeffreys looked around. "Same as before," he decided. "Mark and I will take point, you two flank. You probably will have to stay pretty close on these trails though. Keep an eye on the sky at all times. If our friends show up, holler and run. Split up if you can. It depends how many trails are on this island. Run as far as you can and then find cover and hunker down. Don't go out in the water, that's a killing field. When the coast is clear, meet back here at the boat."

"How will we know if the coast is clear?" Juan asked.

"When it's gone," Jeffreys answered. "That's the best I can tell you. But be patient. Don't rush out." They tied off the boat and Jeffreys and Mark headed up a path into the trees, with Juan and Charles following nervously. It was a clear summer day with a deep blue sky and no clouds. Hardly a day you would expect disaster to strike. Mark felt the incongruity as he walked up the hill, waiting any moment to hear the loud electrical buzz-snap sound that would signal an attacking cat. He was so tense, he jumped when Juan stepped on a twig.

"Calm down," Jeffreys whispered, although it was obvious that he was also tense.

"I can't see the sky," Juan called ahead. "The trees are too thick."

Mark glanced up. Sunlight streamed through the treetops, but they blocked any meaningful view of the sky. "Do the best you can," Jeffreys called back as quietly as he could. They came across several other paths and at each one Jeffreys would pause and let Mark choose the direction. Nearing the top of the island they came across another path. As before, Jeffreys paused. Mark did also, a confused look on his face. "Problem?" Jeffreys asked quietly as Juan and Charles stopped behind them, the path being too narrow for them to walk abreast.

"It's up this way," Mark said slowly, pointing up the hill. "But something has changed. It doesn't feel the same anymore. It's like... muted. Mark shook his head. "I don't know. But something is different." Jeffreys started to go forward and Mark grabbed his arm. "I know what it is! Someone has it! It's the same feeling I had from the local in the karst formation. Someone has found it."

Jeffreys picked up his pace. "Stay alert everyone. This could get entertaining." They traveled another 200 feet and entered a clearing at the top of the island. There was a small pagoda about 50 feet into the clearing and places for picnickers. But what caught everyone's attention were the bodies lying in and around the pagoda. Jeffreys dropped into a crouch, motioning everyone to get down. "The cats have already gotten here," he whispered, glancing nervously around.

Mark seemed frozen, his heart pounding in his ears. "They didn't get the cube," Mark whispered. "I can still hear it. It's coming from the pagoda."

Jeffreys motioned Juan and Charles to stay where they were as he slowly crept towards the pagoda. He reached the first body and knelt down to examine it. Looking back, he motioned Mark to come forward. Mark had to forcibly will his legs to move into the clearing.

With each step Mark imagined a searing lightning bolt blasting him in the chest. It wasn't hard for him to imagine. One of the blue-grays whose memories he had relived had been killed by a cat in the same fashion. The shock of that death had caused Mark to go into cardiac arrest and it was only the efforts of the ship's doctor that had resuscitated him. Now he was afraid it would happen again, but this time for real.

After a seeming eternity, Mark crouched down at Jeffreys' side. "He's alive," Jeffreys whispered. "Not a mark on him." Mark looked at the unconscious Chinese man.

"Sleeping?" he asked.

"Odd position to be sleeping in," Jeffreys remarked. They moved forward together, checking each of the bodies as they went. There were about fifteen people, men and women in their twenties or thirties, Mark guessed. All were sprawled out as if they had fallen where they stood without any warning. They had to step carefully over the bodies when they entered the pagoda.

"Where is it?" Jeffreys whispered, as if afraid to wake anyone up.

Mark looked around and then closed his eyes. Opening his eyes, he stepped over another body to get to the center of the pagoda. "The guy in the blue shirt," he whispered, pointing to the prone figure. "It's coming from him. There it is!" he said louder. "Look in his right hand. He's holding it." Jeffreys started to move forward. "Remember, you can't touch it!" Mark commanded urgently.

Jeffreys paused. "Maybe I can pry it out with a stick or something," he whispered as he glanced around the pagoda for a suitable tool.

"Maybe you can..." Mark finished the sentence with a shocked yell as the man with the blue shirt suddenly opened his eyes and jumped to his feet, yelling something in Chinese. Immediately, all the others woke up as well, scrambling to their feet while yelling in Chinese. The scene was mass confusion. Jeffreys pushed Mark out a low window and quickly followed him out. But the people outside the pagoda had awoken and surrounded them.

Juan and Charles rushed into the clearing yelling something back in Chinese. Suddenly, on command from the blue shirted Chinese, all yelling stopped. He stepped to the front of the raised pagoda and the other Chinese lined up in front of him. He started speaking in Chinese and Charles translated. "He says, 'What are you doing here? What are you trying to do?' "

"Tell him we are just tourists," Mark answered quickly. "Come to enjoy your beautiful country."

Charles translated and the blue shirt spoke back. "He says, 'Why are you trying to rob us?' "

"Tell him we thought they were hurt, we were trying to help them, not rob them."

Charles dutifully translated. Back and forth the questions and answers went, but Charles made no headway in calming down the Chinese, who denied that they had been asleep and kept accusing Mark and Jeffreys of trying to rob them.

"We're not getting anywhere here," Jeffreys whispered to Mark while Mr. Blue Shirt was speaking again.

"They are under control of the cube," Mark said. "All of them. They very likely will attack," Mark added, remembering how the blue-grays had controlled the velociraptors in one of his shared memories and trained them to attack.

Mark and Jeffreys were slowly edging away from the Chinese as Charles translated another message from Mr. Blue Shirt. In the middle of the translation, Charles cell phone started to ring. He glanced down, reaching for his phone, but Jeffreys glanced up into the sky.

"RUN!" Jeffreys yelled, pushing Mark towards the path. Mark saw a streak of light in the sky out of the corner of his eye as he bolted out of the clearing. "Split up," Jeffreys yelled and Mark turned right at the first path and ran for all he was worth, trees and bushes a blur as he ran recklessly down the path. He rounded a turn and slid to a stop, barely stopping before the edge of a cliff. He looked down. He was on top of the 50-foot cliff they had seen from the boat. He glanced back into the sky and noted an eerie red light. 'The cat ship, blazing from its fiery entry into the Earth's atmosphere, must be hovering above the clearing' Mark thought. Without any further hesitation, Mark turned and leaped off the cliff. The fall took forever and Mark clearly heard the snap-buzz of the cats' weapons as his hair stood up with static electricity.

Mark hated heights. Worse, he hated falling. Once he had been cajoled into jumping off a three-meter board at school. But only once. He hated the heart-in-your-throat feeling of falling and the slamming impact into the water even more. The leap off the cliff was all of this and more as he knew he would be struck by the cats' lightning bolt before he hit the water. He heard himself screaming as he fell. Somehow he managed to get a breath of air a split second before hitting the water. Even more miraculously, it wasn't knocked out when he hit. Stunned, he sank in the cold water.

One hundred feet, he remembered Jeffreys had said as they passed this point in the boat. One hundred feet. He couldn't hold his breath for a hundred feet. The thought jarred him into action. Opening his eyes, he started to swim for the surface. His clothes dragged on him as he struggled, the light far above. His lungs ached, crying out for air. He kicked hard and pulled frantically with his arms, heart pounding in his ears. He wasn't going to make it. His clothes were pulling him down. His chest was bursting. He had to breathe!

His head burst out of the water and he gasped for breath. He knew he should look up, probably take a deep breath and swim back underwater to safety. But he couldn't stop gasping that sweet, wonderful air as he tread water. Finally, he forced himself to slow his breathing and look around. The red light was gone. He was treading water ten feet from the cliff edge. The water was cold, but relatively calm. Mark forced himself to relax. He was a good swimmer, so the water didn't bother him. His summer weight clothes were a nuisance, but nothing more. He would have to lose the hiking boots though if he was going to swim any distance. He looked at the cliff. There was no getting out there. At best he might find a handhold, but staying still for too long in this cold water would be fatal.

He started to swim around the island, watching the waterline carefully for a place he could climb out. He remembered the island was about a quarter mile long. It would be an easy swim for him once he removed his boots. He still hesitated in removing them, wondering how easy it would be to find replacements. 'You will not need replacements if you drown,' he chided himself, and reluctantly unlaced his boots and let them sink. As the second boot sank he realized he should have tied the laces together and carried them. But it was done.

Swimming was easier after that so he started an easy crawl stroke, pausing every so often to check his position and look for a way onto the island. He swam routinely at the local YMCA, usually swimming a mile at lunch, so this swim, even with his clothes on, did not bother him. He paused, treading water as he studied the island. He could climb up on the rocks here, but he couldn't see a path onto the island afterwards. Better to get to a beach area, even if that meant swimming around to where they had docked the boat.

He continued swimming, falling into a regular rhythm, pausing occasionally to scan the island for an easy access. When none appeared, he kept swimming. The unmistakable sound of a boat engine resonated through the water. He switched over to breaststroke so he could keep a lookout. 'Would not do getting run over by a boat after having survived the cat and the jump off the cliff,' he thought. He swam a little farther before the boat came into view. It was their boat, Jeffreys at the helm and Juan and Charles in the bow searching the island with binoculars. Mark's heart leaped. He had been trying not to worry about them until he got out of the water, but now that they were safe, a great weight lifted off him.

Mark yelled and waved. Jeffreys spotted him first and quickly motored over to him. Juan and Charles pulled him aboard and Jeffreys turned the boat and headed for the mainland as fast as the boat would travel. The wind was cold and Mark started to shiver. Juan pulled a silver space blanket out of his daypack and wrapped it around Mark to break the wind. It did the trick. Soon Mark was warm and sitting up to see where they were going. They were headed straight to the nearest land. When they got within 100 yards, Jeffreys turned and followed the coast towards the Marina, but at a slightly slower pace.

"What happened?" Mark asked loud enough to be heard over the engine.

Jeffreys put his finger to his lips and Mark swallowed his questions. When the island was far in the distance, Jeffreys pulled up next to a little stub of an island that was clearly deserted and turned off the engine, letting the boat slide up onto a little beach area. After making sure the boat was secure, he said quietly, "Now remember that sound travels over water."

"What happened?" Mark asked quietly.

"Cat arrived," Jeffreys said quietly. "We all ran and hid. Heard the cat attack. After the cat ship left we met at the boat. I went back up to the pagoda to see what happened. It was blasted and everyone was dead. Cat must have used the ship's gun, as the damage was much worse than that poor local at the karst formation. Bits and pieces everywhere. No sign of the cube. The cube is gone, isn't it?"

Mark paused and closed his eyes and listened. In all the excitement he had forgotten about the cube. Opening his eyes, he stated, "Yes. It's gone."

"What happened to you?" Juan asked.

"We heard you scream," Charles added. "Thought the cat got you."

Mark looked embarrassed. "You know that cliff we saw on the other side of the island?" They nodded.

"Well, just my luck. The path I took ended at a very scenic spot on the top of that cliff." Mark paused, enjoying the dramatic effect. "I jumped."

"I would have screamed too," Charles stated and the others nodded.

"So what do we do now?" Juan asked. "Last time we called the cops." He let the statement hang in the air.

"Yes," Jeffreys said. "And they interrogated us all night and kept us locked up three days. And that was for four deaths, but only one local. Can you imagine what they will do with this massacre?"

Mark considered it, trying to put himself in the position of the local police or prosecutor. "No," he finally said. "If we report a lightning strike and they link us up with the other one, then we are going to be detained. Lightning doesn't strike the same people twice. And as Jeffreys pointed out, this is a police state. Who knows how long they will hold us? Even if they ultimately let us go, our mission will be over."

"Can't we just let the cats destroy all the cubes? They seem to be doing a good job of it," Juan asked.

"That is tempting," Mark agreed. "It would certainly be less hazardous to our health. But let's decide that later, rather than having the Chinese decide it for us by holding us in a jail cell till they make up their minds. For now, we just need to get out of Dodge."

"How's this story?" Jeffreys asked when Mark had finished. "We had a wonderful time exploring the lake and some of the islands. Our friend here," he motioned to Mark, "got a little too careless looking at a fish and fell overboard. But otherwise it was a great trip. And no, we didn't see or hear anything out of the ordinary. Everyone got it?" They all nodded their heads in agreement. "Then we go to the hotel, pack up and leave."

They pulled into the Marina and started off loading their gear. The manager was surprised to see Mark all wet and Mark took all their jokes in good nature and swore he had the best time ever, promising to come back next time to go Scuba diving. Twenty minutes later they were checked out and driving away as fast as they dared.

CHAPTER 10

"I better check in and let the agency know what has happened," Charles said, pulling out his laptop while Juan drove out of Chun'an.

"Are you sure you should do that?" Mark asked, getting everyone's attention. "I heard your conversation last night about satellites and stuff. Wouldn't it be bad to have the Chinese discover an encoded transmission so near this disaster? It's not like we need anything from them right now, is there?"

Charles considered Mark's remark and then closed his laptop. "Better be safe than sorry," he agreed.

"We're going to have to decide where we're going pretty soon," Juan commented. "Are we going back to the airport at Tunxi?"

"There's an airport at Hangzhou," Jeffreys said, studying the map. "It appears to be closer and is certainly a more direct route than Tunxi."

"Hangzhou is a major city," Charles explained. "It is serviced by Xiaoshan International, which is a major airport. Probably one of the top ten airports in the country."

"I'm all for getting lost in the crowd," Mark stated.

"Okay, Hangzhou it is. We'll be able to get better connections there too," Charles agreed.

"It looks like it's about a hundred miles away, say about two hours drive time, give or take," Jeffreys intoned. "You take a left when you get to S thirty-two, and that puts you on G twenty-five east. It looks like the highway goes right to the airport."

"Do you have somewhere on that map I can get some shoes so I don't have to traipse all over China in these sandals?" Mark asked.

"We pass through Qiantanzhen," Jeffreys said, studying the map. It looks big enough on the map that we should be able to find something there. Then there's Tonglu."

"Stop, just stop," Juan interjected. "You are just butchering the language. It's Qiantanzhen and Tonglu."

"That's what I said. Qiantanzhen."

"Agh, that is horrible."

"Then I guess you don't want me pronouncing the next cities: Fuyang and Wenyanzhen?" Jeffreys said with a laugh.

They found some shoes for Mark in Tonglu, although it was difficult as he wore the equivalent to an extra large in Chinese sizes. They spent the rest of their drive trying to plan their next move.

"It looks like Chengdu is probably the closest big city to the western target," Jeffreys read from one of the maps.

"Chengdu is the capitol of Sichuan Province," Charles remarked. "It's quite a big city. That's a prosperous area, part of China's breadbasket, although it has a lot of industry and is mineral rich as well.

"Are you a walking encyclopedia of Chinese trivia?" Mark asked.

"I'm assigned to China," Charles defended. "It pays to know the details of your assignment. Helps you analyze information."

"Our target is just north, northwest of that," Jeffreys broke in. "So how do we get there? Can we get a flight at the last minute? Or will we have to take a train?"

"A train wouldn't work," Charles said. "China has a good train system, but with this distance, the train ride would be twenty-four to thirty-six hours. We need to fly. Fortunately, it is very common for the Chinese to book flights at the last minute, so we shouldn't have a problem. We can check when we get to the airport. Or I can do it online once we get closer to a bigger city, or we can have the agency book it for us, again once we get closer to a big city so my signal will blend in with the local traffic."

"When you report in," Jeffreys spoke up with a barely suppressed chuckle, tell them that Mark's plan worked."

"What plan?" Mark asked.

"Run like hell."

Mark laughed. "Yea, but next time you run off the cliff and I'll run down to the beach." They all started laughing. "I never was good with details," Mark choked out.

When they had finished laughing, Jeffreys commented, "But seriously, I would still like an assault rifle. Can't you James Bond types get me one?"

"I don't think even an assault rife would have done any good this time," Charles remarked.

"Not against that cat ship, it wouldn't," Jeffreys admitted. "But it would still feel good having it."

"So what happened to those people at the pagoda?" Juan asked.

"The cats got them," Jeffreys stated.

"No, before that. They were all unconscious and then suddenly jumped up. It was straight out of a zombie movie," Juan continued.

"Scared the daylights out of me," Jeffreys admitted. "So, what do you think happened?" he asked Mark.

"Clearly the guy with the blue shirt had accessed the control cube," Mark began. "My guess is that he probably did it just before we got there. That's when the signal seemed to change. It probably knocked him out while the cube... programmed him, for lack of a better term."

"And then he woke up when we were standing next to him?" Jeffreys added.

"Correct," Mark agreed. "Woke up, but under blue-gray control."

"Is it control, like we control a drone? Real time?" Jeffreys asked.

"No. It's like they plant a goal and the individual uses their knowledge and skill to obtain that goal. Although the blue-grays can also provide a method to obtain that goal, I've seen that before," Mark explained, referring to the blue-grays teaching the velociraptors how to hunt.

"But what about the others? Were they all under the cube's control? They were all out and then jumped up together," Charles asked.

"I don't know," Mark admitted. "I don't know why they were all out."

"You think they all accessed the cube, that they all were genetically compatible?" Jeffreys asked.

"But some were fifteen to twenty feet away," Mark objected.

"The blue-grays sent you visions from the submarine," Jeffreys pointed out. "You weren't in physical contact with a cube then."

"You're right," Mark agreed. "The blue-grays probably perfected their technology."

"Would that happen to us if we touched the cube?" Juan asked.

"Maybe," Mark said. "I don't know. It would if I touched it though." Mark paused, then added. "But Blue Shirt was clearly the leader, he had the cube."

"The alpha male," Jeffreys said.

"They did seem to act directly from what he said, almost robot like," Juan said.

"I wasn't sure if that was from the cube or if that was typical of Chinese culture?" Mark commented.

"No, that wasn't typical, not even for Chinese," Juan answered.

"North Korean, maybe," Charles interjected. "But not Chinese."

"You thought they were going to attack us before the cats arrived?" Jeffreys said.

"It sure looked like it. We weren't getting anywhere with conversation," Mark noted.

"They were paranoid!" Juan interjected.

"They were probably programmed to protect the cube," Mark reasoned.

"Fifteen to four," Jeffreys muttered. "That's why I want a weapon. Those are not good odds!"

"I'm sure after you took out the first fourteen, we three could have taken out the last one," Juan said with a chuckle. The joke broke the tension as they considered the 'what ifs.'

"Right," Jeffreys said. "You better find that entrenching tool for me. In the meantime, we need to see if we can come up with a better plan on how to approach the next cube, particularly now that we know that any humans touching the cube will be hostiles and that the cats are hot on the trail." They traveled in silence as each pondered the possibilities. Mark also couldn't help wondering what the Chinese authorities would do when they found the bodies on the island. He mentioned it to Charles, wondering how good their cover was.

"If the Chinese authorities place us at the lake, then they will detain us," Mark reasoned. "Heck, I would if I were the prosecutor. Two 'lightning strikes' in two different locations out of a clear sky, with the only common denominator being four Americans. Then if they find the encrypted messages, they will assume we are testing a satellite death ray or something."

"That is pretty paranoid if you ask me," Charles replied.

"Isn't this supposed to be a paranoid country?" Mark said.

"That's North Korea. Although China does have its share of paranoia," Charles said. "But how are they going to place us there?"

"That's easy," Mark said. "The hotel recorded our passports."

"Let's take this step by step," Charles said calmly. "First, sooner or later, hopefully later, the Chinese discover the destruction on the island."

"Probably sooner," Jeffreys interjected. "I don't think many people would have missed the cat's ship streaking down. Someone is bound to investigate."

"Ok, sooner," Charles conceded.

"They discover the bodies. If enough people saw the cat ship come down, which you say looks like a meteor, then that may be what they conclude and we are in the clear. But," Charles continued when Mark was about to object, "If they want to investigate, what do they have? Just a bunch of dead bodies apparently hit by lightning."

"And a mystery boat leaving the island after the meteor strike," Mark added.

"How do they find out about our boat?" Charles asked.

"Someone always sees something," Mark answered.

"Ok, so someone reports a boat leaving. They still have to find the boat. There are hundreds of hotels, marinas and private boats out there."

"So they canvas the area," Mark continued, "and find out we were there."

"No," Charles corrected. "They canvas the area and if they get to our hotel's marina, they find out that some Charles Meador rented a boat that day. I wasn't with you during that last attack so I won't be linked with that incident. End of investigation."

"Unless they track down who you work for and see that it is the same travel agency that we used, or if they have you listed as the person who came to get us."

"That's still a lot of ifs."

"What if someone got the registration number off the boat or they check the hotel registrar. We all had to record our passports when we checked in and then they will find out that we left right after the attack."

"If all those things occur, then yes, we are in trouble," Charles conceded.

"Maybe we should disappear," Mark suggested. "Take a train rather than a plane to Chengdu. That way they can't trace us."

"Nice try," Charles said. "But boarding a train is the same as a plane in China. You have to show your passport and it all goes to a central booking computer. Besides, a train ride to Chengdu will take something like thirty-six hours, while a plane will take about three."

"Ok," Mark finally conceded. "So I am being paranoid."

"Yes, you are," Charles said. "You handle the aliens, I'll handle the locals."

When they arrived at Hangzhou, Charles went ahead to obtain tickets. After thirty minutes of waiting, an eternity to Mark as he kept expecting the Chinese police to swoop down on them, Charles finally waved them all to the ticket counter. "You have to show your passports to get the tickets," Charles explained as each handed over their passport. I have four tickets on the last flight to Chengdu, which leaves at 19:15, which is 7:15 p.m. As they were leaving the ticket counter with their new tickets,

Charles said, "Chengdu is the closest I could get tickets for today. There is actually a much closer airport to our destination, but we are in high tourist season, and I could not get us tickets tonight. I thought you probably wanted to leave here as soon as possible." The last comment he directed to Mark, who quickly agreed.

"I know they have our passports recorded," Mark said. "But I just can't help feeling that physical distance is an advantage.

While they were waiting for the flight, Charles logged on with his computer and sent an encrypted update to the agency, informing them of events to date. He waited for a reply and then closed up the laptop. "Did you know," Charles told the group. "That this airport has an interesting history?"

"What's that?" Jeffreys asked.

"On July 9, 2010, the airport was shut down for four hours during the day because they spotted a UFO from the tower."

"You're kidding," Mark stated.

"No. It's true. It never showed up on their radar, but they saw it in broad daylight and shut down the whole airport. They never did figure out what it was."

"Could that be one of our friends?" Jeffreys asked Mark.

"July 2010?" Mark considered the time frame. "I guess it's possible. In my visions the ships came through the wormhole and then came to Earth. Thinking back, I can't say that they immediately came to Earth. They may have been out there for years, perhaps sending scouting missions. I don't know."

"And we don't know if it was a blue-gray ship or a cat ship," Jeffreys reasoned.

"Or a different one?" Juan asked.

"Just what we need," Mark snorted. "A third alien species messing with the Earth. Do you have any more information on that UFO?"

"No," Charles answered. "That's all they have."

Their flight was called before they could continue the conversation. Soon they were all on Sichuan Airlines flight 3U8920 to Chengdu. In another three hours, Mark thought, they would start this all over again. He had to come up with a better plan.

CHAPTER 11

Although they landed in Chengdu at 10:15 p.m., it was almost midnight before they finally arrived at their hotel and Mark gratefully collapsed on his bed. But sleep eluded him as the calls from the three remaining cubes poked at his consciousness and he worried how they were going to find all of them in time. Jeffreys was right, they had been lucky so far with the cats, but they couldn't count on luck the whole time. The attack at the lake emphasized their precarious position, both with the cats and the Chinese. And even if they destroyed the last three cubes, what would keep the blue-grays from launching three more, or five, or fifty for that matter. They had to come up with a better plan, but what? The unsolved problems swirled in Mark's mind until he finally succumbed to sleep.

The next morning the four of them ate a western style breakfast in Mark's room while considering their next move.

"So what's the plan for this one?" Juan asked the group, although really looking at Mark. "Same as last time?"

"Plan?" Jeffreys interjected. "We don't have a plan! No offense, Mark. But find the cube and run like hell is not a plan."

"I completely agree," Mark said. "I've been trying to come up with a better one. But given the parameters that we are under, I haven't come up with anything."

"At the very least we should have a full tactical squad, with air defense capability and air force back up," Jeffreys commented.

"I don't think the Chinese would allow us to do that on their soil," Charles said.

"Who said it had to be our team," Jeffreys argued. "It could a Chinese team supporting us. This is a war against Earth, not the U.S."

"Tell that to the Agency," Charles said.

"I think we should," Mark interjected. "Jeffreys is right. We are going about this all wrong. It's not the U.S. against the blue-grays or the cats, it's us versus them. And 'us' is the Earth. Continuing like we are is unacceptable."

"Are you serious?" Charles asked.

"Absolutely," Mark said. "It was actually discussed in the very beginning, before I flew here. But at that time it was rejected because we didn't have any proof. I wasn't even sure what was going on. Well now there is plenty of proof. We need to get the Chinese on board."

"I can ask," Charles said without any great conviction.

"No. Let me." Mark said. "Can I send a message on your laptop?"

"Sure," Charles said. "Here," he added, turning the laptop over to Mark. "You type it up in clear text and I'll encrypt it and send it. Juan and I need to go out and get some supplies and check on flights anyway. It will take us an hour, maybe two. Can you do it in that timeframe?"

"Sure."

"Ok. You two stay here, we'll be back in about an hour." With that Juan and Charles left and Mark worked on his message to Washington, while Jeffreys consulted the maps and tried to strategize. It took Mark the better part of two hours to draft up a recommendation to his satisfaction. When he had finished, he read it to Jeffreys for his reaction.

"I think it's good," Jeffreys commented. "Direct and to the point. I just don't know if Washington will buy it. They're a pretty secretive lot over there and they don't trust the Chinese."

"But we don't have a choice," Mark argued. "The way we are doing this is going to get us all killed."

"Whoa. You don't have to convince me," Jeffreys defended. "I couldn't agree with you more. I'm just saying how Washington will look at it."

Their conversation was interrupted when Juan and Charles entered, carrying a couple of boxes.

"I hope you have an M-60 in one of those," Jeffreys said.

"I wish," Charles agreed as they emptied the boxes on the bed. "I did get you a collapsible camping shovel, the most lethal looking one I could find," Charles said with a chuckle. "The salesman said it would cut through brush and small trees."

Jeffreys picked up the small metal shovel and eyed its serrated edge. "It's a start," he conceded.

"I also got a machete," Charles said. "Although we may be pushing it a little with the Chinese if they find it.

Jeffreys hefted the Machete. "This is more like it," he said appreciatively.

"You won't touch a cat with that thing," Mark remarked.

"No. But I can intimidate a local with it. It's better than nothing."

Mark shrugged.

"We also have protein bars, water, various food items, topographical maps, and a bunch of tourist pamphlets. We may be headed to some rural areas, where we can't count on restaurants or vendors," Charles explained.

"What? No McDonalds?" Mark laughed.

"No," Charles laughed. "We also have two small tents and four light sleeping bags."

"L.L. Bean!" Jeffreys exclaimed looking at a dome tent. "How did you get L.L. Bean here?"

"Are you kidding," Charles replied. "Everything is made in China."

"Oh yea, I forgot," Jeffreys said sheepishly.

As Juan and Jeffreys started dividing up the new purchases, Charles reviewed Mark's memo, encrypted it, and sent it with his next update. The Agency's download followed and Charles reviewed it. "We have a problem," Charles said as he read from his computer.

Mark's heart seemed to stop. "Are the Chinese after us?"

"No. Not that," Charles answered. "They sent an article from the BBC. Evidently one of their news teams was stopped trying to get into Tibet. Has caused a bit of a stir."

"Why, what happened?"

"Certainly you are aware of the political turmoil between the Free Tibet Movement and the Chinese?" Charles asked.

"I've heard something about it," Mark answered.

"Well, it has flared up again. The Tibetans are protesting and the Chinese are reacting in their usual militaristic fashion by clamping down."

"So how will that affect us?" Jeffreys interjected.

"We are right next to Tibet. Previously, the Chinese were restricting movement of the Tibetans," Charles explained. "But now they are restricting all foreigners from the region. In their typical fashion they are blaming the unrest on foreign agitators. That's always easier than admitting that their internal policies are screwed up. It says that foreigners aren't allowed to take any bus tours now except for Juizhai Gou National Park, which is north of us."

"But we aren't taking a bus tour, are we?" Mark asked.

"No," Charles explained. "But it will still affect us. The only way foreigners can travel is by bus tours. They are not allowed to rent cars. We rented one because Juan has a resident I.D., which allows him to rent cars. But if we are stopped, then our passports will give us away and the travel ban will apply. Yesterday, I tried to get a flight to Sichuan Juzhai Huanglong airport, which is just north of Songpan, the closest airport to our target area. But that airport is a tourist airport for Huangling and Jushai Gou, just like Tunxi serviced Mount Huang, and at this time of year I couldn't get four tickets.

"Remember, we wanted to get away from Hangzhou as soon as possible. But it's too bad we couldn't get the tickets since our target area is just west of Songpan and it would have made the trip much quicker. We couldn't get tickets this morning either. Charles looked back down to review his email on his laptop. "It says here they have set up roadblocks, primarily on the main road into Tibet, which fortunately is south of us, not north. Although we can expect that they have roadblocks north of us also. That area still borders Tibet. It's just not considered a main entrance. We could have a problem if we run into one of those roadblocks, particularly if they think we are journalists."

"All the more reason to get the Chinese on board with this," Mark stated.

"If they send it up channels, we'll get a decision some time next year," Jeffreys commented as he divided the new supplies between their backpacks.

"I'm open to suggestions," Mark said. "It was never my intention to run this show. I can tell you where the cubes are, the rest is up to you." They all looked at Jeffreys.

"Why are you looking at me? I'm just here to keep Mark out of trouble."

"Right," Juan said. "And you are the only military person here."

"But you are the spooks," Jeffreys said. "The military solution is to come in at Regimental strength and blast everything."

"I'm all for that," Juan stated.

"But in the meantime," Charles interjected. "We are going to have to revise our approach. Fortunately, our target area is northwest of us, actually more north, than west. We can head north, ostensibly to visit the Juizhai Gou National Park, since that area is still open to foreign tourists. We can modify our cover story to be more outdoorsy, bird watching and the like. We are driving because we couldn't get a flight, which is true. We need to play dumb on the whole Tibetan issue. Don't know, don't care, attitude."

"So what happens if we run into one of their roadblocks?"

"Hopefully, they let us through. Worst case would be what they did to the BBC crew."

"Which was?"

"They detained them for a while and them let them go."

"A while?"

"Says here nine hours," Charles read. "The Chinese security got a little ugly trying to get confessions from them."

"Sounds familiar," Mark said.

"Yes," Charles agreed. "The BBC refused to sign confessions and were finally released. But they were followed after that and detained again when the Chinese didn't like where they were going and who they were talking to."

"Friendly people," Jeffreys noted.

"The Chinese people are very friendly, it's the security people who are not known to be friendly," Charles pointed out. "That's why it's best not to attract their attention."

"This is just getting better and better," Mark repeated.

"And you thought this would be easier than near the nuclear sites," Juan said with a laugh.

"Foolish me," Mark agreed. "And I was worried about the Chun'an police. Speaking of which, what happens if they put two and two together and get us four?"

"Our people are monitoring the situation. They should be able to give us a heads up if the Chinese start getting interested in us for that little incident."

"But what would we do then?" Mark asked. "They would catch us at the airport when we showed our passports."

"Leave that to us," Charles said. "We have our ways."

"Oh, I keep forgetting you're the James Bond people," Mark said.

"Right," Charles said.

"Maybe we could get in a cleaning pod and jet out of China in their version of the trans-siberian oil pipeline, like James Bond in *Living Daylights*," Jeffreys piped in. "That would be the ultimate Disney ride!"

"I think I would just vomit," Mark remarked.

"You have no sense of adventure," Jeffreys chided.

"No sense of adventure?" Mark retorted. "I've been shot by aliens, dangled from helicopters, climbed a mountain, jumped off a cliff, and am probably being hunted by the Chinese police as we speak. I think that's enough adventure for anyone. Don't you agree Juan?"

"Sounds good to me," Juan answered.

"We really need some weapons," Jeffreys repeated. "Preferably a rifle."

"I told you, we can't have weapons," Charles answered. "We get stopped with a weapon and we will be spending a long time here. You might even get a chance to learn Chinese. But for now our cover story is that we are here to explore the Juizhai Gou region, which is known for its hot springs and colored ponds, much like Yellowstone Park in the U.S. In fact, the geological characteristics are very similar. I have a pamphlet here for you to review," he added, as he pulled a pamphlet out of the pile. You can study it in the car. For now, we probably should get going. We have a car waiting on us.

"In light of recent developments, we will head due north towards the park. When Mark tells us that our target is West of us, then we'll find some back roads to get us over there. That should minimize our chances of running across a roadblock. Hopefully, our target is not too far west, both for the roadblocks and the mountains. We are at the edge of the Tibetan Tableau. Judging from your comments on Mount Huang, I don't think you have much interest in climbing up over sixteen-thousand feet."

"Sixteen-thousand feet!" Mark remarked. "Are you kidding? Isn't that the height of Mount Everest?"

"Mount Everest is about twenty-nine thousand feet," Juan answered.

"Good heavens, we'll be halfway there," Mark complained.

Jeffreys rolled his eyes. "I told you he's not happy if he doesn't have something to complain about. So your plan is to head up two-thirteen towards Juizhai Gou?" he asked Charles while studying the map.

"Right," Charles replied. "We should get to about Songpan before we have to head west. It's not the most direct route, but it will have to do under the circumstances."

"Okay," Jeffreys said hunched over the map. "Songpan looks to be about... say two-hundred miles north. So, three or four hours?"

"It's two-hundred miles, actually two-o-two on the street calculator. But because of the road conditions and the route across the mountains, driving time is estimated at about six and a half to seven hours," Charles answered.

"Then we better get going," Mark said, although he was not looking forward to a seven-hour drive, even if it was scenic. With that they finished packing, loaded up the car and headed north on Route 213 towards Juizhai Gou.

"This is what I expected when I came to China," Mark said when they stopped for lunch near Diexi Lake. "Rural, mountainous, peasants. Not the modern cities, major tourist resorts, and four star hotels that we have been visiting."

"This is rural," Charles agreed. "We are in the foothills of the Tibetan Plateau. Very mountainous, with harsh conditions in winter. Not many people here. The eastern part of China is the more heavily populated portion."

Mark looked out at some Tibetan monks walking down the street and noted that the dress was very different here than in the eastern portions of China. "So this is Tibet," he said.

"No," Charles corrected. "Those are Tibetans, yes. But we are still in Sichuan Province. But, as you can see, there is a large Tibetan population here."

"They are easy to spot."

"Yes, they are not assimilating very well. They are very proud of their heritage," Charles continued.

They got back into the car and headed north, each lost in their own thoughts. Mark interrupted the silence, "Charles, I forgot to ask. What did the agency say about the lake incident?" Did they see it on the satellite?"

"NORAD tracked the ship in," Charles responded. "Lit up the sensors with the heat it generated. But they lost it when it left the island. The heat had dissipated and they have never been able to pick up the ships on radar."

"What about the massacre on the island? Any word on that yet?" Mark asked.

"Nothing, yet," Charles replied.

"I'm surprised it hasn't hit the news," Mark said.

"Nothing hits the news if the authorities don't want it to," Charles explained. "Although with the internet and cell phones, that's starting to change."

"So where are we now," Mark changed the subject.

Jeffreys shifted the map that he seemed to be continuously studying. "We are here," he said pointing. "Still south of Songpan, which is probably another two to three hours north of us. According to NORAD, our target area is here, slightly northwest of our current position. But to get there in these mountains, we really need to go north of Songpan and then west along this route," he traced out a road on the map. "Assuming that agrees with your sense of direction when we get there."

"This is getting quite mountainous," Mark noted with apprehension.

"This is just the foothills," Charles explained. "Songpan is only at eighty-two hundred feet, the airport north of it is at eleven-thousand feet. Some people get oxygen sickness at that height and they have oxygen bottles at the airport. Of course if we start heading west..." he let his statement hang.

"Hopefully, we can avoid doing that particular tour," Mark commented. Thereafter he watched the map while Jeffreys dutifully traced their progress.

"I thought that ride would never end," Mark complained as he climbed out of the tiny car and stretched his cramped legs when they finally arrived in Songpan.

"Unless you tell us the cube is here," Jeffreys said, "our drive is far from over."

"Always the optimist," Mark deadpanned as he stretched. He closed his eyes and felt the cube's call. It's not here," he continued. "It's in that direction," he added, pointing.

Jeffreys took a quick bearing on his ever-present map. "That's northwest of us," he said. "We'll have to take two-thirteen."

"That's outside our safe route," Charles said. "It's no longer en route to Juzhai."

They found something to eat and then all too soon climbed back into the tiny car and headed northwest on 213. They traveled another hour before Jeffreys said, "We'll have to decide which way to go pretty soon since two-thirteen veers to the right to Zaige. If we turn left, we go to Huangyuan. The intersection is coming up."

They stopped at the 213 intersection so Mark could get his bearings and choose which direction to continue. Mark stepped out and stretched, his body sore from riding in the car so long. He closed his eyes and concentrated on the call.

"It's harder to hear," Mark said when he opened his eyes. Pointing, he added, "But it's this way."

"That's towards Huangyan," Jeffreys said.

"Huangyan is closed to foreigners," Charles pointed out.

"That's where it is," Mark repeated. "Or that direction, anyway."

"You said it was harder to hear," Jeffreys said. "Shouldn't it be louder now that we are closer? Have we passed it?"

"We haven't passed it," Mark replied. It's still in this direction," he pointed and Jeffreys took a quick compass bearing. "But it's not as strong."

"We are just in our target area," Charles remarked.

"Not as strong as in it is farther away? Or not as strong in that someone has it?" Jeffreys persisted.

"I can't tell from this distance," Mark said. "All I know is that it is not as strong."

"Then we have either passed it, or someone has it," Jeffreys said.

"So we have to hurry and find out," Mark said.

"Going this way, we probably will run into a checkpoint before too long, so remember our cover story," Charles said. They climbed back into the car and continued.

Twenty minutes later Charles asked if they were getting any closer as they were in the middle of their target area.

"No, Mark replied. "I can still feel it, it's not here though, it's ahead. We need to keep going." Soon they were outside the estimated target area and relying solely upon Mark's instructions on where to turn. "We need to head in this direction," Mark said, pointing slightly to his right.

Jeffreys studied his map. "Assuming what we are on is a main road," Jeffreys said, referring to the unpaved road they were traveling. "Soon we are going to have to get off it onto some mountain trail. Turn right up here," Jeffreys instructed. They traveled some more with Mark pointing out the direction.

"Our target is moving," Charles commented after the last turn.

"It seems to be," Jeffreys concurred. "Are you getting a different feeling from it?" he asked Mark. "Like you did on the island when they picked it up and it changed?"

"I can't tell," Mark said. "I think we're still too far away. On the island I was within a hundred feet or so of it. It is softer though. I can't tell if it's different."

They were traveling a winding road up a mountain. Rounding a corner, Juan suddenly swore and hit the brakes. Ahead of them was a barrier across the road, manned by several machine gun toting Chinese soldiers.

"Is this one of your roadblocks to stop the Tibetans?" Mark asked, trying not to panic.

"No," Charles replied. "This looks like a permanent barrier."

"It's a secure area," Juan explained, pointing to a sign. The soldiers were watching the car, which had stopped about 50 yards away. "What do I do?" Juan asked as the soldiers talked among themselves. "Should I turn around?"

"If we turn, we arouse their suspicions," Charles said. "Drive up to them, slowly," Charles instructed. "We are tourists. We got lost in these roads. We'll ask them directions, remember, we're headed for Juizhai Gou." Charles continued as Jeffreys quickly erased the markings off the map.

"We're way off the route for that," Jeffreys objected.

"Right," Charles agreed. "We are stupid tourists who took a wrong turn at Songpan."

They drove slowly up to the roadblock and stopped as two of the soldiers approached them. Mark was relieved to see that none of them had slung their machine guns off their shoulders, although all were watching them with interest. Probably not much going on up here, Mark thought to himself. Must be boring duty. Let's hope it stays that way. Juan started talking with one of the soldiers with Charles adding questions, while pointing to the map Jeffreys was holding.

The soldiers motioned them out of the car and Juan and Charles kept talking animated with them, showing them the map and then giving them travel brochures that they had picked up in the hotel. Although Mark couldn't understand a word of the Chinese, he thought the scene looked like a bunch of hopelessly lost tourists. A number of other soldiers had come over and joined the conversation, all gesturing and pointing, but none of them, to Mark's great relief, appeared hostile or had pulled their weapons off their shoulders.

While they discussed the proper route, Mark stepped apart from the group and stared out in the distance. Jeffreys noticed and stepped over. "It's moving," Mark said quietly to Jeffreys as he stared down the road. One of the soldiers noticed them to the side and stepped over and asked them something in Chinese. Mark responded, "Ich verstehe nicht. Ich spreche kein Chinesisch." The soldier responded in Chinese and motioned them back to the others. A few minutes later they evidently had exhausted the soldier's knowledge and they all climbed in the car, turned around and left.

As they drove out of sight of the checkpoint Jeffreys asked Mark, "What was with the German?"

"Oh, that," Mark answered sheepishly. "In a hostile country, I always figure it is better to be German than American, not as many enemies."

Jeffreys chuckled. "Unless you're in France."

"Well, yes," Mark agreed. "That was close. So what was it?"

"It was a secure location," Juan said.

"What's here?" Mark asked.

"It might be near an entrance to one of those underground tunnels we heard about," Jeffreys suggested.

"Whatever it was, who ever has the cube has access to it," Mark commented. I could sense the cube moving past that point. Let me see the map," he added. Jeffreys spread out the map and Mark studied it. He asked a few questions of Jeffreys to confirm what he was looking at before commenting. "As near as I can tell, the cube travelled down the road past that barricade and then travelled off road. So either whoever has it started hiking off road, or they were in a tunnel that's not on the map."

"Or on a road that is not on our map," Jeffreys corrected.

"I can get a download from our satellites and we would know if there are any roads not shown," Charles suggested.

"If we are this close to a secure nuclear facility, should we be uplinking to a satellite?" Jeffreys asked. "What if they are sweeping the area for transmissions?"

"Can we approach this area from a different direction?" Mark asked.

"If it is a secure area, it will still be sealed off," Juan objected.

"But if we can get an overlook from two or three positions, we might be able to at least triangulate its position," Mark said. "Then we can determine how to get to it."

They stopped and studied the map, trying to figure out the best approaches and avoid being stopped.

"There are not many roads in these mountains," Jeffreys commented. "At least not on this map. We may have to go hiking."

"That sounds like my idea of fun," Mark replied sarcastically.

"Here's what I propose," Jeffreys said. "We drive to this point, then hike up into this range. Judging by the topographical marks on the map, the climb should not be that bad and we should get enough of an angle that we can triangulate a little better on our target. And," he added, "the view shouldn't be too bad either." They all laughed at the last part.

"I'm kind of partial to views from cable cars," Juan said.

"That was Mount Huang," Charles answered. "You don't get that luxury here."

They climbed back into the car and drove to the spot suggested by Jeffreys. Parking the car off the winding road, they shouldered their backpacks and picked a trail up the mountain. Although he had complained earlier, Mark really enjoyed the hike, although he did feel like he was breathing harder than usual. Juan, on the other hand, seemed to be dying for lack of air.

The view, once they reached the top, was spectacular as row upon row of mountain peaks rose higher and higher in the distance towards the Tibetan Plateau. At the top, Mark closed his eyes and pointed out the direction of the cube so Jeffreys could get the bearing and mark it on the map. They returned to their car and repeated the process another ten miles away. By then it was getting quite late, so they decided to spend the night on the mountain. The thought of driving the narrow mountain roads in the dark was not appealing and they could recheck the location of the cube in the morning.

"Good thing you brought tents," Mark said as he pulled the tent out of his backpack.

"I hope someone knows how to set them up," Juan replied nervously.

"You don't?" Mark asked, a bit surprised.

"Camping was never one of my strong points," Juan admitted.

"Mine either," Charles said, looking at Jeffreys.

"I guess it's you and me then," Mark said to Jeffreys.

"You know how to camp?" Juan asked surprised.

"I'll have you know I was a Boy Scout," Mark said proudly. "Camping merit badge and everything. I used to camp all the time. Loved it." With that, Mark and Jeffreys set up the campsite. "Do you think we should set up a campfire?" Mark asked after he had set up his tent. "Or will that draw too much attention?" They pondered the question and decided against the fire. Fortunately, it was a warm summer night and their food did not need cooking. After they ate, Mark lay out and stared at the stars, which shone with fierce brilliance in the high mountain air. "I could sleep out here," Mark said, admiring the stars above.

"You forget how incredible a night sky can be," Juan admitted.

"I've always preferred stars over city lights," Mark said.

"I'll take the city lights anytime," Charles said, slapping a mosquito. "And air-conditioning, and room service."

"City boy," Mark joked.

After slapping at a few more bugs, Juan and Charles climbed into their tent. Jeffreys and Mark stayed out, staring at the sky.

"It's a little different looking at the stars when you know hostile aliens are out there," Jeffreys said quietly.

"Man, I was thinking the same thing," Mark admitted. "I always assumed there were aliens somewhere. That Earth is the only planet with life seems a bit conceited. But the thought was always in the abstract. Not that the aliens were about to send an asteroid crashing down on us."

"Kind of takes the fun out of star gazing, wondering which one is the approaching asteroid," Jeffreys said.

"Exactly."

"Do you have any ideas on how to proceed with this cube once we get a good bearing on it?" Jeffreys asked after a period of silence.

"I really don't," Mark said. "I've been playing it over and over in my head and I can't come up with a good solution. I'm assuming who ever has it is either military, or a civilian with military clearance. Either way, unless they come out of the tunnels, assuming that is where they are, we can't get near them. And unless they come out soon, I'm not sure what we can do. I don't think we can camp out here too long without someone catching on. They probably have military patrols. We also don't have a lot of supplies and Juan and Charles don't seem to be the outdoorsy-type."

"What about the cats?" Jeffreys asked.

"Since the cube has moved from its original landing spot and is now underground, I think whoever has it is safe from the cats. Of course, I'm assuming the cats can't hear it like I can. That may be a wrong assumption."

"So if whoever has the cube comes outside the secure area and we can get to them, what then?" Jeffreys continued.

"If we could catch them away from the soldiers, I suppose we could overpower them and take the cube," Mark answered. "There is no reasoning with them, we learned that on the island. But even if we do that and destroy the cube, we still have to deal with them. We can't kill whoever has it. And once we take it, what will keep them from reporting a mugging. Particularly since they probably have military connections. It certainly wouldn't be hard to track us down out here. So then the Chinese have us and we go to jail. That's not a good solution."

"No, it's not," Jeffreys agreed.

"What are your thoughts on it?" Mark asked.

"Basically same as yours," Jeffreys said. "Although one of my scenarios was not as polite to the Chinese who has the cube as yours. But then we would still have the problem that he would be missing. That would cause a commotion, how big a commotion would depend on who he is. Either way, our position out here is extremely tenuous and I have some real concerns about our ability to successfully complete our mission."

"We can't successfully complete the mission," Mark said emphatically. "Not with the parameters we have to follow. Even if we find and destroy the remaining three cubes, and I say 'if' because I have no idea how we can do that, what prevents the blue-grays from sending down fifty more tomorrow? Eventually we lose. Either to the cats, or Chinese security, or by someone finding the cube and following its commands. We may have lost that one already. We don't know what is going on over there right now." Mark waved his hand in the direction of the nearby cube.

"So, what do you suggest?" Jeffreys asked.

"What you suggested earlier and what I sent to Washington this morning, we need to get the Chinese on board."

"You have two problems there," Jeffreys said. "First, you have to persuade our side to confide in the Chinese, which is no little feat. And second, you or Washington have to convince China that aliens are attacking. You will recall that a lot of our people didn't believe the alien theory last year."

"And I was one of them," Mark said. "But if we don't, we lose."

"Do we?" Jeffreys asked.

"What do you mean?" Mark asked.

"Do we lose if the blue-grays win?" Jeffreys asked. "I'm not arguing with you," Jeffreys added quickly when Mark tensed up. "You and I have been together in this thing from the very beginning and I believe you. I just want to consider all the possibilities."

"Okay," Mark said, trying to keep the edge out of his voice.

"Let's look at what we know," Jeffreys said. "Neither alien species cares anything about us, whether we live or die. You learned that last year. The blue-grays want to use us to help them fight the cats. If we die in the process, they don't care as long as they don't die. The cats don't care about us unless we become a threat by helping the blue-grays."

"Right, which is why we need to prevent that from happening," Mark interjected.

"Correct," Jeffreys agreed. "But what if we can't prevent it. Like you said, maybe we have failed already. What if whoever has the cube right now follows its commands and helps the blue-grays."

"To do what?" Mark asked.

"We don't know. But we know that they are around nukes, so let's assume that they give the blue-grays a nuke."

"Okay."

"And the blue-grays nuke the cats," Jeffreys continued. "End of cats, end of alien war. Why should the blue-grays stay here on this backward planet now that the threat of the cats is gone? They leave. We all live happily ever after."

Mark considered for a moment. "What if the blue-grays get us to shoot a nuke at the cats? Then we become the hostile and the cats take out the Earth with an asteroid like they did last time."

"No, won't work," Jeffreys answered. "We don't have anything that can deliver the nuke. We can't hit a cat ship with a nuke. We can't target it. We can't even see it. The blue-grays can't be relying on us to shoot the cats."

"Okay," Mark countered. "We give the blue-grays a nuke. They try it on the cats and fail. Now the cats are pissed at us and take out the Earth with an asteroid so we can't give the blue-grays any more nukes."

"Granted," Jeffreys said.

"So that's a fifty-fifty chance of Earth getting wiped out," Mark said. "Personally I don't like those odds. And that's assuming our scenarios are correct. We are doing a lot of guessing."

They lay in silence, staring at the stars. "What if we prevent the blue-grays from getting their nuke, or whatever they are trying to do? That will really piss off the blue-grays. What will they do to us?" Jeffreys asked. "Can't they send asteroids through wormholes also? We know they have wormhole technology."

"They do have wormhole technology. But they are in a science vessel, not a military vessel. That's why they were hiding here in the first place. I don't know if they have the technology on their ship to transport asteroids to Earth. Also, until they get rid of the cats, they're not going to be prancing around the solar system in the open. And between the two species, I put my money on the cats. They are one mean species. Of the two, I rather have the blue-grays mad at us than the cats.

"You're just saying that because the cats shot you," Jeffreys said in a joking tone.

"Shot me twice!" Mark retorted. "Don't forget they shot me in one of the visions also."

"Are you going to quibble about how many times you were shot?" Jeffreys said with a chuckle.

"I guess that is being picky," Mark laughed. "But seriously, I would love to raise the white flag over the Earth and declare us neutral in this war of theirs. Make the whole world Switzerland. But since that won't happen, I think the best thing is to keep the blue-grays from controlling us. If the blue-grays control us, then we become a threat, just like the velociraptors. And we know what the cats did to them. Wiped out the whole species."

"And half the life on Earth," Jeffreys added.

"Right. And the only way to keep the blue-grays from controlling us is to get the Chinese on board."

"The trick," Jeffreys said, "is figuring out who is the common enemy. If it's the blue-grays, then we team up with the Chinese. If it's the blue-grays and the cats, we also team up with the Chinese. But if the common enemy is the cats, then we should team up with the blue-grays."

"I know," Mark sighed. "Don't you know I've been agonizing over that. My problem is that I have been a blue-gray, felt his thoughts when I accessed his personal cube. And the blue-grays are not friendly either. They have no concern about Earth or anything or anyone on it. They look at us with the same concern we have for an ant bed. Step on it or not, who cares? As long as you don't get bit."

"Now I know I'm going to sleep well tonight," Jeffreys responded.

"Welcome to my world," Mark said. "And the worst part is that since I'm now the 'alien expert,' if Earth doesn't survive this little adventure of ours, it's my fault!"

"Well, look at the bright side," Jeffreys deadpanned. "If you are wrong, you will never know it and no one will be around to blame you."

"Thanks. That's comforting," Mark snorted.

"Anytime," Jeffreys said. "And now we probably should get some sleep."

Mark agreed, hoping that he wouldn't dream about asteroids crashing into the Earth. He had seen it happen once already, he had no interest in reliving it.

CHAPTER 12

Chattering birds awoke Mark. He lay there, savoring the cool morning air, before reluctantly climbing out of the tent. Stretching, he gazed over the incredible vista. The sun was just coming over the mountain peaks to the East as the early morning fog nestled in the valley below. The air was crisp and cool, not yet too hot. He listened to the chirping birds and the faint buzz of insects. For just a moment he was at peace with the world, a world of nature and breathtaking beauty, devoid of any evidence of man or his problems. And then the call of the cube invaded his awareness, distant but insistent, and all the worries of the world descended upon him, threatening to engulf him like the fog below.

"You're up early," a voice behind him said. Mark turned and saw Jeffreys approaching from a nearby ridge line, his binoculars slung over his neck and the machete hung on his belt.

"Obviously not earlier than you," Mark said. "Just finish another five mile hike?"

"No, took the opportunity to do a little reconnoitering before it got too light."

"What did you find?"

"Not much really. I didn't want to get too far away," Jeffreys answered. "The checkpoint that we stopped at is over that way," he said pointing. "There is another checkpoint over the hill over there to our right. It's about three clicks away, but you can see it from the ridge. I really don't think we can get much closer and I would not advise running into too many checkpoints. The next time they may not be as friendly. Has the cube moved?" Jeffreys added after a pause.

"No, it's still there," Mark said and closed his eyes to confirm the direction. "It's over..." His voice trailed off. He concentrated and turned slowly back and forth while Jeffreys waited patiently. Puzzled, he opened his eyes. Jeffreys was looking at him expectantly. "It's still there," Mark answered the unasked question. "But one of the others is gone. I can only sense two of them now."

"Is it gone, as the cats got it? Or is it subdued like someone found it? Can you tell?" Jeffreys asked.

Mark closed his eyes and concentrated some more. "I've never been this far away when someone accessed a cube, so I can't tell for sure. But I can't feel it at all, so I would guess it's been destroyed. We need to check and see if NORAD has any recent meteor sightings. That would certainly answer the question."

"We better get back to civilization then," Jeffreys responded. "I don't think it would be a good idea to run a comm link to a satellite this close to a nuke base. They probably have some type of monitoring going on."

"Let's rouse our city slickers and get going," Mark said. "We can't do anything more here anyway. I would like to see if Washington has come to their senses about getting the Chinese to help."

They walked over to the other tent and woke up Juan and Charles. Twenty minutes later they had eaten a rudimentary breakfast, broken camp, and were packing the last items in their packs. As they were about to leave, Juan looked over where they had camped. "Hey, I can't see any evidence that we camped here last night, not even the dry spot where the tent blocked the dew. Is that something you did Jeffreys?"

"No, that was Mark."

"You're kidding. Where did you learn that?"

"That's Boy Scouts again," Mark replied with a laugh. "We used to compete with other troops and one of the categories was to leave no sign that you had been there. My patrol was particularly adept at that. I thought it would be a good idea to do it here."

They finished loading their packs and started hiking down the mountain towards their car. Even going downhill, it took them over an hour to get to their car. As they were loading their packs into the back of the car, two military vehicles came bouncing around the corner.

"Heads up, we have company," Jeffreys warned. They all looked up.

"You think it's the same group of soldiers?" Juan asked.

"Remember our cover story," Charles said urgently. "We got lost and decided to spend the night here rather than trying to find our way back out in the dark." There wasn't time for any more conversation as the vehicles slid to a stop and Chinese soldiers poured out.

'This does not bode well,' Mark thought as the soldiers approached with their weapons held ready. Mark glanced over at Jeffreys and was relieved to see that he no longer had the machete strapped to his belt and had wiped the grease pencil marks off the map with the palm of his hand. 'Nice job,' Mark thought. 'Wouldn't want the Chinese finding marks on their map pointing to their underground bunker.'

The Chinese leader, identified by his radio and a handgun on his hip, was having a heated discussion with Charles, while the others surrounded Mark's group. It was frustrating not knowing what was being said, but from the tone of the leader's voice, it did not sound like it was going well.

"Are they under control of the cube?" Jeffreys asked Mark quietly.

"No, I don't think so," Mark replied. "I don't feel anything from them..."

The nearest guard yelled at them in Chinese. Although unintelligible, the import was clear and both Mark and Jeffreys raised their hands in submission. A few moments later Charles called back to them, "Pull out the large map, will you?"

Mark was closest to the door so he reached in and pulled the map out of the door pocket and stepped towards Charles with his hand out. A mistake. The nearest guard slapped the map out of Mark's hand. Reflexively, Mark quickly bent down to grab the falling map. Pain shot through the back of Mark's head and he hit the ground.

Mark was nestled on a wonderfully comfortable pillow. He savored the moment, not wanting to wake up, but his arm was in an odd position and threatening to cramp. He tried to ignore it, to snuggle back into this comfortable sleep, but the pillow smelled like dirt. No, it was dirt. He was lying face down in the dirt. If he wasn't in bed, then where was he? The memory came back unbidden. He had been hit, knocked down. So this would probably... HURT!

Pain filled Mark's head. He tried to move, but his hands were tied behind his back. He moaned. Voices filled his ears. Unintelligible Chinese voices. Then he recognized Juan and Charles, both talking urgently in Chinese. Someone rolled him over and tore open his shirt to get to the money belt where he kept his passport and other documents. He opened his eyes and the world swam. He quickly closed his eyes, fighting off a wave of nausea. He waited a while longer and tried opening his eyes again. The world stayed still.

Slowly he glanced around, not wanting to make any sudden moves for fear the nausea would return. Jeffreys was lying on his side next to him, arms tied. Juan and Charles were over to one side, surrounded by soldiers, as they continued to argue with the Chinese leader. Mark wondered what he should do. He finally decided he could do nothing. He hurt too badly. Besides, he reasoned, this had nothing to do with aliens. This was Charles' arena, he was the spook, he needed to handle it. Mark closed his eyes and tried not to concentrate on the pain in his head.

After an eternity, Mark was roughly pulled to his feet and leaned over the hood of the car. He willed himself not to vomit from the sudden movement. The soldiers roughly cut off his binds and left him leaning against the car. They did the same to Jeffreys, who looked at Mark questioningly, but did not say anything. A minute later Juan was pushed over to them. "They want us to get in the car," Juan said. He and Jeffreys assisted Mark into the car. Juan got in the driver's seat and Charles climbed in the front as the soldiers went to their vehicles.

"Are you okay?" Jeffreys whispered to Mark as the Chinese soldiers stepped away.

"I could use an aspirin, or six," Mark said. "But I'll live. What's going on?"

Charles answered from the front. "We are being escorted back to the main road and then we have to check in with security at Songpan. We are forbidden to travel anymore."

"We're not going to jail?" Mark asked, surprised.

"Not unless they change their minds," Charles said. "I hate to say it, but that blow to your head may have saved us. Things were going poorly as we were being accused of everything from espionage to inciting the

Tibetans. The leader is only a sergeant, no offense Jeffreys, and was on a real power trip. But after that overeager private hit you, I really played up the American card, threatening them with going to their commander and our embassy and anything else I could think of. I think threatening him with his commander had the greatest effect. In any event, he finally agreed to let us go on the condition that we return to Songpan and not come back."

"I'm glad I could help," Mark said ruefully while carefully rubbing his head. "How about that aspirin?" he added.

"Want anything stronger?" Jeffreys asked as he reached into a backpack for a first aid kit.

"I would, but I don't think you're supposed to take anything stronger after a head injury. I'll settle for aspirin right now."

"I don't think you're supposed to take aspirin either. I've got some Tylenol here, I think that's safe," Jeffreys said as he searched through the first aid kit.

"That will work," Mark said. The trip back to the main road seemed to take forever as one Chinese vehicle lead and the other followed their car. "Don't miss any of those potholes," Mark complained when they hit a particularly big bump. "Not like any of us are hurting back here." Trying to distract himself from the pain, Mark turned to Jeffreys. "Aren't those humvee's that the Chinese are driving?"

"No," Jeffreys answered. "But they are close. The Chinese liked the style and since they are not real big in obeying patent law, they built their own. Actually, a lot of them are made with GM parts. They call them *Eastwind*."

"That must be tough identifying friend or foe on the battlefield," Mark noted. "At least with the Russians, you could tell the difference between their vehicles and ours immediately."

"Yea. It can be a problem," Jeffreys agreed.

"Tell me what happened after I got hit," Mark asked.

"I thought Jeffreys was going to tear them apart for hitting you," Juan interjected from the front. "They must have thought so to from the look on his face, because they all leveled their guns on him and then one of them knocked him down and tied him."

"Are you all right?" Mark asked, not realizing that Jeffreys had been hit.

"Only thing they hurt was my pride," Jeffreys said.

"Ten soldiers with automatic weapons. I don't think you have to worry about your pride," Mark responded.

"Only nine of them had automatic weapons and four of them were distracted," Jeffreys remarked.

"Okay, next time you can play Rambo and take them all out," Mark said.

"Thank you," Jeffreys said. "And I hope it's this same squad. I would really like to teach them a lesson."

"If it is, can I help?" Mark said, rubbing his head. "I have a score to settle with one of them."

"Agreed."

Their escort stopped when they got to the main road. Their passports and travel papers were returned to them and they were instructed to head straight back to Songpan and check in with the Songpan officials, who would be expecting them. With that the Chinese patrol headed back to their base while Mark's group headed east towards Songpan. "Why aren't they escorting us the rest of the way to Songpan?" Mark asked as the soldiers turned back.

"I think they are worried about hitting an American. They don't want to be there when you report. That's the only explanation," Charles said. "We really lucked out, because they usually don't care who they rough up."

"They detained the British journalists," Mark said.

"Yes, but they didn't beat them up, and besides, they were journalists. Journalists are open season," Charles explained.

"What will happen when we check in?" Jeffreys asked Charles.

"Hard to say with the Chinese," Charles answered. "I'm really surprised that they let us go. They don't normally care about beating people up. Not like in the States. Who's going to sue them? And there is no freedom of the press to create public outrage. I really think we just lucked out with that sergeant. He might not have called Songpan. He may have been bluffing. Or, he just didn't want to mess with having to escort us anymore. I really don't know. But we can expect a tight leash in Songpan."

"So the mission here is done," Jeffreys said.

"Pretty much," Charles agreed.

"We could fly up to the other site," Juan suggested. "The one the cats haven't gotten yet."

"We probably would have as much luck there as we did at this site," Charles said.

"Is there an American Embassy in Chengdu?" Mark interjected.

"There's a Consulate, yes," Charles answered, a bit surprised.

"We need to go there, directly there," Mark said. "We can't play this game any longer. If the cats don't get us, the Chinese will. It's been too close too many times. I need to talk to Washington, the President if necessary. I'm sure the Consulate will have a secure line. We have to get the Chinese on our side."

"So we're not going to check in at Songpan?" Jeffreys asked.

"Should we?" Mark asked.

"No. It won't get us anywhere and would only delay us more," Charles answered. "If we are going to go to the

Consulate, we should do it directly." They discussed various options, but none could come up with a better way to complete their mission. "We're going to arrive in Chengdu around seven p.m.," Charles calculated.

"Is that a problem?" Jeffreys asked.

"The Consulate hours are nine to five," Charles answered.

"You're CIA," Mark said. "Certainly you can get us in after hours. Can't you just call them and tell them we're coming in?"

"The Chinese soldiers confiscated our phones and laptop," Charles replied.

"Oh," Mark said. "What about the programs you had on them?"

"They should be okay," Charles said. "On the surface there is nothing out of the ordinary. It would take a pretty good computer tech to even discover the hidden programs, let alone crack them. We also have some self-delete programs written into them, so that part is probably okay. But it has taken out our means of communication."

"What about land lines?" Mark asked.

"Calls to the embassy go through the Chinese system. They are monitored. Don't worry, I can always call the World Wide Tours number and get assistance there, although the Chinese may be monitoring outgoing calls to that number after the Kunming incident. No, what I was thinking is that we have to get past Chinese security to get onto the Consulate grounds. It would probably be safer during normal business hours so we can blend in with the crowd. If we make a special appearance after hours they will pay a lot more attention to us."

"I've had enough special attention for one day," Mark said. The others readily agreed so when they finally arrived in Chengdu, they found a hotel near the Consulate for the night.

The next day they walked to the Consulate. "You don't drive a car into the Consulate. Not in these days," Charles explained.

They had decided to leave their backpacks in the hotel with Juan, since hiking to the Consulate with backpacks would make them more conspicuous. Juan stayed away from the Consulate, since being recognized there could blow his cover, assuming it was not already blown. Charles promised to send a message to him once they had decided upon their next step.

When they arrived at the Consulate they had to pass through Chinese security first, which kept asylum seekers from making a run for it. Their U.S. Passports got them past the Chinese. After some delay, they were finally allowed into a large room filled with people of all nationalities seeking Visa's and other paperwork. "Stay here," Charles instructed before he cut to the front of the line at one of the windows.

"It's like a bank in here," Mark commented to Jeffreys as he stared at the bulletproof glass and Marine guards. "But with better security."

"It's pretty elite duty, being a Marine guard at an embassy," Jeffreys commented.

A few minutes later Charles motioned for them to come to a side door. There they presented their passports again and were escorted down a hall into another, much smaller room. They stayed there for another fifteen minutes while Charles went ahead. Finally they passed through yet another metal detector and were taken into a very nicely furnished reception area.

"Judging by the surroundings," Mark said, "I think we are inside now."

"I agree," Jeffreys said.

Charles returned, accompanied by another individual who was introduced as John Sterling. "I have explained that we are on a highly classified mission and we need a secure link to Langley," Charles said.

"I need to talk to someone higher than that," Mark protested. "I don't want to get caught up in the bureaucratic shuffle."

"Start with Langley," Charles requested.

"You forget," Jeffreys interjected. "Mark is used to talking to the President personally. I've seen him do that to the Commander in Chief of the Pacific Fleet and the entire Pentagon. So you better tell Langley that they need to set up a conference call with the White House."

Charles and John Sterling looked taken aback. "I don't think I can set that up right now," John Sterling said.

"Can we talk to Langley right now?" Mark asked.

"Yes," Charles said.

"Okay, I'll talk to them first, if we can do it right now," Mark said. With that they led Mark and Jeffreys to a secure communications room. As they set up for the call, Mark turned to Jeffreys. "Do you have the map handy? It probably would be best if you briefed them on the coordinates, you're much better at that." A few minutes later the conference call was established. On the China side was Mark, Charles and Jeffreys. On the Langley side was a Jonathan DeMarito, although Mark suspected a number of others were watching off screen.

"What information do you have?" Mark asked as he wondered where to start.

"I have Charles' written reports as of two days ago," Agent DeMarito responded. "Nothing after than."

Mark provided Agent DeMarito a summary of what happened the last two days with Charles and Jeffreys filling in any missing details. Jeffreys pulled out the map and retraced the headings he had taken, showing the suspected location of the cube and asking whether that area coincided with a known tunnel area. The agent said he would have to check. Mark also asked whether NORAD had detected any meteors in China in the last couple days. Again the agent said he would have to check. The agent asked for a detailed report of the last several days before they had arrived at Chengdu. Mark swallowed his initial irritation, rationalizing that Washington had previously received cryptic email messages and it was only natural that they would want a detailed verbal report. So the three of them provided as much detail as they could of events since arriving in China.

During the briefing it appeared that Agent DeMarito was receiving questions from others outside the camera, probably through his earpiece, since he would suddenly get a distracted look before asking a new line of questions. The questioning started to remind Mark of the endless briefings that occurred on board the *Ronald Reagan*. When the questions became repetitious, Mark asked whether a decision had been made about getting the Chinese involved. Again the agent stated he would have to check on it. 'I'm getting the runaround,' Mark thought. To check his theory, Mark asked again whether NORAD had picked up a meteor. When the agent repeated that he would have to check, Mark got irritated.

"We've been talking for over an hour," Mark complained. "Certainly someone could have gotten the information from NORAD by now."

"It's after eleven at night," the agent responded.

'Wrong answer,' Mark thought, but did not say. "What, NORAD is closed at night?" Mark asked, sarcasm dripping from his comment. "I know that you're not the only one there. Certainly someone has picked up the phone and called for that information. The last time we asked, we had an answer back in less than ten minutes. I will make this real easy for you. Call NORAD and find out if a meteor was detected in the last twenty-four hours near Malan, that's in the Sinjiang Autonomous Region," Mark added, looking at the map Jeffreys had been using. "If there were any other meteor sightings, that would also be useful. I'll wait for the answer."

With that, Mark pushed his chair away from the table and the camera. Turning to Charles, he asked, "Do you think you can find a coke or something, I'm awfully thirsty." He then just leaned back and watched the agent, who sat uncomfortably in his chair, clearly listening to instructions over the earpiece.

"Someone's working on that," the agent repeated. "While we are waiting, perhaps you could explain how you…"

"You give me the information from NORAD first," Mark interrupted. "Or you can just patch me through to NORAD. I'll show you how easy it is to get this information."

"I don't have that capability," the agent protested.

"Nonsense. My iPhone has that capability," Mark said. "Why don't you have someone with some authority call me back," Mark suggested and then reached over and disconnected the call.

As Mark got up to leave a stunned Charles said, "You just hung up on Langley. You can't hang up on Langley."

"Sure I can," Mark responded.

"He hung up on the President last year," Jeffreys said laughing. "Langley is quite a step down from that. So what now?" Jeffreys asked Mark as they walked out of the secure conference room.

"I don't know," Mark replied. "We're wasting time, that's for sure."

"Bureaucracy, I warned you about it," Jeffreys said.

"Yea, you did. We need to get to a decision maker," Mark thought out loud. "And in this case that will ultimately be the President. So how to get to him?"

"There could be a power play going on over there," Charles added quietly. "But you didn't hear that from me."

"You're right," Mark agreed. "Damn stupid time to have a power play, but probably right." Mark thought for a while. "Ok, if they are having a power play, let's use it. Charles, can you put me in touch with whomever is the highest ranking person from the State Department over here?"

"That would be Scott Weatherby," Charles replied. "Why?"

"I'll explain to him that we have a message for the President that Langley is holding up and give him the opportunity to get it to the President through his channels. That will give State a point and Langley a black eye. Isn't that what they like to do in Washington?"

"I try to stay as far away from Washington as I can," Charles responded. "But you are probably right. Let me see what I can do."

Forty-five minutes later Mark, Jeffreys and Charles were sitting in Mr. Weatherby's office. Mark had been debating how to run this, particularly the part about the aliens, since that aspect usually immediately labeled him as a nut. Instead, he came up with a modified version.

"Mr. Weatherby. We need your assistance. As you probably have been informed, I am here on a top-secret, clandestine mission at the personal request of the President. Jeffreys and Charles, along with another agent who is waiting for us offsite are assisting me. Unfortunately, we were detained and the Chinese confiscated our communications gear, which is why we came here. Here's the problem: we just had a secure conference call with some underling at Langley. For some reason, Langley is dragging their feet. I have a message I need to get to the President and I am afraid that by the time Langley runs through channels, we will be too late. I need you to go through your channels and get a message to the President for me."

Mr. Weatherby looked at his watch uncomfortably. "It's almost midnight, eastern time," he said. "And I don't have any knowledge of your mission." Mr. Weatherby turned to Charles. "What are your people doing about this?"

"I'm only a field agent, Sir," Charles answered. "I don't know what is going on at Langley."

"I realize that you're in the dark," Mark said, expecting this reaction. "Unfortunately, my initial briefing was with the President personally," Mark explained. "I don't know who else has clearance on this mission." Mark paused as if considering his next comment. "I will tell you this. We are investigating a very dangerous..." he paused for effect, "...group that we tracked to China. The Chinese were not notified as we did not have sufficient proof. Instead, our team was sent to investigate.

"We arrived in country fifteen days ago. The opposition killed three of our team members and we barely escaped being killed in the same attack. There have now been three attacks by this group, resulting in at least sixteen Chinese deaths that we know of. The Chinese are investigating, but I don't believe they realize what they are up against. Unfortunately, my team has been compromised with the Chinese, so if we leave the Consulate, Chinese security will probably pick us up.

"Two days ago I made a recommendation that we notify the Chinese of our findings. We haven't received a response since our laptop was confiscated and it looks like Langley is dragging their feet. Maybe they are trying to cover their tracks before they send it upstairs. I don't know. But here is why we can't wait." Mark paused again. When he had Mr. Weatherby's undivided attention, he continued.

"We have been trying to figure out what this group's goal is. Yesterday, we tracked one of their agents into the mountains west of Songpan. We tracked him to the underground bunkers housing the Chinese Second Artillery, which as you probably know, controls the Chinese mobile nuclear missiles. He is inside the bunkers and has been now for over thirty-six hours.

"We were stopped at a Chinese checkpoint, but Charles talked our way out. Then after conducting surveillance from a nearby mountaintop, we were caught by another Chinese patrol as we were leaving the area. They roughed us up and confiscated our equipment, but somehow Charles managed to talk them into letting us leave. We were not in a secure area when they caught us and we played dumb, lost tourists. Anyway, we are supposed to check in with the Chinese security, which obviously we have no intention of doing. I need to get this information to the President before that agent has the opportunity to do something with the Chinese nukes. And he already has a thirty-six hour head start."

Mark could tell that his story had the desired effect and was glad that he had not mentioned aliens. "What message do you want delivered?" Mr. Weatherby asked.

"Let me write it down," Mark said. He stopped to think of the most concise message that had the best chance of being delivered immediately. He wrote:

> *Mark Williams is at the Chengdu Consulate. 36 hours ago he tracked control cube to an underground bunker housing Chinese mobile nuclear missiles. Imperative that China be warned of danger immediately. William's team unable to complete mission alone as team compromised while leaving area. Williams requests immediate conference with President.*

Mr. Weatherby read over the message. "What's a 'control cube'?"

"That's our code for the agent," Mark answered easily. "Add whatever contact information you need to that and get it to the President. I suspect he will be calling back shortly."

"I'll get your message sent," Mr. Weatherby said as he buzzed for an orderly to escort them out.

They were taken to a very comfortably furnished waiting room, complete with iced water decanters, bowls of fruit and exquisite Chinese paintings on the wall. Mark asked the orderly if they could get a meal and was informed that arrangements would be made shortly. As they waited, Jeffreys traded unit information with their attending Marine guard, who had been stiffly standing by the door. Naturally, there were a number of units that they had both been assigned to and several Marines who were mutual acquaintances.

That was the easy part, Mark thought as Jeffreys chatted with the Marine guard. The hard part is yet to come. The orderly was bringing in a tray of food, when a messenger arrived saying that Mark was needed for an important call.

"Thirty-five minutes," Mark said to Jeffreys. "You wonder why Langley couldn't do that." They were escorted back to the secure communications room where a videoconference link had already been established. Mark, Jeffreys and Charles sat at the conference table across from a large flat screen TV monitor and a remote controlled camera. On screen a technician was doing the last sound check. When he saw Mark sit down, he quickly moved out of the camera and the President stepped into the view and sat down.

"Hello, Mr. Williams," the President said. Mark noted the President was dressed in casual pants and a polo shirt, not the usual presidential attire.

"Mr. President. They tell me that it is past midnight your time. My apologies for disturbing your sleep."

"Comes with the job," the President responded. "Tell me what's happened."

"Yes, Mr. President," Mark began. "And so I know where to begin, I gave someone at Langley a detailed briefing about an hour or two ago. Do you have that? Or should I start from the beginning?"

"No, I don't have that," the President said with a hint of irritation as he glanced off camera, and Mark thought he heard a chair scrape and some scrambling emanating from the speakers. "I do have written reports which were sent from your team up until about two days ago," the President continued.

"Okay," Mark said. "Let me bring you up to date." Mark went through the events since arriving in China, but focused on his impressions of the cube and the effects it had on him and the Chinese on the island. He wanted to convey to the President the power of the cubes. He stressed how the cube's 'sound' changed once it had been found and how they had tracked the last cube into the mountains. Here he interrupted his narration to introduce Jeffreys. "You may not recall, Mr. President, but Sergeant Jeffreys was my Marine escort back on the *Ronald Reagan*. He was with me the whole time and was actually the one who saved me from being killed by the cat."

"Hello, Sergeant Jeffreys," the President said.

"Hello, Mr. President," Jeffreys said in his best Marine fashion, sitting at attention in his chair.

"Jeffreys," Mark continued, "is a wizard with a map and compass and he took compass headings of the directions that I felt the cube's call coming from. He's the one who triangulated the position so we could get close enough for me to find it. I'm going to ask him to explain the compass headings I received in the mountains north of us."

Mark had alerted Jeffreys that he would probably do this so Jeffreys already had the map marked. He held it up for the camera and explained the position and the lines, noting where the Chinese checkpoint was located and where the call left all marked roads, leading them to the conclusion that the cube was in an underground bunker.

"I asked Langley if they could confirm the location of the bunker," Mark interjected at this point. "They said they would check on it, but I haven't heard back yet."

Jeffreys concluded with the results of his reconnaissance that morning on the mountaintop, noting that the other checkpoint he located would put the cube between the two checkpoints.

Mark finished with a cursory description of the incident with the roving patrol, ending by saying, "So you see, we have been compromised. We can't do anything else on the ground here without Chinese assistance and have some real concerns about being detained by Chinese security if we step foot outside of the Consulate. But the real problem is that someone under the control of the blue-grays is inside a Chinese nuclear facility and has been now for upwards of thirty-six hours."

"Can you tell if he is still there?" the President asked.

Mark closed his eyes for a moment. Opening his eyes, he responded, "It's hard to tell from this distance, Mr. President. The call is coming from the same general direction, but I can't tell if it has moved a degree or two. And I can't distinguish distance very well unless I'm real close. I..." Mark trailed off.

"Mr. Williams?" the President asked after several seconds of silence. "Mr. Williams?"

Mark shook his head as if snapping out of a trance. "Mr. President, I just lost the other call."

"The what?"

"The other cube," Mark explained. "There were two remaining cubes. Or there were. I just lost the second. I can only sense one, the closer one that we have been talking about. The other one is gone. It should be the one near..." Mark asked Jeffreys to show him the larger map. "This one, near Delingha, in Qinghai Province. Sir, can you call NORAD right now and see if they detected a meteor in this vicinity. It could be the cats." The President motioned to someone off screen. "And Mr. President, I lost the call to the other, the third cube, the one near Malan, yesterday. I asked Langley to check on a meteor at that location also, but I have not heard from them. If they detected meteors, that would be the cat ship coming in. It's the same thing they detected for the original cube near Kunming and the one on the island. As I understand it, the only thing that registers on our satellites is the heat from their entry."

"You think both of those cubes were destroyed by the cats?" the President asked.

"The call from the cubes is gone," Mark said carefully. "When someone touches them and the cube controls them, the call changes. I have felt that three times now. When the cube is destroyed, the call disappears. I felt that when we destroyed two of the cubes and the cats destroyed the third. Now these two cubes have stopped calling, so I would have to conclude they were destroyed, either by someone on Earth or by the cats," Mark explained. He was about to continue when someone off screen distracted the President. Mark could hear a voice, but could not make it out.

"NORAD confirms a meteor near Delingha," the President said. He listened some more to the unseen speaker. "Ok, it did not impact, they tracked it in and then it disappeared. No impact observed."

"Have them watch that area," Mark said excitedly. "They may see what happens next." They all waited for the next report. A speakerphone was set up in front of the President. After a minute a voice on the speakerphone reported fires on the ground. Then nothing for several minutes. As the minutes passed and it appeared no new information was coming, the President asked about the other site, 24 hours earlier. A minute later a report came in that a meteor had been tracked in that area at 03:09 a.m., local China time. "That confirms it," Mark said. "The cats got both of them. We should find out what damage was done. If anyone else was killed," Mark added, flinching at the grisly memory of the first cat attack.

When nothing further came from NORAD, the President continued the conference with Mark. "What exactly are you recommending, Mr. Williams?"

"We need to tell the Chinese the blue-grays are trying to get their nukes."

"They won't believe it," the President said.

"Let them see the video from the *Ronald Reagan*. Then ask them to explain Kunming, the island, and now these two incidences. They can't. A freak lightning bolt might explain one. But four? And we won't be asking them for anything. I'll need to go and point out where the cube is. But I'm nobody, a civilian. They can blindfold me if they want, so I don't see anything. All I have to do is tell them where it is so they can destroy it. And they have already gone public about the existence of these bunkers, bragged about them to their own people, so I won't be compromising some national secret. I think they will be very concerned about someone around their nukes. What would you do if they told you that a person under someone else's control was in one of our nuclear sites?"

"Good point," the President responded. "If we do nothing," the President asked, "do you think that the cats will destroy this cube like the others?"

"We have been discussing that very issue," Mark said, gesturing to Jeffreys. "My opinion is no. I am assuming that the cats observe the entry the same way we do and that they cannot hear the call afterwards. I have to assume that the blue-grays would not create a device that could be heard by their enemies. So once the cube leaves the landing site, it is harder to find. So far, all the cat attacks have been at the landing site. Unless NORAD tells us that the last two meteors were not located at the original sites. Why it is taking the cats so long to attack and why they take out each site separately, I don't know." Mark paused while the President consulted with someone off screen.

"The last two meteors have been at the estimated impact points," the President confirmed.

"Mr. President, here is why we have to get the Chinese involved. The blue-grays sent down one cube. The cats destroyed it. Three days later, the blue-grays send down six more. Five have been destroyed, three by the cats and two by us. What's to keep the blue-grays from sending down fifty next time? We are being dragged into this war. And by we, I mean the Earth, not just the United States. We, the Earth, need to act together to stay out of it."

The conference continued for a few minutes more before the President said, "I will consider your proposal, Mr. Williams. I need to consult with some people here and then I will get back with you. In the meantime, I assume you will be staying in the Consulate?"

"Yes, Sir."

As the President was about to get up, Jeffreys interrupted, "Mr. President?"

The President looked back at the screen. "Yes, Sergeant Jeffreys?"

"Sir, if you accept Mr. Williams' proposal about him going with the Chinese, I would request being sent with him. I have been with him from the beginning and am very familiar with how he reacts around these alien cubes. There are times that he can become... disorientated, even disabled for a period of time. I think it would be very important to have someone with him who knows the signs and knows how to take care of him during those times. As an example, Sir, in the karst formation Mr. Williams was knocked out when the cat destroyed the cube. If I had not pulled him to safety, the cat would have killed Mr. Williams then, just like Chin, Hwang and Bob."

"That is true," Mark conceded.

"I will consider both of your proposals," the President said as he turned and walked off camera.

"You don't have to do this," Mark said to Jeffreys as they left the secure conference room. "You don't know what you are getting into."

"I probably know more than you do," Jeffreys responded. "At least as far as the Chinese are concerned."

"That's probably true," Mark said. They were escorted back to the lavish waiting room. "Now where did they put that food?" Mark said. "I'm starving."

Jeffreys pointed to the tray sitting on a coffee table. "Better enjoy it," Jeffreys said. "If you go with the Chinese, this will be the last American meal that you have for a while."

"As long as it is not my last meal, I can live with that," Mark joked, hoping that it was in fact a joke.

CHAPTER 13

It took a day for the President to make a decision and another day for the Chinese. During that time Mark and Jeffreys remained at the Consulate to avoid being picked up by Chinese security. Their packs were delivered, but Juan made a point of staying away from the Consulate. They were treated well, but the delay was frustrating and monotonous. Mark did take the opportunity to finally call his wife.

"I'm surprised you didn't try to call earlier," Jeffreys remarked as the embassy staff were placing Mark's call. "I remember last year you were always trying to call home."

"That's true," Mark said. "But last year was very suspenseful. We didn't know what was happening. This time we knew it could be dangerous and then on that first contact, four people were killed. How could I call Beth then? I couldn't tell her about that. It would have been too stressful. And I couldn't lie, she would see right through it."

"So silence was better?" Jeffreys asked.

Mark was saved from answering as the call connected. "Hey honey, it's me."

"Are you all right? Why haven't you called? What's going on? I've been worried sick. You haven't called since you left."

Mark was always amazed how many questions Beth could fit into one breath.

"I'm fine," Mark said. "I am at the American Consulate in Chengdu, China. We made a bit of a whirlwind tour of some very remote areas, so I was not able to call earlier." Mark punched at Jeffreys when he rolled his eyes at that comment. "Anyway," Mark said, trying to recover his momentum, "the President is talking with the Chinese. The plan is to get them involved."

"So you were right. They are back," Beth said.

"They are," Mark said.

"I thought they were all dead," Beth said.

"I did too. I don't know what is going on now."

"Have you seen them? Talked to them?" Beth asked.

Mark considered for a moment and then realized that there was no censor at his side. The technician that had placed the call had left, although Mark felt sure someone was probably monitoring the call. "No. We are pretty sure the blue-grays are sending down cubes. Several of them. We are trying to locate the cubes. Most of them have been found, but there is one left that we need the Chinese help in locating."

"That's what you dreamed about? A cube? That is what you were hearing?"

"Yes."

"So once the Chinese are involved, then you can come home?" Beth asked.

"I have to show the Chinese where the cube is, and then, hopefully, I can come home," Mark hedged.

"What aren't you telling me?" Beth asked.

"Damn," Mark cursed under his breath. Jeffreys just shook his head. "The blue-grays keep sending more cubes," Mark said. "We destroy them, and they send more. I don't know if they will send more after this."

"So what. Why do you have to stop that? What's wrong with the memory cubes?"

"They are not memory cubes," Mark said. "They are… they're bad news. I can't explain over the phone. But we have been destroying them. They're not dangerous unless you touch them," Mark added hastily. "And we have been very careful not to touch them. But not everyone has been that fortunate. Which is why we have to get to them first and destroy them."

"Because you don't want to help the blue-grays."

"Right."

"So the war is still on?"

"Apparently," Mark said, not liking where this conversation was going.

"And the cats, what are they doing?"

Mark paused. "They are destroying the cubes also."

Beth paused while she considered this information. "You promised me no heroics," she said.

"My idea of heroics is to run like hell," Mark said, prompting another raised eyebrow from Jeffreys.

"Are you safe?"

"I'm in an American Consulate surrounded by guards. Yes, I'm safe."

"Then I'm coming over to be with you," Beth said. "We can do this together."

"There isn't time," Mark extemporized. "The flight here takes twenty-four hours by itself. Hopefully, we will be done by then."

"Unless they send more cubes," Beth argued.

Mark paused. "True. Okay, I'll make a deal with you. We get this last cube. If the blue-grays send more after that, I will make arrangements to have them bring you here."

Now it was Beth's turn to consider. "Okay. But you be careful. And call me."

"I will. But, I probably won't be able to call while I'm with the Chinese. They are not the most cooperative people. So just be patient."

"Easy for you to say," Beth complained. "You don't have to stay up worrying."

They talked for a little while longer before hanging up.

"Boy, she saw right through you," Jeffreys remarked after they hung up.

"Yes. She's smart. And when you've been married forever, you get to know each other pretty well. No secrets."

"She knows about the control cube?" Jeffreys asked.

"Okay, not many secrets. It just never came up," Mark explained.

The rest of their stay at the Consulate was occupied by conference calls to Washington requesting further details. Mark learned that the two northwestern cubes had been destroyed near their points of landing, presumably by the cats. The Chinese were being tight lipped about any further details, but rumors had surfaced about some strange deaths by lightning and an unexplained explosion near a manufacturing plant.

They were told the President had contacted the Chinese leader personally, after which it was finally agreed that Mark would assist the Chinese in locating the last cube and Jeffreys would be allowed as Mark's escort. Charles and Juan left the country on the next flight as their covers would be blown once the Chinese matched them up with Mark. Mark was relieved, as he did not want to be responsible for their welfare. He was nervous enough being responsible for Jeffreys, but that was not his decision and he was glad Jeffreys would be with him.

A Chinese representative, whose name Mark never could manage to pronounce, met with Mark and Jeffreys at the Consulate the next day. The meeting was stiff, formal, and very brief, prompting the phrase "inscrutable Chinese" to rise unbidden in Mark's mind as he could not read the Chinese representatives at all.

"You will meet with Colonel Liu Jiang," one of the Chinese said to Mark in surprisingly good English, while ignoring Jeffreys, whom they had been informed was a Marine Sergeant, attending solely to take care of Mark's needs. Jeffreys played the part well, spending most of his time standing at attention. "You will follow his orders. Follow me."

They walked out to the Consulate's parking lot where two Chinese flagged cars waited. "You will ride with them," the Chinese delegate said, pointing to the second car, before walking to the first car. A Chinese soldier jumped to attention and quickly opened the car door for the delegate.

Mark glanced at Jeffreys and then walked over to the second car. Two Chinese soldiers sat stone-faced in the front seats, making no move to get out. Jeffreys jumped in front of Mark and opened the back door while Mark climbed in. Jeffreys had climbed into the car before both cars accelerated out of the Consulate grounds into Chengdu traffic. After a few turns the lead car turned off, while the car carrying Mark and Jeffreys continued straight.

"Where are we going?" Mark asked the driver as he watched the first car disappear down a side road. "Aren't we supposed to be following them?"

The Chinese ignored Mark's questions. When it became apparent that no response was forthcoming, Mark leaned back in his seat and turned to Jeffreys. "I guess we should just enjoy the ride."

"Yes, Sir," Jeffreys responded, staying in character.

They sat in silence as the car traveled through the streets of Chengdu. When city sights gave way to more rural vistas, it became apparent that they were traveling outside of Chengdu. Mark was completely lost, as he had not paid much attention to the maps of this area. But this certainly did not look like the route they had taken coming here from Songpan. They were traveling on a two-lane road surrounded by fields when they pulled over and stopped behind a convoy of three Chinese humvee's.

The Chinese soldier in the front passenger seat turned to Mark and said in perfect English, "You will go with them," before turning back to stare out the front window.

Mark looked at Jeffreys in surprise and then shrugged his shoulders. "Thanks for the lift," he said as he climbed out of the car and headed over to the convoy. Another Chinese soldier escorted them to the middle humvee and motioned for them to climb in the back. Two soldiers climbed in the back with them, one on each side, while two more soldiers rode up front. It was a tight fit. Mark figured it would be a long ride if they were going back up where he had sensed the cube and wondered if they would blind-fold him. That would certainly make the trip even more unbearable.

"How long is this ride going to be?" Mark asked. His question was met with stony silence. "Just let me know when we get there," he added, before resigning himself to sitting back and just waiting. The humvee was cramped and the springs were tight, making the ride almost unbearable. Mark glanced at Jeffreys, who just sat there as if he did not have a care in the world.

They rode in silence for about an hour before pulling off the main road and driving into a very rural area. After an interminable period of time the Humvee pulled over and stopped. The soldiers got out, motioning Mark and Jeffreys to get out also. Mark climbed out and stretched.

He had stiffened up during the uncomfortable ride. He looked around and noticed they were on a rural road next to a large field. The soldiers from the other Humvees were also climbing out. One soldier, who Mark took as an officer, although he could not interpret the rank insignia, walked over to Mark and Jeffreys. Three soldiers with rifles slung on their shoulders followed. Mark did not like the looks of this.

"You will take off your clothes," the officer instructed in reasonable good English.

"What is going on?" Mark asked, confused and a bit concerned.

"You will change into these clothes," the officer said, handing them some basic Chinese style clothes, including Chinese sandals.

"I think they believe we're wired, Sir," Jeffreys said when Mark made no move to comply.

Mark shrugged, relieved that they were not being marched into the field to be shot. 'You really have watched too many movies,' he told himself. He and Jeffreys stripped naked, handing their clothes to another soldier who took them away. The officer pulled out a metal wand, something like Mark had seen at airport security screening areas, and slowly waived it over Mark.

"Good thing I'm not modest," Mark said as he stood naked on the side of the road, arms and legs spread, while the officer slowly conducted his scan. As usual, his remark was met with silence. The scan was repeated on Jeffreys, before they were handed some Chinese style clothing to put on.

The officer spoke something into his radio, after which everyone stood there in stony silence.

'This is too weird,' Mark thought, wondering if he should have followed Beth's advice and just gone home. "Chinese clothing looks good on you," Mark said to Jeffreys to break the silence.

"Thank you, Sir," Jeffreys replied, his Marine bearing ever present despite his peasant looking clothing.

A few minutes later, Mark heard a helicopter in the distance. As the sound grew louder, Mark spotted a short, squat, helicopter, painted a drab grey. It came closer and finally landed in the nearby field. Three soldiers escorted them to the helicopter, where they were seated, belted, and blindfolded, before the helicopter took off.

Mark resented the blindfold. He had always enjoyed riding in helicopters, especially looking out the window. 'Oh well,' he chided himself, 'I'm not hear for the scenery.' They flew about an hour before they landed and, still blindfolded, were escorted to a ground vehicle, possibly another Chinese humvee by the feel and sound of it. Another trip of indeterminable length followed, punctuated by twists, turns and bumps. Mark tried to sleep, since there was nothing else to do, but the constant bumping made that impossible. He was comforted by the fact that they were going in the same general direction as the cube, which felt like it was getting closer.

A clanging noise filled Mark's ears as they drove over some type of grating. Sounds echoed after that, indicating they were in some type of tunnel. They drove for several minutes without stopping, the engine noise reverberating off the tunnel walls. Finally, they came to a stop and Mark and Jeffreys were taken, still blindfolded, out of the vehicle and marched down an echoing passageway. Mark felt like he was being squeezed through a doorway before he was seated in hard, wooden, chair. Only then was the mask taken off.

Bright light blinded Mark and it took several minutes for his eyes to adjust. He and Jeffreys were sitting in a bare room about 15 feet square with a simple wooden table and four straight backed wooden chairs. Naked fluorescent lights hanging from the ceiling cast a harsh light, while two Chinese guards stood at attention beside the door.

"So much for luxury," Mark mumbled.

They were kept waiting for over an hour. 'Perhaps another reminder of how unimportant they were,' Mark thought. Again Mark's only consolation was that he could sense that they were close to the cube. Mark used the time to try to plan how he would explain the situation to this Colonel Lui. He ran several scenarios in his head, trying to determine which would be best. He finally decided that he would have to play it by ear, as he would have to judge his presentation based upon his reception. Judging by the treatment so far, though, it was not going to be easy. The seats were uncomfortable, particularly after their long ride. Exhausted from the ride, Mark moved to the corner where he uncprestat on the floor. "Wake me up when Colonel Lui arrives," Mark said as he leaned back and tried to rest.

Mark awoke to Chinese voices. He opened his eyes to see the two guards standing stiffly at attention on either side of the door, while three other soldiers, clearly officers from their bearing, were standing in the room. One officer was asking Jeffreys in passable English if he was Mark Williams.

"No, Sir," Jeffreys responded.

Still half asleep, Mark climbed slowly to his feet, brushed himself off and said, "I'm Mark Williams," while stepping forward with his hand out. There was an awkward moment before the first officer shook his hand. The second officer also reluctantly shook Mark's hand. Then Mark held out his hand to the third, which Mark assumed must be Colonel Lui. Jeffreys had told him to look for three stars on the shoulder epaulette. The Colonel hesitated, looking at Mark's hand, then relented and shook hands. The handshake was awkward and

Mark stepped back, flustered. One of the officer's barked something in Chinese and a guard ran over and moved a chair to the other side of the table so three chairs faced one. The three officers sat down and motioned for Mark to sit in the opposing seat. Mark complied and Jeffreys took up a position behind Mark where he stood stiffly at parade rest.

"This is Colonel Lui Jiang," the officer on the right stated in acceptable English. Mark nodded to the Colonel sitting in the center, wondering if the introduction was typical for the Chinese or if the Colonel did not speak English. "You are to explain your mission to him," the officer continued.

"I would be happy to," Mark started. "May I ask if you have been briefed from my government so I am not repeating things?" Mark asked, resisting the urge to speak to the talking officer and instead addressing the Colonel directly.

The two officer's spoke in Chinese before the first responded, "He would like to hear directly from you, rather than indirectly."

"Fair enough," Mark said. "I will try to state it as succinctly as possible. There is a war going on between two alien races, a war that has come to Earth. Last year one alien race, which I call the blue-grays, attempted to make contact with me onboard the aircraft carrier *Ronald Reagan*. I say 'attempted contact' since there was a lot of difficulty trying to be understood. The blue-grays communicate with alien species through the use of a technology that I call the cube, because it resembles a cube slightly smaller than your fist. The technology was not properly programmed so the communication was not very accurate. Finally, when a blue-gray actually landed their ship on the *Ronald Reagan*, the other alien race, whom I dubbed the cats, since they somewhat resemble cats, attacked and killed the blue-grays. The cats then left, taking the blue-grays' ship with them. That was a year ago and we thought both races were gone for good.

"About two weeks ago, we became aware of what we thought was the return of the blue-grays, although we were not sure. Recently we have confirmed that the blue-grays have been sending their cubes into China, probably in an attempt to communicate again. Unfortunately, the cats have not been far behind and they have now destroyed all but one of the cubes. It is our understanding, based upon our communication last year, that the blue-grays are requesting our help in their fight against the cats. Since a number of the cubes have landed near nuclear sites, my government believes that the blue-grays are trying to obtain a nuclear device.

"There has been a debate in my government whether we should help the blue-grays or not. I do not have any details concerning the debates that have gone on. All I can say is that I have been told to find and destroy the cubes so that we don't get involved in the war between these two species. The cats have the ability to destroy the Earth by hurling asteroids at us and my government has decided that we should not aid the blue-grays for fear of becoming the cat's enemy." Mark paused to let the Chinese reflect on his words. Since the officer had not translated Mark's narration, he assumed the Colonel understood English.

"And what are you here to do?" the same officer asked.

"I am hear to help locate the last cube," Mark responded.

"How do you do that?"

"I can hear it," Mark said.

"How?" the officer asked, after a quick conversation with the Colonel in Chinese.

"I don't know," Mark answered.

"Yet, you can tell us where it is?" the officer asked slightly incredulously.

"I can help you find it," Mark said, looking directly at the Colonel. "What you do with it is your decision."

"You expect us to believe your story?" the Colonel asked directly in perfect English.

"No, not really," Mark said, clearly surprising the other officers. "I didn't believe it either at first. Not until I saw it with my own eyes."

"So you expect us to let you inspect our military installation?" the third officer asked accusingly.

"No. I'm a civilian. I probably wouldn't even recognize what I saw. I'm sure your people have already confirmed that. But I can do it blindfolded, if I must. I have no interest in your facility." The officers had a rapid-fire conversation in Chinese that Mark couldn't even guess at what they were saying. At length one of them said, "We will discuss this some more." And they got up to leave.

Mark turned to Colonel Lui and said, "Colonel, may I talk to you privately, please?" The other two officers looked at the Colonel. When he nodded, they left the room. Mark turned to Jeffreys, "We need a moment by ourselves, Sergeant." Jeffreys was clearly surprised, but snapped out a "Yes, Sir," and marched out of the room.

When they were alone, Mark turned to the Colonel. "Colonel, I know where the cube is, and you do too." The Colonel looked at him with surprise. "I can hear it, just like you can. I didn't want to say this in front of the others. They would not understand. You see, I touched a cube. Last year on board the *Ronald Reagan*, the blue-gray handed me a cube. But the cats came and killed the blue-gray and they almost killed me. Have you seen the video from the *Ronald Reagan*? You can see me touching the cube, twice. I kept getting knocked back because the programming was too strong, I couldn't hold it. But I kept trying and would have succeeded if the cat hadn't arrived. And then at the end of the video you will see me shooting at the cat ship, trying to stop them. But I failed. And I have lived with the shame of that failure for the past year. But now the blue-grays have come back and I have an opportunity to redeem myself."

The Colonel was quiet as he considered Mark's comments. Finally, he asked, "Why are you hunting down the cubes? Why are you trying to destroy the cubes?"

"Because my government has decided that we can not help the blue-grays, because they think the cats are going to win and are afraid that the cats will destroy the Earth. So they have decided to destroy all the cubes."

"And you helped them," the Colonel accused.

"I have been pretending to help," Mark argued. "NORAD tracked the cubes here. They were sending a team in. I volunteered to come along in hopes of getting to the cubes first. The cats got to four of them first. We did get to the cube on Mount Hwang first and we had the cube. We were taking it off the mountain. But the others had it, not me. And then they were afraid that the cats would come before we could get off the mountain, like last time, and they destroyed the cube. I couldn't stop them. When I knew that you had the cube, I told the team we had to return to Chengdu and I convinced my government that we should work with you, the Chinese, directly. I knew you wouldn't allow a team in here, so I volunteered to come here alone and assist you. I told them it was the only way."

"How can I believe you?"

"Watch the video. The cat shot me, tried to kill me. And would have if I did not happen to have a Kevlar vest on. You think I want to help the cats? I was trying to kill the cats at the end, I was the first to shoot at them. The others only started shooting after I did," Mark argued.

"You are not alone."

"Oh, the Sergeant? They insisted that I have someone to protect me. But he is to follow my orders. He is not CIA. He doesn't have any authority. He's just some enlisted Marine."

"He could have an accident," Colonel Lui said.

Mark was shocked, but tried not to show it. "He could," Mark agreed. "But then Washington would probably insist on sending someone else, probably some CIA agent, and that would be worse. He is harmless. He will do whatever I say."

"What do you suggest?" Colonel Lui asked.

"The show is yours," Mark said. "You have the cube. I can help, but it is your show now."

There was silence while the Colonel considered Mark's words. "Where is the cube, right now?"

Mark closed his eyes and concentrated. He turned slightly and then pointed. Opening his eyes, he said, "It's this way. I can't tell you exactly how far. But it's not too far away. I could take you to it, if you wanted."

The Colonel picked up the blindfold Mark had worn to the site and placed it over Mark's head. He then turned Mark round and round, till Mark got dizzy.

"Without taking the blindfold off," the Colonel said, "tell me where the cube is." Mark paused while the dizziness subsided and then slowly turned and pointed. The Colonel repeated this two more times and each time Mark easily pointed in the direction of the cube. After the third time the Colonel took off the blindfold. Mark blinked in the light. "I need to consider your remarks," the Colonel said. Mark nodded. With that the Colonel left the room and Jeffreys was sent back in.

Jeffreys played the perfect aide. He walked in and looked at Mark, ensuring that he was okay, then asked, "Anything you need at this time, Sir?"

"No, Sergeant," Mark answered. Jeffreys then took position at the door, standing at parade rest.

About an hour passed and nothing happened, while Mark replayed recent events. After a while he noticed that he was getting quite hungry.

"Sergeant," he said.

"Yes, Sir?"

"See if you can get us some food, I'm starving," Mark instructed.

"I don't speak Chinese, Sir," Jeffreys said.

"You can pantomime," Mark said. "Tell them you are hungry and pantomime eating," Mark said, holding an imaginary cup in his hands while spooning out something to his mouth.

"Yes, Sir," Jeffreys said and turned and knocked on the door. When it opened, he repeated the instructions provided by Mark. The sentry clearly understood, said something in Chinese and then closed the door.

"I hope that meant we'll get some food right away, rather than starve to death you capitalist pig," Mark said. Jeffreys resumed his stance at parade rest near the door.

Fifteen minutes later the door opened and the sentry brought in some food and placed it on the table. "Thank you," Mark said, bowing slightly to the guard and sat down to eat. "Come and eat, Sergeant," Mark said to Jeffreys. "You need to eat too." Thanking him, Jeffreys sat down and joined Mark. Normally they would have joked about the meal, particularly since Mark did not like Chinese food, but under these circumstances they stayed very formal.

Another hour passed before the sentries entered again, this time with army cots and light blankets. "I guess we're spending the night here," Mark said. They pushed the table and chairs against the side of the room, set up the cots, turned out the lights and went to sleep. Mark could feel the cube nearby and wondered what would happen next. But all he could do now was wait. The next morning the cots were removed and a basic Chinese breakfast was delivered. They were finishing their breakfast when the door opened and the Colonel came in alone. Jeffreys jumped to attention. "I need to speak to you," the Colonel said to Mark. Mark glanced at Jeffreys, who quickly stepped outside.

"You brought the cube," Mark said, trying to keep the stress out of his voice.

"You can feel it?" the Colonel asked.

"Yes," Mark answered. "It is your cube, but I can still feel it."

"Would you like to touch it?" the Colonel asked, holding it out in his hand.

Fear raced through Mark. This was the moment he had been dreading. Mark gazed at the cube. He had to destroy it. But he couldn't touch it. And he probably would not be able to take it from the Colonel. If he succeeded in attacking the Colonel, smashing the cube without touching it himself, then what would he do next? How could he explain why he attacked the Colonel? And how could he get out of this facility alive? And even if he destroyed this cube, what would keep the blue-grays from sending more? He would have to bide his time and pick the right moment to act. But in the meantime, he could not touch the cube. These thoughts raced through Mark's mind as he stared at the cube in the Colonel's hand.

"I don't think I should touch it," Mark answered tentatively. "I can hear it. But it belongs to you. It does not call me the same as the other. I already belong to a cube, the one from last year. I don't think I should touch two."

The Colonel paused as he considered Mark's remarks. "Perhaps you are right," he finally decided, pocketing the cube. "I have decided how you can help," the Colonel said, as he sat at the table. Mark sat across from him and listened. "I told my other officers that when you talked to me, you told me that you could help us locate this device, but that you were not as sure of it as you had led your government to believe and you wanted to tell me privately to save face. You can still feel it, but it is further away than you thought. You will lead them to the cube. It will be a false direction. I have brought a map. This is where I want you to lead them. Take your time, go slow. But generally follow this compass heading. Your Sergeant should be able to help you there. I'm sure he can follow basic map and compass directions. Tell him that you are hearing the call from here," he pointed to a valley on the map.

"What then?" Mark asked.

"That's all."

"But when I get there and the cube is not there?" Mark asked. "What do I do then?"

"If I haven't called you back by then, just keep going on that heading. Tell them it is moving," Colonel Lui said.

"You are not coming with me?" Mark asked.

"No. I have other things that need my personal attention."

Mark paused, trying to figure out what to do next. Finding no other alternative, he said, "And this will be helpful to you?"

"It is what I require of you," the Colonel confirmed.

"Then I will do it," Mark said obediently.

"Good," the Colonel said as he stood up from the table. They walked over to the door. Before opening it, the Colonel turned to Mark and said, "Thank you for your assistance." Instinctively, Mark reached out to shake the Colonel's hand. A blinding light filled Mark's mind and he fell back.

Mark's next memory was staring up at the ceiling tiles. He groaned and slowly sat up. The Colonel was lying on the floor across the room, still unconscious. Mark had been concerned about the room being monitored. But the fact that no one had come in proved that it was not. At least not now. Mark got unsteadily to his feet and was reaching down to assist the Colonel, when he realized he probably should not touch him again. The Colonel had the cube and its power had evidently been transmitted through the Colonel's touch to Mark. Touching the Colonel, and hence the cube again, would be more than Mark could take. Mark was turning for the door when the Colonel moaned. Mark stepped away and leaned over the table so that it looked like he was just getting up. He glanced over in time to see the Colonel open his eyes and sit up. Mark straightened up, using the table for support as the Colonel quickly jumped to his feet.

"What are you doing?" the Colonel asked.

Puzzled, Mark started to ask whether the Colonel had felt the impact, but then remembered how the people on the island had suddenly jumped up, totally oblivious to the fact that they had been unconscious. Catching himself, he simple said, "Stomach cramps. I must apologize, but I am not used to your food and sometimes it reacts badly. I will be fine. I just need a little time to rest and perhaps a bathroom."

"The guards will take you. When can you leave on your mission?" the Colonel asked, clearly unaware of the impact of their contact.

"Can you give me thirty minutes or an hour?" Mark asked.

"I will send them to you in an hour," the Colonel decided and then stepped for the door. Mark made a point of bowing, rather than reaching out his hand again. The Colonel acknowledged the bow and stepped out.

Jeffreys came in, a look of concern flashing across his face when he saw Mark standing there, white faced, holding a chair for support.

"Are you okay, Sir?" Jeffreys asked.

"Vision," Mark said wondering how he could tell Jeffreys. He was concerned the Colonel may have stepped into an adjoining room to monitor them. Mark knew that was paranoid, but he was in fact in a police state and as the old joke went: 'Just because you are paranoid, does not mean people are not out to get you.' He sat shakily at the table. "You know how I get visions when I'm very close to a cube?" Jeffreys looked at Mark carefully. Before Jeffreys could respond, Mark continued. "Colonel Lui will be sending some people to us in an hour. We are to take them to the cube. The Colonel gave me this map so you can assist me. The cube is in this direction," Mark indicated the bearing on the map. Jeffreys looked at Mark quizzically. The map had not been orientated to magnetic north. Just to be sure that Jeffreys understood the message, Mark added, "When we go outside, you will need to obtain a compass from our friends, the Chinese, and orientate this map so you can help me go along this route here," again indicating on the map, "we will find the cube in this valley. Do you understand?"

Although Jeffreys did not understand, he repeated the instructions, "Yes, Sir. Once we are outside I will obtain a compass and orientate this map and we will proceed to find the cube down this bearing."

"That's correct," Mark said, wondering how he was going to fill Jeffreys in on what was going on. At that point a Chinese guard entered the room and motioned to Mark to follow. Jeffreys looked at Mark questioningly. "Oh," Mark said, remembering, "I told the Colonel that Chinese food did not always agree with me and that I needed a restroom. He said he would send someone."

Mark stood up to follow the guard. "Come with me," he added to Jeffreys.

They walked down a hall to a door and the guard motioned to it. Mark opened the door and saw that it was a small, single person bathroom, Chinese style. He handed Jeffreys the map saying, "wait right here," before he closed the door. Sweat beading on his brow, Mark took the grease pencil that he had pocketed after the Colonel marked the map and wrote at eye level on the inside of the door: "COL HAS CUBE." A few minutes later he emerged. Mark turned to Jeffreys and reached for the map. "You had better go in there also," Mark instructed. "We have a long trip ahead of us. And try not to write any graffiti on the wall. I know how you enlisted love to do that. We are visitors after all."

Jeffreys stepped in and closed the door. Several minutes later he emerged, poker faced. "I'm ready, Sir."

"You clean up, Sergeant? Didn't leave the toilet seat up?" Mark asked.

"You have to have a toilet to leave the seat up," Jeffreys said. "But yes, Sir, I left it clean."

About thirty minutes later an officer came for them and they were escorted to a waiting truck. Mark and Jeffreys climbed into the back of the Chinese humvee along with a soldier. Two other soldiers were in the front. The officer had a rapid conversation with the driver in Chinese before they drove off. Oddly, they were not blindfolded as they were driven through an elaborate underground tunnel system, finally emerging about an hour later into a valley. Judging from the position of the sun, Mark estimated that it must be before noon. He couldn't check as the Chinese had confiscated his watch. In the valley they met up with another Chinese humvee, this one with a machine gun mounted on the roof. The second humvee pulled behind them as they drove down the mountain road.

"They seem to know where they are going," Jeffreys remarked, when no one asked the Americans for directions.

"They do," Mark agreed worriedly. "Can you figure out where we are on the map?"

Jeffreys spread the map out and started comparing it to their surroundings. "We could be anywhere, he conceded. I can't tell."

"We were supposed to direct them," Mark said.

"Maybe they changed their plans," Jeffreys said.

"We need to stop," Mark said. They both started talking to the soldiers, telling them to stop. It was clear that they did not understand English. They finally persuaded the driver to stop and Jeffreys and Mark climbed out, quickly followed by the three Chinese soldiers. Mark spread the map across the front of the Humvee, while he and Jeffreys poured over it. Two soldiers from the second humvee came up and had an animated conversation with the others in Chinese. It was clear that they wanted everyone to get back in the vehicles and get underway. None of the soldiers spoke English. But by pantomiming, Jeffreys had one of the soldiers show him where they were on the map and even procured a compass, so he could orientate it.

"We are here," Jeffreys told Mark, pointing to the map. "At least that is what I think he is saying," Jeffreys added, referring to the nearby soldier. "I will know after we drive some more, whether the features line up right."

"How far to this valley that they want us to go to?" Mark asked.

"About eight klicks, kilometers," Jeffreys corrected.

"So just under five miles," Mark calculated.

"Right."

They were getting a lot of pressure to get back into the vehicle so finally Mark relented, bowing and shaking hands with all five soldiers before heading back to the first humvee. "Have him sit in the middle," Mark said to Jeffreys as they climbed into the back of the humvee. Jeffreys made an elaborate show of bowing and gesturing and the Chinese soldier climbed in between them and they started back down the road with the second humvee following.

Mark was quiet for a moment and then said, "Anyone here speak English?" There was no reply from the soldiers. He repeated the question, again without any results. He then turned to Jeffreys. "Let me see that map," Mark asked Jeffreys. They spread the map out on the Chinese soldiers legs and Mark pointed to it while he spoke rapidly to Jeffreys, hoping that none of the Chinese could understand English, but figuring he had nothing to lose even if they could.

"We have a problem," Mark said quickly. "When we get to this point on the map the humvee behind us is going to open fire with that machine-gun on their roof and kill everyone in this vehicle."

Jeffreys looked up at Mark in surprise and then glanced at the soldiers sitting with them. None of them reacted, so it was clear they did not understand English.

"You're sure?" Jeffreys asked.

"Yes, the two behind us are controlled by the cube. When I shook their hands I could tell their intentions," Mark explained.

"You could read their minds?" Jeffreys asked.

"Something like that," Mark said.

"So what do we do?" Jeffreys asked.

"I don't know," Mark said. "I was hoping that you would figure something out. And quickly. We are running out of time."

"At this valley?" Jeffreys asked, pointing to the map.

"Yes," Mark confirmed.

"We have about two miles," Jeffreys calculated. "We need a weapon."

"I see three in here," Mark said, glancing at the assault rifle held by the soldier between them and the two rifles in brackets in the front.

"We can't take out all three before we get hit from behind," Jeffreys said, while glancing at the humvee following them.

"We need to do something, and quickly," Mark said.

Jeffreys paused as he analyzed the situation. Looking back at the map, he said, "That curve about a half mile ahead. That turn leads into the valley," he said. "We have to act now." He glanced behind again. "One of the soldiers is climbing into the turret," he said. He sucked in a deep breath, straightened his shoulders, and as if making up his mind said quickly, but calmly, "When we get to the turn, open your door and jump. Head for the woods."

"What are you going to do?" Mark asked, watching the curve quickly approach.

"I'm going to take this weapon and go out my side," he said evenly, smiling at the soldier between them. "Do you have that?"

"Yes," Mark said uncertainly.

"You can do it," Jeffreys said. As they approached the curve Jeffreys continued conversationally, "Ok, get ready, get set, go."

Mark yanked on the door handle while Jeffreys struck the soldier between them with a vicious elbow strike to the temple. The soldiers in the front yelled and the driver hit the brakes, slowing the vehicle, which was fortunate Mark thought absently as he jumped out and rolled, ending in a ditch, stunned.

The second vehicle slid to a stop next to Mark. The sound of machine gun fire filled the air as the soldier in the turret opened fire. Hot metal rained down on Mark, burning him. He winced, waiting for the searing pain of the gunshots, before his brain finally registered that it was hot empty shell casings ejected from the machine gun that were hitting him. He heard the sound of another machine gun firing, faster, but at a higher pitch. It came in short bursts, followed by a scream, and then another burst. Then all was quiet.

Mark lay in the ditch on his stomach, his ears ringing despite the silence. He told himself to get up and run, but his body would not obey. He heard footsteps, light and quick, and his mind screamed for him to run, but still he couldn't move. The footsteps came nearer and then stopped.

"Are you okay?" Jeffreys voice. Relief flooded through Mark as he tried to get up. A helping hand grabbed his arm and lifted. "Are you okay? Are you hit?" Jeffreys repeated.

Mark stood up slowly and looked around. Jeffreys was holding Mark with his left hand. His right hand held the assault rifle in a ready position as he quickly scanned their surroundings before looking back at Mark. Mark shook his head to clear it. "I'm okay," he said, his voice sounding quiet after the gunfire.

"Okay, good. Stay here," Jeffreys commanded. "I'll be right back." Assault rifle at the ready, Jeffreys sprinted around the humvee. Dazed, Mark slowly walked to the front of the Humvee. It felt like he was walking in a dream. He watched as Jeffreys leaned into the first vehicle and came back carrying two more assault rifles, which he put into the back seat of the second vehicle. He searched each of the dead Chinese soldiers, removing all ammunition and their web gear, which he also placed in the back of the second humvee. When he finished, he came back to Mark.

"We can't stay here long," Jeffreys was saying. "We can take this vehicle and put some distance between us. But once the alarm sounds, we will probably have to ditch it. It's pretty noticeable with that machine gun on the roof. Not something we can drive back to Chengdu. Trying to make it back to the Consulate is probably our best shot. Unless we can get a call into the World Wide Tours number and ask them for instructions. What do you think?"

"I'm having trouble thinking right now," Mark said. "Can we get somewhere safe where we can just stop and think for a minute?"

Jeffreys retrieved his map and studied it quickly. "Okay, here's the plan. Help me drag these bodies into the woods. We can't do anything with the hummer, it's toast. So we'll just push it into the ditch. Then we'll drive over to this spot here," he pointed to the map. "I wouldn't call it safe, but it's a bit more secluded. We won't be able to stay there long. The sooner we have a plan and get moving, the better." Mark followed Jeffreys' instructions, surprised at how detached he was as he dragged the bodies into the woods, particularly the three soldiers who had been chopped up by the heavy machine-gun. They climbed into the second humvee and Jeffreys drove, while holding the map in his lap. Fifteen minutes later they pulled off the road and drove up into the woods. Once out of sight of the road, Jeffreys parked the humvee and turned to Mark. "You okay now?"

"Yea," Mark answered, realizing that he was starting to feel like himself again. They climbed out of the humvee. "Sorry about that back there," Mark continued. "Bruce Willis makes jumping out of moving cars seem so easy. It hurts!" he said as he stretched. "By the way, thanks for saving us back there."

Jeffreys nodded. "You want to fill me in on what's going on? We haven't been able to talk since the Chinese picked us up. Although I did get your bathroom graffiti."

"And wiped it off, I hope?"

"Yes."

"Good. Anyway, Colonel Lui is the one with the cube. When I shook his hand when we first met, I knew. I could sense it."

"That's why you gave such a weird briefing to the Chinese," Jeffreys said.

"Yes," Mark said. "It really took me aback realizing that the one in charge of finding the cube, was actually the one under its control. And of course I didn't know who else might be with him. Remember the island, where everyone was controlled? They were all paranoid." Jeffreys nodded and Mark continued. "Anyway, I figured since Colonel Lui had the cube, he would want to protect it and that meant we were now the enemy. He would either send us on a wild goose chase, or if he thought I really could find it, then we were dead. So I decided to change the game. I gave that equivocal briefing and then asked to speak to him privately.

"In private I told him that I knew he had the cube and wanted to help. I told him to watch the video of me on the *Ronald Reagan*. Since it showed me touching the cube, I hoped he would assume I was under its control. I told him that Washington had overruled me and they wanted the cubes destroyed because they were afraid the cats were going to win and didn't want the cats trying to destroy the Earth. It wasn't hard convincing him that I didn't like the cats, since the video showed me getting shot by them. I blamed the destruction of the earlier cube on the CIA and told him that I had talked Washington into sending me here alone, so that I could help him.

"I explained your presence as being solely as an aide, which is why I treated you so brusquely. Even then, the Colonel suggested that you should have an accident to get you out of the way. I managed to talk him out of that."

"Thank you for that," Jeffreys said.

"You're welcome," Mark said. "Anyway, he tried to get me to touch the cube. That was his second private visit with me. The first time he did not have the cube on him. He was afraid to bring it with him in case I really could hear it. The second time he brought the cube. That's how he controls the others, through the cube. I talked him out of having me touch it by saying that I had already touched a different cube and didn't think I should touch both. I stressed that it was his and he was in control. I did not want him to think of me as a threat."

"That doesn't seem to have worked," Jeffreys noted.

"No, it didn't," Mark agreed. "It seems that he came up with a plan to take care of both of his problems, me and Washington. He would use us as a decoy, showing Washington and his superiors that he was actually looking for the cube. He sent two of his controlled soldiers to make sure that we did not survive. In the meantime, he is mobilizing his troops and moving a nuclear missile. He intends to give it to the blue-grays."

"That's what we guessed the blue-grays wanted, a nuke," Jeffreys said. "So what should we do now?"

"Before I try to answer that, let me finish," Mark said. "Remember, on Mount Huang, I promised I would tell you everything."

"Yes."

"Well, the second time I met privately with the Colonel…" Mark started.

"The time he wanted you to touch the cube," Jeffreys finished.

"Yes, that time. He had the cube, but I managed to talk him out of having me touch it. Then stupidly, as he was leaving I shook his hand. It was just reflex. I was so relieved he had put the cube away. I just reached out and our hands touched. It knocked both of us out. Just like the people on the island. I woke up first. He woke up, but didn't know we had been out. Again, just like on the island. But I did."

"That's when you told me you had a vision," Jeffreys said. "You were white as a ghost."

"Correct. I was trying to figure out how to warn you. I did have a vision of sorts when I touched him. It was jumbled though, something like on the submarine. But that's how he controls people. He makes physical contact with them while he has possession of the cube and the cube works through him. He becomes their leader. I don't know if it works on everyone, or just those who are susceptible to the cube. If he shook your hand, for instance, I don't know if you would feel it or not. But I did."

"Are you saying he can control you?" Jeffreys asked alarmed.

"Yes and no," Mark answered. "I feel the control. It's like a pressure, a strong pressure. But I can resist it. At least I think I can. It's like a war of emotions going on inside me. I think the reason I can resist is because I accessed the blue-grays' personal cube last year. So I know what is going on. That's the only explanation I have. But I wanted to tell you, to warn you. In case you think my decisions may be influenced by the cube."

"That's scary," Jeffreys said.

"You think it's scary? Try fighting it in here. Now that's scary," Mark said, pointing to his head. "But to answer your question, what should we do next? I know where the Colonel is. He has the cube and I can hear it. I can get us there like I did all the other cubes. And I know his plans. Let me explain that. I can't read his mind like you read a book. I have a general impression of his intent. It's like a collage of thoughts or feelings or flashes. It's not perfect though. I couldn't read his intent for us. I learned that from the two soldiers in this humvee when I shook their hands. They wanted us dead.

Their plan was foremost in their thoughts, so it was easy to read. The Colonel was different. Much more complex. But I can tell you that he is moving a nuclear missile, one of those on a truck like you see in all the May Day parade pictures. And I sensed, or saw, a bunch of soldiers. He's not doing this alone. He's taking a lot of firepower with him."

"Is he taking a squad, platoon, or company?" Jeffreys asked.

"I really don't know," Mark said. "I would guess, and this is really a guess, that it is several platoons, maybe a company. I can't tell for sure. It's not a squad. And I don't think it's a battalion."

"That's still a lot of soldiers," Jeffreys said.

"It is," Mark agreed. "And the question remains, what should we do about it? Should we stop him? Can we stop him? And how?"

"We've talked back and forth about this before," Jeffreys said. "If the blue-grays get a nuke and blast the cats, so what? They win and then leave."

"Assuming the blue-grays win," Mark agreed. "And if they blast the cats on Earth, we get the fall-out."

"Hadn't thought of that," Jeffreys admitted. "And if the cats win?"

"What's to keep them from chucking a couple of asteroids at the Earth as payback," Mark answered. "In fact, the more cubes the blue-grays send down here, the more likely the cats will stop trying to find each cube and just blast the Earth."

"You paint a very rosy picture," Jeffreys said.

"Don't forget, I personally witnessed the Earth getting wiped out sixty-five million years ago."

"That was a vision," Jeffreys said.

"Yes, a vision of a real event which is now my memory, a memory as real to me as my own experiences."

"So what do you suggest?" Jeffreys repeated.

"Part of me wants to run away and let Colonel Lui give the nuke to the blue-grays. I think that part is coming from the cube. It's also the easier choice. The other part says that we came here to stop the blue-grays and that we should continue our mission."

They sat in silence while each considered the possibilities. Finally Jeffreys asked, "So which part are you going to follow: run or continue?"

Mark sighed. "I never wanted to make this decision. But I can't run. I have to take this thing to the end. What ever that end may be. You don't have to come."

"I hate not completing a mission," Jeffreys said. "Besides, you wouldn't last ten minutes without me."

"That's probably true," Mark said, rubbing his hip where he had hit the ground jumping out of the humvee.

"So where are we going?" Jeffreys asked.

"Let's see that map," Mark answered. They spread the map across the hood of the vehicle and Jeffreys orientated it to their location. Mark closed his eyes and concentrated. Opening his eyes, he said, "Right now the cube is in this direction," Mark said, pointing. Jeffreys drew a line across the map. He also marked where they had first come out of the tunnel system. "I saw a valley in the vision, surrounded by hills, mountains actually. That's where he will go."

Jeffreys started scanning the map looking for a suitable candidate. "It will probably be the opposite direction from us," Jeffreys reasoned. "These valleys would be likely candidates." He circled three valleys on the map. "Less likely candidates would be these," he drew five squares around other valleys.

Mark studied the map. "You can cross off this one," Mark said. "It's the wrong shaped valley. And this one, and this one," Mark said as he studied the map. "One of these two," Mark finally said. "These two look the closest to what I saw. Too bad we don't have Charles' computer so we could get an aerial view, I could confirm it then."

"These two are not too far from each other," Jeffreys pointed out. "We could get close by driving this route here," he traced a route on the map. "We can't drive right up, but we can get close. We would have to hike the last part."

"Of course," Mark said.

"What would we do when we got there?" Jeffreys asked.

"I don't know. We have to play it by ear," Mark said.

"What if we run across the owner of this vehicle on our way?" Jeffreys said, pointing to the Chinese humvee. "We can't fight our way there. We would never make it."

"I guess we keep a low profile and get as close as we can and then hike," Mark said. "You're the tactician, that's the best I can do. And if we run into our friends, we run like hell."

"That was your plan with the cubes," Jeffreys said. "I didn't think much of it then, either. Let's think this through. How many people do you think are in on the Colonel's plans?"

"Hard to say," Mark answered. "It may be a matter of genetics. He may only be able to control those like me, who have the right genetic make-up."

"Or he can control anyone he touches," Jeffreys said.

"True. But the three soldiers in our vehicle weren't under his control. Only the two in this one were."

"Of course he is a Colonel," Jeffreys pointed out. "So all the soldiers will follow his orders unless they get too bizarre. So the question remains, what are his orders regarding us?" Jeffreys paused to consider before continuing. "Since the two soldiers in this vehicle were under his control, he probably has not given general orders to kill us. So we probably would not be shot on sight by a random patrol. But we would be detained. It's a military vehicle and we can't pass as locals."

"But once word gets back to the Colonel that we are alive, he will remedy that," Mark said.

"Correct," Jeffreys said. "So we can't be caught by the Chinese. If we are, we're dead. That means we would have to fight our way out."

"Fight our way out of China?" Mark asked.

"I told you I didn't like your plan," Jeffreys said. "We just have to avoid being captured."

"That sounds easy," Mark replied sarcastically.

"Right," Jeffreys agreed. "So if you are still up for this adventure, we need to travel this route. But you drive," Jeffreys said. "That way I can man the turret gun if needed." They loaded into the humvee and Mark drove while Jeffreys followed their progress on the map, giving directions. They traveled back roads for thirty minutes, Mark terrified that at every turn they would meet up with a Chinese patrol. But the Colonel had evidently chosen this location for its isolation, because no one appeared.

Finally, Jeffreys told Mark to stop so they could consult the map together. "We are here. Your valley, if it's the right one, is on the other side of this mountain. We can get there either by driving around here, which will take an hour or two. Or we can hike over the mountain. If you are correct about the valley and the Colonel is not doing this alone, then they will have checkpoints and security patrols. The odds are very high that if we drive around, we will run into them. In which case, we lose."

"You're just saying that because you want me to be the one to choose hiking over the mountain," Mark said gloomily. "I knew at some point staying with you would involve some serious exercise."

"Can you tell where the cube is?" Jeffreys asked, ignoring the rib.

Mark closed his eyes and concentrated. "It's over there," Mark said, pointing.

"There is a valley on the other side of this mountain," Jeffreys said. "One of the two likely candidates." Mark nodded. "It will take several hours to get over this mountain," Jeffreys continued. "But it will allow us to keep the lowest profile possible, while we try to see what's going on and what we are going to do."

"I think that's our best bet," Mark agreed. "I don't like the idea of the hike, but I certainly don't like the idea of driving into our friends again."

"Okay, then," Jeffreys decided. "According to the map, the best approach is probably here. If you don't mind, I'll drive. I think I have more experience driving these babies off road than you do. I'd like to drive as far up this mountain as we can before we start hiking."

"That works for me," Mark agreed as they changed seats. Jeffreys slowly drove down the road until he found the most likely approach. There he turned off the road and headed up the mountain. They bounced, swerved, and climbed over bushes, rocks and between trees that Mark never thought they could get past. Jeffreys had picked a washout to start the climb and made it a surprising distance before he finally had to admit defeat and abandon the vehicle.

As they climbed out, Jeffreys reached into the back seat and pulled out two assault rifles. "Can you use one of these?" he asked.

"I'm pretty comfortable with weapons," Mark said. "I've fired a Chinese SKS and I'm not a bad shot."

"Good, that will give us two effectives. Let me just walk you through this weapon. Hopefully, we will not be using it, but if we do, you don't want to be looking for the safety for the first time." With that he took a couple minutes to show Mark how to work the safety, replace the clip and work the action. After that he gave one of the assault rifles to Mark and divided up the spare magazines. He also found two pairs of binoculars and a canteen. "Not the best outfitted patrol," Jeffreys remarked. "But it will have to do."

With that he set a course up the mountain, with Mark trudging along behind. They walked in silence, Jeffreys taking point, ever vigilant for a Chinese patrol. At first, Mark watched Jeffreys scan his surroundings and tried to mimic his actions, afraid that at any minute the Chinese would find them. But before long the monotony and fatigue from the climb dulled his senses until he was only focusing on the next step. He even avoided looking up, as the distance to the top of the mountain was too depressing.

After an eternity, Jeffreys stopped. Mark looked up, surprised to see the crest of the mountain not far above them. "Wait here," Jeffreys instructed. "I'm going to reconnoiter before we expose ourselves on the crest." Light headed and exhausted, Mark gratefully lay down on the trail, his heart pounding in his ears and his breathing fast. Jeffreys was back about 15 minutes later. "Nothing moving down there that I can see."

Mark sighed. "This better be the right place," he said. "I don't think I can climb up another mountain." They crawled up to the crest of the mountain, while Jeffreys cautioning Mark not to present a silhouette. Wedged between two rock outcroppings, Mark studied the valley floor with the binoculars. "This looks like the right place," Mark said. "What's on the other side of that mountain," he asked, indicating the mountain rising up on the other side of the valley.

Jeffreys studied his map. "There's another valley, actually more a ravine than a valley. Nothing really flat."

"The cube is over there," Mark said, pointing across to the other mountain.

"On top of the mountain?" Jeffreys asked, quickly scanning the mountain with his binoculars.

"No, I think in it. I think there is a tunnel over there."

Jeffreys studied the terrain again. "Well, either way we have to get off this ridge. We're too exposed in this location. I would recommend going down into the tree line down there," Jeffreys pointed. "There's better cover and still a good vantage point. We can also get to the valley floor quicker if we need to. The downside, of course, is that to retreat we have to climb this exposed area. Under the wrong conditions that could present a problem."

Mark looked over the area. "If we are going to do it, we might as well go all the way," he said.

"Then let's get down there before anyone pokes their head out," Jeffreys encouraged. Despite their desire to get to the tree line quickly, they moved a lot slower as Jeffreys tried to follow natural cover as they moved down the mountain. Mark was surprised how tiring it was going downhill as Jeffreys kept them in a low crouching walk most of the time. By the time he reached the tree line his heart was racing and he could not seem to catch his breath. "Stay here," Jeffreys instructed. "I'll scout out a good observation post."

"Great idea," Mark said as sweat poured off him.

By the time Jeffreys returned, Mark's heart rate and breathing were somewhat back to normal. "This altitude is killing me," Mark complained.

"Not much farther," Jeffreys said. "I think I found a good spot. You can rest there." Jeffreys led him to a depression in the side of the mountain, which had a good view of the valley below, yet provided them some cover. They scanned the valley for signs of movement. None.

"You want to stay here, or move on down some more?" Jeffreys asked.

"Let's stay here for a while," Mark said, still trying to breathe evenly. "I really think this valley is the right place." It was late afternoon and the mountains were casting long shadows across the valley floor.

"I'm glad the sun is behind us," Jeffreys remarked after they had been there awhile. "I wouldn't want it full in our face, giving away our position."

Jeffreys continued to scan the valley and mountain across from them with his binoculars. "There!" he suddenly whispered. "Got you."

"What?"

"There's a team on the mountain across from us. Someone got sloppy and the sun glinted off something." He pointed out the area and soon Mark was able to see the team. "I make out two, three, no five soldiers," Jeffreys was saying. Looks like a firing team. They have an HJ-eight."

"A what?"

"An HJ-eight. It's a tripod based, wire-guided missile. It packs a pretty good punch." He continued to scan and found two more firing teams. "Looks like you were right about the valley. They have some serious firepower here."

"Do you think we should move down farther?" Mark asked.

"We can," Jeffreys said hesitantly. "But you can count on them having some firing teams on this side also. We will have to be careful not to run into them."

"Let's stay here for a while longer," Mark said. They continued to watch, spotting two more firing teams in the process. About twenty minutes later, Mark spotted some movement on the valley floor. "Look over there," he whispered. "Is that a tunnel entrance?"

Jeffreys looked where Mark pointed. "And look what's coming out," Jeffreys said. A truck was driving slowly out of the tunnel, the long cylindrical shape of a missile lying on its bed. "I hope the folks in Washington are watching this."

"You think they can see this?" Mark asked.

"All depends on where the satellites are," Jeffreys said. "That information is above my pay grade." They watched as the truck pulled into the valley and stopped. A second truck, equipped with a crane, followed and parked next to the missile truck. Soon technicians were swarming over both vehicles.

"What do you think they're doing?" Mark asked.

"I'd say they're unloading the missile," Jeffreys answered, after studying the scene below for a while. "What should we do now?"

"I was going to ask you the same thing," Mark responded.

"Tactically, there is nothing we can do," Jeffreys answered. "We can't get near it. We don't exactly blend in with the crowd. And don't get any ideas about running in guns blazing. That's Holleywood, this is real life."

"What if we shot it?" Mark asked.

"Shoot a nuclear bomb?" Jeffreys asked with disbelief.

"Just asking," Mark said.

"Not my area," Jeffreys said. "But my guess is nothing would happen. I recall reading somewhere that getting a nuclear bomb to go off is very tricky science. It has to be done just right. I don't think it's like shooting a stick of dynamite."

"Good," Mark said. "I really didn't like that option, but thought I should ask." They watched as the crane slowly lifted the missile off the first truck and lay it horizontal on a cradle on the ground. "I bet they're removing the warhead," Mark guessed as they watched soldiers swarm over the nose of the missile. They watched for about an hour as the soldiers slowly separated the nose from the rest of the missile. Mark's stomach was knotted with fear as he tried to decide what to do.

Suddenly, a fiery streak shot out of the sky and landed about 100 yards from the missile truck.

"Watch it, cats are here," Jeffreys warned. They lay prone, just their binoculars over the lip of the ledge as they watched the scene below. A number of people were running. Others just stood and stared.

"Where did it go?" Mark asked as he scanned the valley with his binoculars. One person detached himself from the crowd at the missile and walked toward an empty space in the valley. Suddenly a blue-gray emerged, walking towards him. "It's not the cats," Mark said. "The blue-grays are here!"

"Where?" Jeffreys asked, and then said, "Got 'em. Where's their ship?"

"I don't know?" Mark said. "I don't see it. They must have hidden it somehow."

"I bet that's the Colonel walking toward them," Jeffreys said. They watched the Colonel walk up to the blue-gray and then escort it to the missile, which lay open on the cradle, the technicians scurrying away. "This is it," Jeffreys said. "We were right. What now?"

"Could you shoot the blue-gray?" Mark asked.

"With this? From here?" Jeffreys snorted. "Not with any accuracy. And after about my third shot, the fire teams with the HJ-eight's would zero in on us and we'd be toast. I would not recommend that option."

"Then we'll have to get closer," Mark decided.

"We can do that," Jeffreys said. "The blue-grays' ship has to be somewhere over to the left there. We could go down this way and come up between the blue-gray and his ship. You get me close enough and I can take him out. But all bets are off after that."

"Okay, you lead," Mark said. They backed off the ledge, staying prone until they entered the cover of the trees. They made their way down the hill as quickly and quietly as they could. The sun had almost set, so the deepening gloom helped them move unnoticed, yet they still had enough light to see, which was good since they did not have flashlights, nor would they have considered using them.

Jeffreys set a quick pace, his steps remarkable quiet as he almost bounded down the mountain. Mark had trouble keeping up with him without ending up just hurtling out of control. "Slow down," he whispered after he almost fell on his face the third time. Jeffreys slowed slightly. A short distance later he stopped and crouched down quickly. Mark almost ran into him. Jeffreys pantomimed that there was a fire team down and to their right. Slowly, quietly, they angled away to their left, putting a rock outcropping between them and the fire team.

They were about to stand up and move on when another meteor streaked out of the sky. Jeffreys grabbed Mark and they rolled to the base of the rock outcropping. Seconds later the sky lit up with lightning bolts and the sound of automatic fire. Explosions rocked the valley as the fire teams opened up. Mark's skin tingled and his hair stood up as static electricity filled the air. The ground shook and Mark's ears echoed with the sound of gunfire, rockets and explosions. Just as quickly as it had started, the firefight ended and all was quiet, except for the ringing in Mark's ears.

"We need to see what happened," Mark whispered. He and Jeffreys cautiously crept out of their spot by the rock outcropping.

"Wait here," Jeffreys instructed. "I'll do a quick recon and come right back for you." Mark started to object, but Jeffreys insisted. "This is my game," Jeffreys said. "You are out of your element. I'll just check to make sure it is clear and come right back."

Mark reluctantly acquiesced to Jeffreys' logic and waited while Jeffreys silently crept from their position. After an eternity, which was probably less than five minutes, Jeffreys returned and motioned for Mark to follow him. Staying in a low crouch, Jeffreys led Mark back up the hill, around the ledge. Mark realized he was heading for the fire team they had just passed. They found the team 150 feet further, or what was left of the team. Their position was a charred, smoking hole. They looked over the edge, down to the valley floor.

Smoke drifted across the valley as the two trucks and some bushes burned. Nothing else moved. They scanned the valley with their binoculars. "Look at the missile," Jeffreys whispered in Mark's ear. Mark trained his binoculars on the missile, which was sitting on the cradle next to the burning truck. He waited for the smoke to clear. On the ground near the missile lay the blue-gray, his legs blown off. A cat stood over him and appeared to be torturing the blue-gray. Jeffreys was scanning the other mountain and the valley with his binoculars.

"The cats won," Jeffreys whispered. "All the fire bases on the other hill have been taken out. It looks like the cat's ship is intact." Indeed it did. The cat's ship was floating fifty feet off the ground just down from the burning truck. "What do we do now?" Jeffreys asked.

"I wish I knew," Mark said. "Try to convince the cats not to wipe us out?"

"How? We show our faces, they shoot us," Jeffreys said. "I would."

"Would you shoot someone coming out with their hands up?" Mark asked.

"I wouldn't," Jeffreys said. "But a lot of soldiers have. Besides, how do you know they have the same custom?"

Two cats were fighting, fast and furious, fur flying, claws flashing. One was clearly losing. Suddenly it stepped back and straightened up, its arms held down by its side, palms forward. The second cat stopped its attack, turned its back and walked away into the crowd of cat spectators.

The vision cleared. Once again Mark was next to Jeffreys, looking down at the scene of destruction. "They do," Mark said.

"They do what?" Jeffreys asked.

"They have the same custom, hands down, palms out."

"You're serious?" Jeffreys said in disbelief. "The cats tried to kill you once before. A whole company of Chinese just tried to kill them. And, as you pointed out, they care nothing about us. Like ants, I think you said. Just how do you propose to communicate with them and convince them that we mean them no harm?"

"I have to do something," Mark said. "I couldn't live with myself if they leave and drop a couple of asteroids on the Earth as payback."

"If they do that, you're dead. Doesn't matter. If you walk out there now, you're still dead. What if they leave and do nothing to us? It's over. Then you are dead for no reason," Jeffreys argued.

"I know the cat's sign for surrender, that they no longer wish to fight. I have to try," Mark said.

"For the record," Jeffreys said, "I think it's a real bad idea. One of your worsts."

"Duly noted," Mark said. "If the cats kill me, you can be the first to say 'I told you so'."

"Don't think I won't," Jeffreys said. "Come on, let's get down there." They moved back out of the smoking fire team position. As they were leaving, Jeffreys stepped over a case. "Wait, what do we have here?" he said to himself as he pulled a box out of the rubble and opened it up. Inside was an HJ-8. "They had a spare!" Jeffreys said as he pulled it out of the case and expertly looked it over.

"Will you put down your new toy and let's get moving before I change my mind," Mark said.

"I'm going to take my new toy with me," Jeffreys said, packing the weapon back up and hoisting the case over his shoulder. "If the cats get unfriendly, then I'm going to give them a little sting."

"The others did not work," Mark commented. "You'll just be committing suicide."

Jeffreys shrugged. "You're one to talk."

It took them less than five minutes to move down to the valley floor as night descended. They were about to leave the cover of the trees when Jeffreys grabbed Mark's arm. A cat was running across the valley floor and then suddenly disappeared.

"Where did it go?" Mark asked.

Jeffreys put down the HJ-8 and scanned the area with his binoculars. "There," he pointed. "It must be the blue-gray ship. Look, all you can see is the open hatch. The rest of it is cloaked or something. Mark trained his binoculars in the direction Jeffreys was pointing. He could just make out the outline of a hatch and the back of a cat inside. Around the hatch was the faintest shimmer, like heat coming off a hot road, but otherwise he couldn't see anything. The cat jumped out of the ship and started sprinting back to the wounded blue-gray.

A burst of heavy machine gun fire shattered the air as tracers flew out of the tunnel and sprayed across the cat. The cat shrieked as it changed course, charging the tunnel entrance while firing lightning bolts from a weapon in its hands. "I think you just lost your chance to surrender," Jeffreys said as he hoisted the HJ-8 to his shoulder. "If we weren't already, I think we have just become the cat's new enemy. It's probably time to join the Chinese."

"Okay," Mark reluctantly agreed.

"We'll hit the cat as it leaves the tunnel," Jeffreys said, comfortable now that action was required and he was back in his element. "Take position over there by the boulder and I'll set up over by that stand of trees. Make sure to aim," he shouted over his shoulder as he ran for his position, lugging the HJ-8.

Mark slung his assault rifle off his shoulder and ran over to the boulder. He checked to make sure the safety was off and resting the stock on the rock, took aim into the mouth of the tunnel, and waited. He saw a couple of flashes in the tunnel and heard a muted explosion, then silence. Mark glanced over to Jeffreys who was quickly setting up the tripod in a small patch of trees. "Hurry, hurry," Mark whispered to himself as he nervously glanced back at the tunnel entrance.

It was dark inside the tunnel and the valley was getting darker. Mark glanced back at Jeffreys, who was still adjusting something on the tripod. Sighting back at the tunnel, Mark wondered if he would be able to hit a running cat. They were fast. He could not tell whether the tracers had hit the cat. If they had, they did not slow it down any. His assault rifle was switched to automatic, but Jeffreys had cautioned him to shoot in short bursts, otherwise he wouldn't be able to aim and would just waste his ammunition. "Shoot, aim, shoot," he coached himself. He placed two spare magazines on the rock next to him, wondering if he would have time to reload. He sighted back down the rifle.

A few seconds later the cat came bounding out of the tunnel. Mark was trying to track the cat with his sights when Jeffreys' shot streaked at the cat. The cat leaped in the air and fired, while the missile slammed into a small boulder and exploded, spraying the cat with shrapnel. The cat hit and rolled, apparently injured, but not down. The blast slowed the cat enough that Mark could take aim and fire, concentrating on short bursts. Aim, then another short burst. Mark fired until his magazine was empty and then fumbled for another magazine. He slammed the magazine home and took aim again. The cat was not moving.

Mark glanced over to Jeffreys' position. The stand of trees was burning. Jeffreys was nowhere in sight. Glancing one more time at the motionless cat, Mark ran over to the trees, yelling for Jeffreys. He found him sprawled on his back, unconscious, twenty feet away from his firing position. Mark dropped his rifle and bent over Jeffreys, checking for a pulse. There was an ugly burn across his chest and he was bleeding from multiple wounds, but he was breathing.

A noise startled Mark and he looked up in time to see the blue-gray sliding to the ground at the base of the Chinese missile. "Hold on, I'll be right back," Mark said to Jeffreys, not knowing if he could hear him or not. He grabbed his rifle and ran over to the blue-gray, who was now lying on his back on the ground. Unsure what to do, Mark reached down and touched the blue-grays' shoulder.

Pain raced through Mark and he fell back, his legs missing as his life ebbed out.

The connection broken, Mark sat up, heart racing, breath coming in gasps, but his legs were still there. A vision! They communicated by touch. Gritting his teeth for the expected pain, he bent over the blue-gray and touched his shoulder again. Pain raced through him, but he held on, trying to get past the pain to the intelligence behind it.

Anger and hatred welled up in him. Hatred for the cats, hatred for the stupid humans that infested this planet, hatred at the universe for the loss of his species 65 million years ago, hatred of all life. All would die, like his race, none deserved to live...

Mark fell back, the connection once again broken. Emotions as powerful as the cat's coursed through him and then were gone, like lifting fog. He shook his head to clear it as conflicting alien memories rose unbidden through his consciousness. Many were fragments, unrecognizable, but one stood out clear and recent. Triumph. Victory over the hated cats. Victory over the worthless humans. Victory over the Earth. All purged by fire. The blue-gray's last act had been to painfully pull itself up onto the warhead, and arm it.

Mark jumped up and looked at the warhead. Attached to it was an alien device. He tried to pull it off but it would not budge. He grabbed the blue-gray, pushing his consciousness roughly past the pain, searching for the means to disarm the warhead.

Pain. Pain. And laughter. Insane laughter filled Mark's head, threatening to suffocate him, before it receded as the blue-gray gave one last shudder and died.

Mark's vision cleared. He was kneeling down, holding the dead blue-gray's cold shoulder.

"No, no, NO!" Mark screamed, shaking the dead blue-gray. Mark couldn't understand the blue-grays' system of time, but he sensed that there were only minutes before the warhead detonated. Frantic, he searched the blue-gray, until he found his personal cube in a pouch at his hip. Steeling his mind to avoid being overcome, he grabbed the cube, hoping to find the key to disarming the warhead.

Pain, loneliness, anger, welled up in Mark, threatening to engulf him. He pushed back, trying to control the emotions and images that filled his brain like a kaleidoscope. The ship, the cats, asteroids, emptiness, time, time, time.

Mark dropped the cube and shook his head. The cube was too powerful for him to understand quickly. He had barely dropped it before he had been overwhelmed. He would have to try something else. Pocketing the cube, he ran back to Jeffreys.

"We have to get out of here," he yelled frantically to Jeffreys' unconscious form.

'But where?' He did not have time to get far enough from a nuclear blast to survive. The tunnel. The blast would take out the tunnel, probably the whole mountain. He looked around for transport. The two trucks were burning wrecks. The Cat ship hovered fifty feet overhead. It might as well have been fifty miles. The blue-gray ship... The blue-gray ship, Mark thought. Mark reached down and picked up Jeffreys, slinging him over his shoulder in a fireman's carry. He could see the open hatch of the blue-gray's ship 100 yards away. His legs were like lead as he staggered under Jeffreys' weight, wondering every second when the searing fire from a nuclear explosion would consume them. The open hatch teased him from a distance. Heart pounding, he staggered on. He tripped and fell fifty feet away from the ship and had to pick Jeffreys up again, wondering if he would hear the blast or feel the heat.

He finally made it to the ship and looked in. It was a one-person craft, a tiny closet with an upright seat, nothing more. He laid Jeffreys inside the hatch, carefully stepping over him as he climbed inside. He had to reach down to pull Jeffreys' legs inside the hatch. Could he fly this? He had flown the blue-gray ships before, during the visions. But that was the alien host flying it, not him.

He leaned back into the seat and felt his body sink into it as it had in his visions. He placed his hands on the armrests, willing them to sink in as they did for the blue-grays. Nothing. "No!" he cried. He couldn't make it this far and then fail. He tried to dig his fingers into the unyielding material. Nothing. Calm, calm, he told himself ineffectually. How had the blue-gray done it? The first time he had 'flown' a blue-gray ship those doctors had drugged him, he didn't have a clear memory of what the blue-gray had done. But there was another time. Right before the cats attacked. He had sat down and then... spread his fingers!

Mark spread his fingers, keeping two fingers together to approximate the blue-grays' four fingers. The chair responded and his hands sunk into the controls. Alien screens materialized in front of him with symbols flowing across some, pictures in others. He had never understood the alien symbols. One screen showed the warhead. Beneath it was a bright line, quickly shrinking. That must be the time, Mark thought. How to disarm it? As much as he tried to concentrate, he could not affect the disappearing line. There were seconds left. "Stop, Stop, STOP!" he yelled, but the line kept shrinking. He wanted to shake the chair, to yell at the unfairness of life, the unfairness of the universe, he hated the cats, he wanted to stop it all, to quit, to ESCAPE! The bright line ran out.

CHAPTER 14

The *USS Ronald Reagan* was on full alert. NORAD had reported a nuclear explosion in southwestern China, north of Chengdu. The explosion was unexpected, clearly not a test. The *Ronald Reagan's* task force was the closest to China. It was placed on full defensive alert while Washington tried to figure out what was going on. Captain Joseph Peters was on the bridge as additional F-19's were being launched to ensure an adequate air umbrella over the task force. He listened to the myriad reports that came in from all over the ship, announcing the ship's readiness. They had drilled endlessly, enough that the ship was running smoothly, the reports coming in like clockwork. Captain Peters was worried about the situation in China, but pleased with the response of his ship and battle group.

Then he heard a distinct thud, and yelling from the flight deck drifted up to the bridge. He turned, resisting the urge to ask what was going on. He knew he would get a report as soon as it came in. He didn't have to wait long, although the report was confusing. "Casualties on the flight deck."

"What happened," Captain Peters asked.

"Still don't know," an Ensign answered. "A tractor collided with something near the tower with two casualties."

"Who?"

"Don't know, Sir. They were wearing civvies."

Now civvies would not be unheard of as they are authorized while off duty, but no one should be on the flight deck without dressing out. Someone had gotten very careless. That irritated Captain Peters. But he would handle that later. For now, flight operations were continuing and the safety and operation of his battle group was paramount. And then sick bay called.

"Captain, urgent message from sick bay," a young Ensign reported. "They request to talk to you personally."

The Captain picked up the nearby intercom. "Captain Peters," he said.

"Captain, this is Dr. Martins. You're needed in sick bay immediately."

"Why?"

"Mark Williams is here!" the doctor replied.

"Mark Williams?" the Captain repeated, trying to pull the name up from his knowledge of the ship's roster. "Who is Mark Williams?" he grudgingly had to ask when he could not place the name among his ship's company.

"The civilian Mark Williams, the lawyer from last year," came the reply.

The name came up along with the face. "That Mark Williams? I talked with him two weeks ago. He was in Pensacola."

"He is here in sick bay," the voice said.

"In my sick bay, here?" the Captain repeated, not believing what he had heard.

"Yes, Sir. He says he has to talk to you. That it's urgent."

The Captain stared at the wall as events took an unexpected significance. Mark Williams had said the blue-grays were in China. Now there was an unexplained nuclear explosion in China. Was this part of the blue-gray, cat war? "I'll be right there," Captain Peters responded before hanging up the mike. "XO, you have the bridge. I'll be in sick bay if you need me."

"Aye, Aye, Sir," the XO responded, but the Captain was already going out the door. The Captain made it down to sick bay in record time. If this was a joke, someone was going to regret it, he thought. He burst into sick bay and was directed to a room filled with orderlies. Lying on a gurney in the center of the room, wearing Chinese style clothing, and covered with dirt and blood, was Mark Williams. Mark sat up when he saw the Captain enter, wincing slightly as he did. "Everyone out," the Captain barked and the room emptied. He stared at Mark. "What are you doing here?" he finally asked.

"Long story," Mark said. "But the gist of it is that the cats and the blue-grays had their battle in the mountains of China. The cats lost. But in the process, the blue-grays got hold of one of China's nukes and set it off. NORAD probably alerted you to the nuke."

"Yes. We know about the detonation. But not the why."

"It was the blue-gray that set it off. I saw him do it."

"Actually saw it, or in a vision?" the Captain asked.

"No, I actually saw it. I was there."

"Then how are you here now? That nuke went off less than twenty minutes ago."

"The blue-gray ship dropped me and Jeffreys off here."

"Jeffreys is here too?"

"Yes, he was shot by a cat. They're treating him in the next room," Mark replied.

"Why did the blue-grays drop you off here? Why did they save you?

"Probably because we killed the last cat, the one that had been torturing one of the blue-grays," Mark said.

"What are the Chinese doing?" the Captain asked. "Do they know all this?"

"No," Mark replied. "The Chinese that were involved were under blue-gray control and they are all dead, either killed by the cats or by the nuke. I doubt that the Chinese government knows anything at all. They are probably trying to figure out why a nuke just went off in their country."

"And whether this is the start of World War Three," Captain Peters finished. "We need to get online with Washington ASAP."

"I thought as much," Mark replied.

"Are you well enough to get to the conference room?" the Captain asked.

"Yes. I'm tired and sore, but otherwise okay," Mark replied. "Oh, and this probably sounds odd under the circumstances, but I'm starving. I haven't eaten since this morning. Do you think...?"

"Now I know that you are really here," the Captain said with a chuckle as he called up to the XO. This was going to be quite some conference call.

CHAPTER 15

An unbearably bright light filled the tiny ship. Mark closed his eyes and screamed, the light still blinding through his tightly closed eyelids. Time slowed, stopped. The bright light remained. No pain. No noise. Only the light. And then it slowly darkened and was gone. 'I'm dead,' Mark thought, a sense of sadness coming over him. 'I failed Jeffreys. He had saved me so many times, and I couldn't save him even once. At least it didn't hurt.' He had expected an intense searing pain. Instead, he felt cool, comfortable, even like he was enveloped in a... a... an alien chair. Mark opened his eyes. The door to the small craft was closed and holograms floated in front of him. One showed a growing mushroom cloud rising above the mountains in the distance.

Mark awoke with a start, the reoccurring dream fresh in his mind. Covered with sweat, he climbed out of bed and walked into the bathroom to dry off. Looking in the bathroom mirror, he wondered when the nightmares would stop. Although a month had gone by and he was back practicing law in Pensacola, he remembered the events of those eighteen days clearly, particularly that last day. Standing in front of his bathroom mirror, Mark recalled that last day as if it were yesterday.

Miraculously, at the very last second, the blue-grays' ship had shot off to safety. Mark's only explanation was that his final rage had been sufficiently close to the blue-grays' rage to be recognized by the ship. He was not proud of that, since the hatred he had felt from the blue-gray was so foreign to Mark's usual demeanor. But there he was, hovering over the mountains as he watched, horrified, as a mushroom cloud grew in the distance.

His emotions had unlocked the blue-grays' personal cube that was stored in the ship. Alien memories flooded Mark, threatening to overwhelm him as he experienced the blue-grays' life for the past year; trying to hide from the cats, perfecting the cube's programming, coming to Earth... Mark pushed the alien memories aside, keenly aware that Jeffreys was curled up, unconscious, at his feet. He couldn't allow himself to become lost in blue-gray memories. He searched for the logic of the memories and remembered how the blue-grays' personal cube back on the *Ronald Reagan* had provided him information. He stopped fighting the vision, instead trying to channel or direct it. Memories of the ship rose in his consciousness, the controls suddenly making perfect sense. He had to find medical attention for Jeffreys, and fast. But where? Not in China, that was for sure.

The ship zoomed south, leaving the spreading mushroom cloud behind, and was soon over open ocean. Mark searched with the ship's sensors and saw a fleet of ships further south. He increased the magnification and saw an aircraft carrier. Increasing the magnification further, he recognized it as the *Ronald Reagan*. Perfect, he thought. They could care for Jeffreys. He zoomed towards the *Ronald Reagan*, easily avoiding the prowling F-19's. He landed on the flight deck, next to the tower.

He paused. What now? He had to think this through. He always distrusted governments, even his own. He was in a spaceship that possessed technology so far advanced the implications were mind-boggling. Where it could take mankind was unimaginable. The cloaking device that shielded the ship alone would revolutionize the military. And that was the problem. Morality and ethics were already hard pressed to keep up with the quickly evolving technology of present day. What would happen with this leap?

Despite best intentions, Mark feared for the worse. He could not turn over this technology, not even to his own government. But Jeffreys was lying unconscious, possibly dying, at his feet. A bump ran through the ship as something ran into them on the flight deck. He needed to decide and needed to decide now. He thought a moment longer and had his solution. He rolled the small ship so the hatch was facing down. He gave the ship a final command, before disengaging from the command chair and assisting Jeffreys through the opening door, onto the flight deck six inches below them. He crouched down and the ship rose up over him and disappeared, leaving him and Jeffreys exposed ten feet from the tower.

The effect was pretty dramatic. A sailor driving a tractor across the deck hit the invisible blue-gray ship, stopping the tractor. The sailor had gotten out to see what happened, when suddenly two people materialized in front of him. Chinese, judging by their clothing, but not by their looks. They were obviously injured and the sailor's first thought was that he had run them over. Medics were called and they were carried down to sick bay. Once there, fortune smiled on Mark. Dr. Martins, the same doctor who had worked with him a year before, was the trauma doctor. To her credit, she overcame her initial shock at seeing Mark and listened as he described Jeffreys' injuries and requested an immediate conference with Captain Peters.

The effect of Mark's arrival on Captain Peters was even more dramatic, probably because Captain Peters knew, unlike Dr. Martins, that Mark should not be on his ship. As expected, Mark was immediately taken to a conference room where they set up a live video feed with Washington. Mark even kept his bloodstained Chinese clothes on for the call to add a visual confirmation to his report. He was going to have some explaining to do. Although it was 6:57 a.m. Sunday morning, Eastern Standard Time, the President and his security advisors had been up since shortly after the Chinese explosion was reported less than an hour before, so no time was wasted patching Mark through to them.

The President was clearly taken aback when Mark appeared on video, blood stained and dirty. "Good evening, Mr. President," Mark said, referring to China time, rather than Eastern time.

"You are injured," the President said.

"I'm fine," Mark responded. "Jeffreys is hurt much more. They are treating him down in sick bay as we speak."

"You both were in China. How did you and Jeffreys get onboard the *Ronald Reagan*?" the President asked.

"The blue-grays' ship brought us here," Mark answered truthfully. "But let me tell you what you probably want to know first, and then we can get into the details." The President nodded and Mark continued. "The final battle between the blue-grays and the cats was held in China. The cats lost. They are all dead. And the blue-grays are gone. And this time I can say it with absolute confidence. I received this information directly from the blue-grays."

"What happened in China?" the President asked.

Mark closed his eyes and took a deep breath. Opening his eyes, he said, "It's a long story. Let me try the *Reader's Digest* version first. When we left the

Consulate, Jeffreys and I were assigned to a Colonel Lui of the Chinese Second Artillery, the officer in charge of finding the cube. Unfortunately, Colonel Lui was the one who had the cube. He was under the control of the blue-grays. I realized this the moment I met him and came up with a story that I was trying to help him and that it was Washington that was trying to destroy the cubes. My attempt at subterfuge did not work and he sent Sergeant Jeffreys and me on a decoy mission, while he prepared to deliver a nuke to the blue-grays. Five soldiers, two of whom were under Colonel Lui's control with orders to kill us, escorted us on our decoy mission.

"I'll give you the details later. Suffice it to say that we escaped solely because of Sergeant Jeffreys combat skills. Sergeant Jeffreys then got us to a mountaintop overlooking the valley where the transfer of the nuke was to take place. Late this afternoon Colonel Lui brought a mobile nuclear missile out of a tunnel into the valley. It was on a truck, like those you see in all the communist May Day parades. They were dismantling the warhead when the blue-grays arrived. We saw the ship streak in, and NORAD may have picked it up. But once on the ground it had some type of cloaking device, so it was invisible to the eye. One blue-gray got out and met with Colonel Lui, who took him over to the disassembled nuke. At that point Sergeant Jeffreys and I moved out of our observation point to get down to the valley floor. That move probably saved our lives. As we were passing a rock formation, basically under a ledge, the cats attacked.

"The Chinese were prepared for a cat attack and had a number of fire teams stationed on the mountains around the valley. They had some sort of wire-guided missiles. Sergeant Jeffreys could tell you what they were. Anyway, all hell broke loose. We heard machine gun fire, rockets, explosions and the unmistakable sound of the cats' weapons, like arcing electricity. The battle ended pretty quickly. When we climbed back to an observation point, we realized the cats had won. All the Chinese were dead and a cat was standing by the nuke, where a blue-gray lay wounded.

"We didn't know what to do. This was our worst fear; that humans would help the blue-grays, the cats would win anyway and now probably consider us their enemy. The only option I could come up with was to try to contact the cats and explain that we, humans, were not their enemy. We climbed down to the valley floor to attempt to contact the cat, but before we had a chance, a Chinese survivor in the tunnel opened fire on the cat with a heavy machine gun. The cat charged into the tunnel firing. I figured at this point that we, and I mean humans, had probably just made it to the cats' number one enemy list, since we were now attacking the cats directly. So now we had to take out the cats.

"Sergeant Jeffreys had us set up two firing positions, with the plan that we hit the cat as it exited the tunnel. The cat came out fast, real fast. Jeffreys had acquired one of the Chinese wire-guided missiles and he shot at the cat. The cat jumped fifty feet in the air to avoid the shot, but was hit by some of the shrapnel. That slowed the cat down enough that I could hit it with the assault rifle Sergeant Jeffreys had given me. In the process, the cat shot Sergeant Jeffreys, which is why he is being treated down in sick bay right now.

"While this was going on, the wounded blue-gray placed an alien detonator on the nuke. After the cat was down, I checked on Sergeant Jeffreys, who was unconscious, and then ran over to the wounded blue-gray. Blue-grays communicate by touch telepathy. When I reached down and touched the blue-gray, we finally fully communicated. I first had to get past the pain, because the blue-gray was dying, but when I did, it was anger and hatred that I found. Hatred against everything, cats and humans. It was the dying blue-gray that detonated the nuke, to get back at the cats and us for his death."

"How did you and Jeffreys get out?" the President asked.

"Sheer luck," Mark admitted. "The blue-gray died in my arms. From my vision while holding him, I knew I didn't have much time left before the nuke detonated. I tried to take the alien detonator off the nuke, but I couldn't detach it and didn't know how it worked. So I looked for a way to escape. The only option I had was the blue-grays' ship. The cats' ship was still hovering fifty feet above the ground and the trucks were all burning. So I picked up Jeffreys and carried him to the blue-gray ship."

"I thought it was invisible," the President asked.

"It is," Mark answered. "As one of the sailors here can attest to. But when the hatch is open, you can see inside it. The open hatch was facing me. I picked up Sergeant Jeffreys and ran for the open hatch. I put him inside and climbed in. Seconds later the nuke detonated and we shot away. To me it seemed like we left the second the nuke detonated." There was silence while they considered Mark's account.

"Why did the blue-grays drop you off at the *Ronald Reagan*? the President asked, breaking the silence.

Mark had been waiting for this question. 'Careful. Stick as close to the truth as possible,' he told himself. Aloud he said, "I never communicated with a blue-gray in the ship," Mark answered truthfully. "Only with the one that was dying. A guess? I would say it was because we took out the last cat and it appeared I was trying to help the dying blue-gray. The ship took us to the place we had met the blue-grays before, the *Ronald Reagan*. Remember, they know who I am by my DNA."

"But why didn't the cats take out the blue-gray ship? Or the blue-gray in the ship attack the cats?" the President asked.

"There was only one cat left. I learned that from the dying blue-gray. The original cat ship was a two-person, or two cat, fighter. Last year it separated and one cat and one half the ship was lost to the collapsing wormhole. The remaining cat had been waiting for a year in the other part of the ship for the blue-grays to expose themselves so it could attack. As for the blue-gray ship, it was unarmed," Mark explained. "And the cats didn't kill the blue-grays because they wanted something from them. That's why the blue-gray was wounded, not killed, and probably why the cat didn't destroy the blue-gray ship.

"Let me back up. Last year, I thought the blue-grays and the cats were gone, killed or lost in the collapsing wormhole. I never could figure out how they came back. Well now I know. And this is from the dying blue-gray, this is not me guessing. Two ships were transported to Earth in the wormhole sixty-five million years ago, one blue-gray science vessel and one cat attack ship. The blue-gray science vessel, I'll call it the Mothership, contained two smaller vessels; I'll call them a transport and an escape pod, for lack of better terms. The transport, incidentally, appears to be the same type of ship that I flew last year in one of my visions, the one where they were fleeing the Earth when the cats attacked with asteroids. The transport was the blue-gray ship that landed on the *Ronald Reagan* last year and was sucked into the collapsing wormhole. The dying blue-gray believed that ship was either destroyed or lost as well.

"The cat attack ship is actually two ships joined together, but they have the ability to separate and fight independently. When they attacked the blue-gray science vessel and were caught in the wormhole sixty-five million years ago, they were joined together. Last year they separated and one came down to attack the *Ronald Reagan*. That ship was also lost in the collapsing wormhole. That left one blue-gray mothership and one cat attack ship. For a year, the blue-grays hid from the cats while they perfected their control cube technology. This year they sent the control cubes to Earth, their goal to obtain a weapon to fight the cats: a nuke. The ship the blue-grays sent down today was the escape pod, while the mothership stayed hidden somewhere up in space. The cats wanted to find the location of the mothership so they could destroy it."

"So now that all the cats are dead, what are the blue-grays going to do?" the President asked.

"The blue-grays are gone," Mark answered. "The blue-grays have no use for us, for what they consider a backward planet."

"But you said the dying blue-gray detonated the nuke because of hatred for the cats and us," the President said. "So what will keep the surviving blue-grays from crashing asteroids into the Earth?"

"The dying blue-gray set the detonator before we killed the cat," Mark said. "I can only assume that I would not be here talking to you if the blue-grays intended to destroy the Earth."

"So it's over?" the President asked.

"Yes, it's over," Mark agreed.

"But we have to clean up the mess they left behind and avoid World War Three," the President added.

"Yes, Mr. President," Mark said. "But Sir, that's your job. My job is over. All I want to do now is to get back to my wife and family in Pensacola."

The questioning continued, but not as long as Mark had feared since the President had to contact the Chinese and address the nation. Mark wondered what type of spin the politicians would put on this story. He knew there would be no mention of aliens and at this point he really did not care.

When the President concluded the conference, Mark headed down to sick bay to check on Jeffreys. The Captain accompanied him, which allowed him to get past the orderlies and, along with Dr. Martins, into Jeffreys' room. Jeffreys was covered with bandages and hooked up to an I.V. and monitoring equipment, an orderly by his side. "Is he going to make it?" Mark asked Dr. Martins.

"Sure I am," Jeffreys responded with a slur.

"Jeffreys!" Mark said. "You scared me to death. Are you okay?" Even as he asked the question, Mark realized how stupid it sounded, but he did not care. Jeffreys was alive.

"Can't let a little cat take me out, can I?" Jeffreys said softly.

Mark reached down and squeezed Jeffreys' left hand, which seemed to be the only part not covered with some type of bandage. "Well you look like hell," Mark said.

"I never did care for cats," Jeffreys said. "Did we win?"

"Yes, we won," Mark said. "The cats are dead and the blue-grays are gone."

"I don't remember anything after the cat came out of the tunnel."

"He needs to rest," Dr. Martins interrupted. "He has a concussion, a nasty burn on his chest and multiple lacerations. I've administered morphine, so he might not remember this conversation when he wakes up."

"Get some sleep," Mark said to Jeffreys. "I'll tell you all the details when you wake up."

Jeffreys said something in response, but his words were too slurred to understand.

"He is going to be okay, isn't he?" Mark asked Dr. Martins as they left the room.

"He should be fine," Dr. Martins assured him. "He demonstrated good cognitive function when I examined him and his wounds, although ugly, are for the most part superficial. The burn is the most serious, but it is not deep, mostly second degree burn. I think we can avoid having to do any skin grafts. He is in a lot of pain, but with time he should make a complete recovery."

"Can I stay with him?" Mark asked.

"He needs to sleep. He will probably be out for at least twelve hours, maybe more," Dr. Martins said.

"Can you contact me the minute he wakes up?" Mark asked. "I imagine I will be here for a while."

"With the Captain's permission, sure," Dr. Martins said.

"Why don't you come with me and give me all the details of your little adventure before Washington starts calling back," the Captain suggested. "The doctor can contact us when Sergeant Jeffreys wakes up." They went to the conference room where Mark had given so many conferences last year. This time it was only him and the Captain.

"What have they told you so far," Mark asked when they had arrived in the conference room.

"Nothing since I convinced them to send Sergeant Jeffreys with you," the Captain replied.

"How did you know about that?"

"Originally, they were talking about using the *Ronald Reagan* as a staging area, so I was in the loop. When they changed their minds, I heard nothing else. Although I assumed that you had gone to China with Sergeant Jeffreys."

"That little piece of advice saved my life," Mark said. "The CIA agents didn't have a clue what was going on. They weren't even briefed. So Jeffreys helped me there. And of course his combat skills at the end. We would not have made it without him. You order us something to eat, and I'll tell you the whole story." Mark then provided a detail account of his whole trip to the Captain.

"You really think they are gone for good?" the Captain asked when Mark finished his account.

"I do," Mark said. "Last year I was guessing, based upon the visions and what we had seen. This time I had direct contact with the blue-grays, not filtered by the memory cube or control cube. The blue-grays believe that the all the cats are dead, one from the collapsing wormhole last year and one now. And the blue-grays don't want anything to do with us. We are just too primitive to be of any interest to them."

"And they are not interested in dropping any asteroids on us?" the Captain asked.

"No. They don't have an ax to grind with us. Their sole concern was avoiding the cat ship."

"What will they do now that the cats are gone? They can't go back in time, can they?"

"No. They aren't time travelers. And I don't know what they will do. They can still travel by wormhole. Maybe they will go back to their home planet. They could do that," Mark said.

"That's sixty-five million years in their future. The blue-grays that they knew would be long dead."

"Their species may be long dead. Or evolved," Mark said. "Can you imagine what changes would occur in sixty-five million years? On our Earth, what species have stayed the same for sixty-five million years? Sharks? Turtles?"

"Crocodiles," the Captain added.

"Right. And other than that, the world is totally different." They paused while each considered the ramifications.

"The bottom line," the Captain broke the silence. "Is that this time you really think they are both gone."

"I do."

"It's a lot to think about," the Captain said. "I guess I'm relieved. But the concept is fascinating, alien beings, alien technology. So much to learn."

"Sounds like you wish the blue-grays would stay."

"Don't you? Look how much we could learn."

"But are we ready to handle that type of technology?" Mark asked.

"What do you mean?"

"To make that technological leap. Their technology is light years beyond ours. Look at our history. Every time we have come across a technologically inferior race, they have lost. And lost big. The American Indians. The Aztecs. Just to name some more recent examples. And in this case we are the inferior race."

"But there are just a couple of blue-grays," the Captain said.

"And they have the control cubes," Mark objected.

"You really think they could control the whole world with the control cubes?"

"Yes, I do. You don't realize how powerful they are."

"But what about the people who are not susceptible to the control cubes," the Captain asked.

"I think they have resolved that with this newer model," Mark said. "I think that whoever is controlled by the cube, has power over others. I'm not certain. But that is my impression."

"Okay, that is scary."

"Since we are on this topic," Mark continued. "Let me run a hypothetical by you that I have been debating with Sergeant Jeffreys. And this is strictly a hypothetical." The Captain nodded, so Mark continued. "Let's assume that the blue-grays don't care about us. That they decide just to leave. But first they give us their technology, or some of it. Do you think that mankind as a species is ready to handle that type of technology. Gene splicing, space flight, that type of thing."

"We already do that," the Captain said.

"Yes, but not like they do. It's like comparing a baby's fist steps to a marathon runner. Don't you think we need to learn to walk first, before we start doing marathons among the stars and bio-engineering and who knows what else they can do?"

"I think I know what your answer is," the Captain said.

"Granted the technology is enticing," Mark continued, ignoring the Captain's comment. "But we are having trouble handling the ethics for the science we are already developing. Not to mention the obvious military possibilities. Remember, the blue-grays bioengineered to create the ultimate warriors for them."

"But with that technology we could stop war. No one could stand against it," the Captain objected.

"You really don't believe that," Mark said. "First, you are assuming that whoever controls it, handles that power wisely. History has proved that wrong time and time again. At some point it falls apart. Second, you are assuming that no one else obtains the secrets. Look at the atomic bomb. It wasn't long before we no longer had the monopoly on it and then it was a nuclear race with 'mutually assured destruction' being the only thing that prevented a nuclear war. And today we are worrying about terrorist states and terrorists obtaining nuclear weapons."

"You have a rather pessimistic view of the world."

"I think realistic. Look at all the conflicts going on in the name of religion, or politics, or ethnicity. And look at our own government. We couldn't even control those NSA doctors from trying to control me last year. I think the blue-gray technology is a Pandora's box that we are better off avoiding. Just being around the control cubes was enough for me."

The talked for a while longer before the Captain received word that Washington wanted another conference with Mark. "You are on again," the Captain said to Mark. "You ready for another round?"

"As ready as I'll ever be."

Mark stared at his reflection in the bathroom mirror. He had lied to his government, to the President of the United States, and he could still look himself in the eye.

Mark had told the entire story over the course of several conference calls to Washington as he insisted on staying on the *Ronald Reagan* until Jeffreys woke up. He was then debriefed in Washington before returning home. His story remained the same throughout. Which was easy, because it was all true. All except two facts which he kept to himself.

One fact was that he had piloted the blue-gray's ship himself, before sending it off. He did not think that information would endear him to Washington, certainly not to the military folks, as they probably did not share his opinion that the U.S. should not have the power to unilaterally control the world. Fortunately, Jeffreys had been unconscious when Mark carried him to the blue-gray ship, so no one could contradict Mark's story. Mark simply maintained that he was too injured and exhausted to provide any details about the trip in the blue-gray ship, that it was all just a blur.

The other fact he had learned from the dying blue-gray, the mothership was empty as all the blue-grays were dead. Only four blue-grays had made it to the mothership before it was forced to flee from the attacking cats 65 million years ago. Three blue-grays were killed by the cats on the *Ronald Reagan* last year, one on the flight deck and two in their transport ship. The blue-gray in China had been the sole survivor, having stayed on the mothership.

The blue-gray had worked on the control cube technology alone for the past year in order to exact vengeance against the cats. He had come down to Earth in the escape pod as it, and it alone, had the cloaking technology and was more maneuverable than the mothership. Right before Mark disengaged from the escape pod's command chair after landing on the *Ronald Reagan*, he 'saw' the location of the mothership as it hid in space, programed to wait for the return of the escape pod and the now dead blue-gray.

EPILOGUE

Mark lay wide-awake in bed, the night sounds of chirping frogs filling his ears, while moonlight bathed the room. The clock on his bedside table read 1:35, but he could not sleep. Quietly, he slipped out of bed, pulled on a pair of shorts and headed down the hall. Ever since his return from China, Mark found late night walks in his fields very comforting. The warm summer air, the fireflies, and the constant symphony of frogs from the pond soothed his mind. He even found the moon and blazing stars overhead oddly comforting now that they no longer hid an alien menace.

Mark found that he was more contemplative. Before he had only focused on work. Now he was more philosophical, although he did not think he had any more answers. It felt odd being back at work as if nothing had happened. Jeffreys was also back on duty, having made a full recovery from his injuries.

The story provided to the public was that a terrorist group had tried to steal a nuclear warhead and Colonel Lui was a hero for stopping them from escaping with the nuke, which detonated in the process. A huge multi-national effort was established to handle the fallout, which although in a very remote area, was spreading to some degree in the prevailing winds. Perhaps the only good thing coming out of the whole event was renewed talks on limiting nuclear weapons. Once again word of aliens did not make the press.

The warm summer night air blew gently as Mark continued to slowly walk through the fields, gazing up at the blinking stars, his eyes easily adjusted to the night. He walked for an hour, before heading back to the house, taking a detour at the barn that sheltered his tractor and hay from the elements. Walking through the perpetually open double barn doors, he smelled the sweat scent of freshly cut hay. Three rows of freshly cut round hay bales were visible in the moonlight that streamed through the doors. He walked between two rows, absently counting the bales stored for the winter. In the very back of the barn, past the last hay bale, the pale moonlight shimmered, like heat off hot pavement. Mark walked over and reached out with his hand, touching the shimmering light.

The hatch to the blue-gray's escape pod opened.

THE END

Made in the USA
Charleston, SC
17 October 2014